THE
SHADOW
MAN

F. M. PARKER

THE SHADOW MAN

NAL BOOKS

NEW AMERICAN LIBRARY

NEW YORK
PUBLISHED IN CANADA BY
PENGUIN BOOKS CANADA LIMITED, MARKHAM, ONTARIO

PAR

For information address New American Library.

Published simultaneously in Canada by Penguin Books Canada Limited.

NAL BOOKS TRADEMARK REG. U.S. PAT. OFF. AND FOREIGN COUNTRIES
REGISTERED TRADEMARK—MARCA REGISTRADA
HECHO EN CHICAGO, U.S.A.

SIGNET, SIGNET CLASSIC, MENTOR, ONYX, PLUME, MERIDIAN and NAL BOOKS are published *in the United States* by NAL PENGUIN INC., 1633 Broadway, New York, New York 10019, *in Canada* by Penguin Books Canada Limited, 2801 John Street, Markham, Ontario L3R 1B4

Library of Congress Cataloging-in-Publication Data

Parker, F. M.
  The shadow man.
  I. Title.
PS3566.A678S48   1988   813'.54   88-12476
ISBN 0-453-00619-1

Designed by Guy Ramsey

First Printing, November, 1988

  2   3   4   5   6   7   8   9

PRINTED IN THE UNITED STATES OF AMERICA

To Louise

To Louise

Without a family, man, alone in the world, trembles with the cold.

—Andre Maurois

The Making of the Land

A Prologue

The first mountains, ancient beyond imagination, were created so long ago that even the sun forgot it had ever shone upon their birth. They were formed a billion years in the past by a mighty, compressive force that thrust up great blocks of the earth's crust into a giant east-west mountain range.

In the last paroxysm of mountain building, molten grantie magma welled up from subterranean reservoirs deep in the bowels of the earth and intruded, replacing broad zones of the older rocks of the mountains. Hot mineral-bearing solutions and gases were injected into fractures and ruptures in the rock. In rare, isolated locations, copper, silver, and gold precipitated out in rich concentrations.

Finally the mountains ceased growing and rested. For six hundred million years only the rain and snow and the sigh of the wind were upon the face of the huge mountains.

Bit by minute bit, the mountains were eroded away. The high cloud-brushing peaks wore away to low hills. The valleys of the land were invaded by a shallow sea,

9

and the hills became a chain of small islets surrounded by salty brine.

Seventy million years ago, the seas retreated to the south as a tremendous force again crumpled the mantle of the earth. The rocks arched up in gigantic folds with a north-south axis. The force continued to torture the rocks, overturning them to the east. Then one added inch of movement exceeded their strength, and deep faults of unbounded energy sliced through the layers of stone. In places the earth's crust was lifted upward, in other locations there were down-warping and subsidence. Stupendous rift valleys were formed.

One such rift valley was fifty miles wide and hundreds of miles long. A tall range of mountains bordered it on the side where the sun rose. In the depths of the five-mile-deep chasm, a grand river came to life, fed endlessly by the countless streams pouring down from the mountains. The strong current of the river rushed away to the south until it reached a far-off sea.

Over the aeons the great fault valley began to fill with rubble from the mountains, boulders, and gravel washed down from the highlands. Once a thick lava flow dammed the river, but the prodigious torrent of water hammered a gorge through the tough rock and surged onward.

On the east side of the mountain range a myriad of streams tumbled with awesome violence down from the high ramparts. As the grade flattened on the lower reaches of the streams, they slowed and wandered in meandering courses, dropping their load of eroded mountain debris. The valleys of the streams became choked with swamps and shallow lakes as thousands of cubic miles of sediment were spread in ever-thickening layers for great distances over the land.

The millennia passed, score after score, adding to millions of years. During the long epoch a broad plain formed at the base of the mountain and extended to the east for many hundreds of miles. So flat was the land surface that the larger animals could see each other for great distances, to the limits of their vision.

Twenty million years ago, near the mouth of the grand river of the north, a hungry lizard raced down the bank to capture a fish that was stranded and floundering in a shallow pool of water. The lizard's tail left a small scratch in the mud. From that tiny scar in the dirt, during the next rainstorm, an incipient streamlet was born.

The rivulet had inherited the hunger of the beast that had created it. Within a foot, the rivulet cut into the course of another trickle of water and beheaded it, adding that miniature flow to its own body. Then it captured another streamlet, and another. Swiftly the rivulet grew to become a creek.

The new creek greedily ate its way north along the base of the tall mountains, encountering the channels of many streams. A battle was fought each time to determine which stream would die. The hungry offspring of the lizard won every battle and survived.

The creek grew to become a river, flowing in a wide, swampy valley. Its headwaters lay on the very summit of a high mountain far to the north. Now there were two large rivers, with a mighty mountain range rearing into the sky between them.

That is the way a tribe of man found the land when they arrived, migrating from a far and distant place in the north. The people liked the land of rivers and mountains, and they stayed, their numbers increasing.

Thirty thousand years later, barely a tick of time as measured on the geologic clock, a second tribe of men arrived, creeping timidly and cautiously up from the south. They also liked the two rivers and the mountains. The men gave them names, the Rio Grande, the Rio Pecos, and the Sangre de Cristo Mountains, and they settled there with their women and children.

Time ticked away again, and a third tribe of men came hurrying into the land. They came from the east and their numbers were many. They made savage war upon the first two tribes.

The events of this story happened during the days of that war.

CHAPTER 1

Culebra Mountain, Mexican Territory,
February 27, 1846

The storm came straight from the hunting ground of
blizzards. Jacob Tamarron could see the seething
dark clouds through breaks in the forest, pouring
in a mile-thick avalanche down from the high backbone
of the Sangre de Cristo Mountains.

A mighty blast of frigid wind roared out ahead of the
storm, careening across the mountainside and whipping
the giant pine trees like blades of grass.

The thick mass of clouds, riding upon the back of the
frontal winds, charged in to hide the weak winter sun
from the earth. The forest was filled with dark, gray
shadows, as if the evening dusk were arriving with deep
night but minutes behind.

Jacob increased his pace to a trot. He moved effortlessly with a rolling, spraddle-legged stride to keep his
bear-paw snowshoes from tangling together. His .50-cali-
ber Hawken rifle swung easily in his hand. The pack of
wolf skins and his buffalo sleeping robe rode lightly upon
his back.

His camp lay an hour away at the base of the tall
Culebra Mountain. Already he could catch glimpses of

the bottom of the valley lying a thousand feet below him. His partner, Daniel, would be at their bivouac. He would have a hot fire burning and an elk haunch roasting.

Three days before, the mountain had lost some of its deep freeze, and the pale winter sun now coasted on a cloudless blue sky. Jacob had taken his rifle and tramped around the flank of the mountain to a broad thicket of bitter brush. The browse was the favorite food of deer, and the winter-hungry animals had come for miles across the snowy shoulders of Culebra to congregate there and feed.

The wolf packs also stole through the forest and gathered. The powerful predators stalked and killed many of the deer. In turn, Jacob stealthily stole up on the wolves and slew five of them. All the pelts were prime, with long luxurious guard hair and a soft, dense undercoat. The fur would bring a premium price.

Daniel had remained behind at the cabin. He was getting old and did not like camps in the snow. But he was a staunch and hardworking partner. Each day he traveled the long, difficult miles of the trap line and removed the night's catch of mink, otter, fox, and marten, and reset the crushing steel jaws of the traps.

Jacob halted abruptly. The short hairs on the back of his neck twisted and rose as some instinct warned him he was not alone in the woods. He stepped sideways to stand against the trunk of a large tree and swiftly scanned ahead toward Saruche Creek, along every snowy aisle among the thick-boled pines.

He pivoted slowly to the rear, his eyes probing all the openings. On one of the curving passageways, his fresh tracks lay plain in the white blanket of snow covering the ground. An enemy could track him at a run.

Jacob waited, pushing the limits of his senses outward, straining to determine consciously what some ancient instinct had detected at a primal level. He didn't question the feeling that unseen enemies were near. Once he had made that mistake, when he had been very young in the mountains, and a long scar remained from the wound that had almost killed him.

The forest grew dimmer and the falling temperatures sent cold, probing fingers through his fur coat and buckskins. Still he did not stir, letting the minutes pass, his eyes constantly roaming and his ears straining to pierce the moan of the rising wind.

The frigid front of the storm overran Jacob. A mighty wind pounded him. All around him, the pines groaned at the onslaught, bucking and bending. A mammoth pine creaked under the strain. One of its high limbs broke and fell crashing to the ground.

Icy sleet began to fall in long, slanting diagonals from the swollen bellies of the clouds. The hurtling ice pellets stung like fire, and Jacob ducked his head to protect his face.

The storm intensified. The sleet became a white torrent. Visibility lessened to a few yards. A hissing strumming filled the forest as billions of sleet pellets struck the pines, drummed on the limbs and tree trunks, and bounced down to roll on the ground. The noise was deafening, pressing in upon Jacob from all sides like an invisible force.

The wall of sleet thinned. In the white curtain, not twenty yards distant, five Arapaho warriors on snowshoes glided as soundlessly as phantoms along the border of the creek. The leader lifted his hand and the band stopped instantly.

Jacob moved a few inches to shelter behind the trunk of the tree. He stared past the rough bark and watched the Indians standing motionless, the sleet swiftly collecting on their fur coats. Each man was warily scrutinizing the valley bottom and the mountainsides.

The warriors were lean and hard, not old, not young, seasoned fighting men. They wasted not a word or motion, as if they had fought together before and each knew what was expected of him. The leader carried a rifle, and the other men strong war bows. The Arapaho would be tough to kill.

The sharp eyes of the Indians ranged the limits of their vision, searching the forest to detect something that should not be there. The warrior in the rear stared directly up the slope toward Jacob. An arrow was nocked in his bow and half drawn.

The man raised his face, almost black against the sleet. He pulled in a breath of cold air, testing with his keen nostrils for an alien scent. His tongue ran out, as if he were tasting the wind.

Jacob knew why the Arapaho were here in the valley. Over the years they had developed a successful tactic for killing and robbing the white trappers that invaded their land. Before the spring arrived and the trappers loaded their pelts on packhorses and left for Saint Joseph or Santa Fe and the fur buyers there, the Indians would leave their winter camps on the low, warmer plains lying to the east and come up into the mountains. Ranging in small war parties along the creeks, the Arapaho would ambush the white men and carry off their winter catch of fur.

The leader of the band of Indians made an almost imperceptible signal with his hand. The Arapaho moved as if they were all part of one large, hungry hunting animal, disappearing up the creek and into the masking sleet.

Jacob hastened down the remaining stretch of slope and off along the trail of the Arapaho. His partner would not expect an attack in such foul weather, and Jacob could not call out or shoot to warn him for that would turn the warriors back upon himself. He had to follow close behind and he prepared to join Daniel in the fight, to strike and kill the moment the battle began.

He hurried faster through the thrashing trees and stinging ice pellets. The cabin was a quarter of a mile up the creek and on a south-facing meadow. It would be easy for the Indians to locate.

A rifle crashed close ahead. A second boomed an instant later.

"Damnation," cursed Jacob. The battle had started too soon. He darted forward. As he ran, he untied the leather strap that held his coat shut around him, putting his five-shot Colt revolver and skinning knife ready at hand.

The dark figures of several men took form in the streaming sleet near the wall of a small log cabin. Two forms lay partially buried in the deep snow. An Indian was leaning over one of the still bodies.

Jacob recognized the fallen man as Daniel. Before he fell, his tough old partner had shot one of the Indians.

Jacob lifted his rifle, sighted along the iron barrel, and squeezed the trigger. The long weapon jumped in his hands like a live thing. The Arapaho bending over Daniel was slammed down onto the snowy earth. Jacob swung the rifle into his left hand. His right snatched the revolver from its holster.

He cocked the gun as he extended it. His finger pressed the trigger.

With amazing swiftness the Indians had pivoted toward their attackers. One, faster than the others, jerked up his bow and bent it. An arrow sprang toward the trapper.

Jacob heard the whizzing flight of the shaft and felt the feathers of the fletching brush his cheek. You're a brave bastard, Jacob thought, but you missed. He fired the revolver.

The Arapaho stumbled. He caught his balance and started to reach behind his back for a second arrow from the quiver. His fingers fumbled at the arrow. He fell to his knees and collapsed onto the snow-covered ground.

During Jacob's short fight with the second Indian the remaining warriors had sprung away into the storm. Now Jacob hastily backed away until he could no longer see the crumpled forms of the men in the snow. The Indians probably thought he'd go and investigate the condition of his partner and they could circle and steal up on him. But he would not make that mistake. Daniel, old friend, if you're still alive, hold on for a few minutes longer.

Jacob sheltered his rifle from the falling sleet with his body as he hurriedly poured a measure of powder down the barrel and rammed home the greased patch-and-lead ball. A fresh firing cap was pressed firmly upon the nipple. There were still four rounds in his revolver, and he didn't take the weapon apart to reload the one empty chamber.

Jacob knelt, hunkered low as the wind and sleet swirled around him. He waited, staring intently into the blinding whiteness.

Jacob knew that too much time was passing. He leapt erect and lunged into the storm. Indians almost always liked to have the enemy far outnumbered. The three Arapaho were not going to continue the battle. They would be searching for the trappers' horses.

Jacob crossed the narrow meadow and the frozen channel of Saruche Creek at a dead run. He veered slightly left, aiming to enter the downstream edge of the aspen thicket. That was where the horses would most likely be, for they liked to feed upon the tender, sweet sprouts and limbs of the trees. When he caught the first glimpse of the grove of aspen, he slowed.

Two horses burst from the trees. One animal carried two riders, the other the remaining Arapaho. The single Indian saw Jacob running to intercept their course. He began to shout at his companions.

The Arapaho had found only two of the horses, but that had been accomplished more quickly than Jacob had thought possible. Already the running horses and the men clinging to their backs were disappearing into the wall of white. Jacob slid to a halt, jerked his rifle to his shoulder, and snapped off a shot at the hurtling figure of the lone rider.

Horses and men vanished into the turmoil of the storm.

Jacob followed cautiously along the deep tracks of the running horses. His shot had been hurried; still, he felt it had been close to its target. He badly needed the cayuse to haul out the catch of furs.

The horse stood beside the body of a man on the ground. It looked back the way it had come and caught sight of Jacob slinking forward. It nickered as it recognized its master.

"Well, it 'pears you still belong to me," Jacob said to the horse.

The Indian stirred and groaned. He weakly struggled to a sitting position and propped himself up with his hands. His eyes were full of pain.

The eyes hardened to black obsidian as they came to rest on Jacob, standing not three paces distant, so close that the white man could reach out with his rifle barrel and touch him.

The Arapaho saw the pitiless anger in Jacob. The battle was over and he had lost. There would be no mercy.

The wounded Arapaho sat more erect and placed his hands on his knees. He squared his fur-clad shoulders and raised his face up to the falling sleet. He began to chant in a clear tenor voice.

Jacob listened to the warrior's death song. Let him prepare himself for the journey into the world of the dead. Had Jacob been defeated, he would have appreciated that privilege from his victor.

With hooded eyes the Indian stared upward, seeming not to feel the stinging sleet pellets striking him. His voice was strong, with a fine, almost musical timbre.

Jacob drew his long-bladed knife and leapt forward. His hand lashed out as swiftly as the snapping end of a whip. The sharply honed steel blade sliced into the warrior's neck, cutting deeply, grating off the bony vertebrae of the spinal column. As the Indian fell backward, Jacob plunged the knife through his rib cage and into his heart.

If he had lost, Jacob would have wanted a quick death from the victor.

CHAPTER 2

"The mountains are like whorés," Daniel said, his voice frail and far away.

Jacob did not reply. He leaned farther over his friend to protect his face from the falling sleet. Daniel was gravely wounded. Blood oozed steadily in a red stream from a gaping hole in his chest. He was dying, and there was nothing Jacob could do. His sorrow clutched at his throat until he could not speak.

Daniel struggled for words again. "The mountains draw us to their cold beauty. Every fall we climb up into one of their hidden, secret valleys, hoping it will be virgin and has never felt the intrusion of a man before. The mountains charge a heavy price for what they give. They take their pay in the precious years of our youth. Then they kill us in one of a thousand ways.

"Do you hear me, Jacob? The whorish mountains have killed me. Not the Indians but the mountains!" Daniel's voice rose in a lamenting pitch. "Do you hear me, Jacob?"

"Yes," Jacob said, choking.

"Get down from the high country to the low river valleys or the plains and find yourself a woman. It's not too late for you to do that. Your beard is mostly white and there's a touch of white in your hair, but you're still strong and quick as any man I've ever seen. You'll live long enough to raise a family. Maybe you'll even die in bed. Take all my furs. You'll need the money."

Jacob had long reflected on having a wife and children, and that at his death perhaps a grave would enclose him. But he had always thought it more likely that when he died, his body would rot and waste away in some wild and lonely place.

"I hear you, Daniel," Jacob said.

Daniel's voice came as a gasping whisper. "Bury me deep, Jacob."

Jacob buried his comrade in the unfrozen ground of the floor of the cabin. He finished and stood staring down at the grave.

He recalled Daniel's last words and recognized the truth in them. The solitary life in the mountains was missing something very valuable.

With a surging sense of urgency driving him, he hurriedly packed all the furs in bales. The fresh skins he bundled by themselves. They would still need to be fleshed and dried. The horses were brought up to the cabin door. Two packhorses were loaded with furs and one with camp gear, and his riding mount was saddled.

Jacob carried arm load after arm load of firewood into the cabin, all the fuel that had been cut for the winter, and piled it over the grave. Kindling, rich with pitch, was placed in the center of the mound. Taking a fiery brand from the fireplace, he ignited the wood. When the fire was burning strongly, he went outside.

The roaring fire touched the rafters. Red flames broke through the clapboard roof and dense smoke soared up to meet the falling sleet.

Jacob climbed astride his cayuse. He rode a few yards then halted, sitting his saddle and staring back at the burning cabin. He felt the hollow ache of his sadness. Life was without tang and very bitter.

Jacob reined his pony away into the lonely gloom of the storm.

At some unknowable hour of the gray day the rattle of the sleet pellets on the skeletal branches of pine died away. Fine, flinty snow began to fall, and the air became smoky, filled with the wind-swirled flakes.

Jacob turtled his head down more deeply between his shoulders and strained to peer through the icy mist. The string of packhorses, tied nose to tail with short lengths of rawhide, trailed behind, crunching a path through the deep snow crusted with two inches of brittle sleet.

On a large, twisting bend of Saruche Creek, he crossed the tracks of the stolen horses. The imprints were getting old, partially filled with new snow. Yet Jacob could tell that one Indian rode and one ran behind the cayuse. He would make no effort to overtake the Arapaho. However, if he should come upon them, they would die, for Jacob's anger at Daniel's death still seethed within him.

The cavalcade of horses was forced to cross the frozen creek at a place where the slick ice was exposed. The horses' hooves slipped and skittered. One animal fell, nearly pulling its adjoining mates down with it. The upright beasts patiently waited as the fallen horse carefully gathered its legs beneath itself and heaved erect.

The valley gradually widened, the flanks of the mountain drawing back a hundred yards or better. Long, narrow meadows began to appear, separated by stretches of fir and pine.

The evening dusk came swiftly. Jacob veered aside, leading his animals up a tightly curving tributary of Saruche Creek. When he had passed around two bends that would hide his fire from the main valley, he halted.

The horses gathered close about him, as if wanting to be near. Jacob became wreathed in swirls of steam from his own breath and that of the ponies. He brushed at the formless vapor to no avail. He gently slapped the horses away and stepped out to where he could observe his surroundings.

Jacob saw nothing except the steep sides of the mountain and the dense woods. Nearby up the creek lay a large, wind-fallen pine. He led his animals there and tied them to separate trees.

With his small single-bit ax he cut aspen branches and piled a quantity of the sweet fodder before each horse. Soon the sound of contented munching was joined with the noise of the storm.

Jacob dug the fire-starting materials, flint and steel and a pouch of dry grass and pieces of punk, from his pack. At the edge of the windfall he collected small pieces of wood. He screwed a piece of the punk into a nest of the grass and struck the flint and steel over it. Sparks sprang from his blows. A hot, twinkling fragment of steel fell upon the punk.

Jacob cupped the grass and punk in his hand and blew lightly and carefully on it. A tiny coal came to red life. A curl of smoke arose. He coaxed the incipient fire to bright, glowing life and fed it shavings of dry wood. Then larger and larger pieces of fuel were added.

He cooked elk meat and ate, washing the strength-giving flesh down with a quart of hot tea.

As the night deepened, the snow stopped and the clouds thinned. From time to time he saw the stars, glittering like ice shards flung across the ebony sky.

He sat gazing at the leaping flames of the fire, watching the sparks chasing smoke into the sky. As the last yellow blaze began to flicker and weaken, Jacob cut fir boughs and laid them thick and overlapping on the snow. His tanned buffalo-hide sleeping robe was placed upon the soft mattress.

The horses began to stir and stomp. One snorted, frightened, and jerked at its tether.

Jacob turned. Three pairs of eyes glowed red just beyond the horses at the far edge of the circle of fire-light. Wolves had crept in close to investigate the intruder in their domain.

Jacob grabbed a flaming brand and flung it in a looping, fiery arc at the beasts. The eyes vanished. There was

a swift scratching of clawed feet on the snow crust, and
then the wolves were gone. There was plenty of food for
the predators this winter. They would not be back to
bother the horses.

The fire dwindled down to a small bed of living red
embers. The darkness pushed in from all sides. Jacob got
up and walked past the horses to stand in the gray,
snowy night.

Through holes in the clouds he caught sight of the
moon, round and frozen and wintry wan. Its light glowed
gray-blue on the long snowdrifts. He heard the fast wind
high on the mountainside whistling to the North Star. In
the trees, all around, the night lay cold as iron.

He reflected upon where he was in life. He had spent
most of it in the mountains. At first they had been a
joyful new world to play in. Now the mountains contained only emptiness, an aloneness all around him. And
in the future? He could not see, so it, too, was empty.
But then, maybe not completely empty. He would go
and see.

Jacob returned to his bed. He wrapped himself and his
rifle in the thick fur of the buffalo robe. It encased his
body snugly, soft as heavy velvet. He covered his head
and lay on his back, thinking about the violence of the
day and the terrible loss of his partner.

He shoved away his sorrow and for a long time pondered what the next few days would bring. Then he
pushed even those thoughts aside. He listened to the
arctic wind moaning an endless dirge as it wandered the
dark world. Felt its cold fingers clawing at his protective
covering, searching for an opening so it could come inside with him.

Jacob pulled the robe in closer around his shoulders.
He went to sleep in the black, arctic night.

In the uncertain light of early dawn Jacob threw aside
his frost-cloaked robe, pulled on his moccasins, and stood
up. The air had a static crackle of cold. The clouds were
heavy and hung close to the earth. They had spilled snow

again during the night, and all around lay huge white drifts, carved and hardened by the wind of the blizzard.

Without making a fire, Jacob loaded his mustangs, mounted, and left the camp. The clouds threatened more snow. He had to reach lower country quickly, or he might be trapped in the mountains for many days by impassable snowdrifts.

The horses labored mightly, lunging through the high snow ridges blocking the route. Large plumes of mist exploded from their nostrils. Sweat began to dampen and darken the long winter coats of the brutes.

At noon Jacob came out of dense timber and struck the main stream of the Purgatorie River near its headwaters. He had dropped two thousand feet in elevation. The snow that had been crotch-deep along Saruche Creek, now reached only to his knees.

Jacob turned to make his way with the watercourse, buried under snow and ice and winding down a valley studded with giant pines. He pushed hard, often jumping down from the saddle to help the tiring animals break trail.

Half a score of miles later, Purgatorie River swerved directly east. Jacob had traveled that path, a rapid descent through a narrow, rock-walled gorge down to the great plains lying five thousand feet below. He turned aside and continued due north, passing over a low saddle and finding North Fork of the Purgatorie River. By dusk he had climbed up and over a second rock-choked divide and found the tiny creek that was the beginning of the Cucharas River.

A silent camp was made in the edge of the night. It began to snow.

When the cold morning arrived, three inches of new snow lay on the ground, and icy mist filled the valley of the Cucharas River. Vision was shortened to a range no greater than a long rifle shot. Yet Jacob knew when he passed beneath Spanish Peak, towering fourteen thousand feet unseen on his right hand.

When the Cucharas River veered to the northeast, Jacob angled away from it and went northwest. He began to climb the steep, heavily wooded slope. By noon he had reached Veta Pass, crossed over, and was tramping south beside Sangre de Cristo Creek. He did not stop to rest at all.

Jacob hurried down from the mountains with snow frozen to his back and the wind clouting him. He made camp on the south end of a low range of frozen hills fifteen miles east of the deep lava gorge of the Rio Grande.

All day Jacob held course toward Santa Fe, traveling south between the canyon of the Rio Grande and Taos Mountain. Clouds hid all of Taos Mountain above a couple of hundred feet. Snowflakes, large and soggy, sifted down through the piñon trees to pile upon the packs and the backs of the ponies.

He crossed the Rio Pueblo de Taos on thick ice and halted his string of horses at the edge of the ancient Indian settlement of Taos. The weary ponies hunched their backs, let their heads droop dejectedly, and stood stock-still in the wind and snow.

Jacob surveyed the adobe homes of the Pueblo. The buildings rose one, two, and in a few sections three stories high around a large, open plaza. Pole ladders led up from one level to the next. Gray wood smoke climbed from chimneys, vanishing almost immediately in the hanging overcast.

An old Indian woman with a blanket wrapped around her and a fold of it thrown hoodlike up over her head came out of one of the dwellings. She shuffled across the snow in an aged, stiff-legged waddle and drew near half a score of dome-shaped ovens. She stopped at the one round structure that had its snow cover melted away.

Jacob stepped down from his mustang and walked quietly toward the woman. Intent on her task, the woman didn't see or hear his approach. She lifted aside a thin slab of rock to open the door of the oven. Then, with a

slat of wood, she reached into the hot interior and brought
out a big loaf of brown corn bread. It immediately began
to send short streams of steam into the cold air.

Jacob caught the aroma of the fresh bread wafting
toward him on the wind. He breathed it in slowly, savoring the tantalizing odor. He had not tasted bread for
months, and his craving turned his mouth moist.

"Mother, I will give you a Mexican peso for half of
that loaf," Jacob called.

The woman flinched back at the sound of his voice.
She whirled to face him.

Her old eyes ran over the white man, searching quickly
for any danger that might lurk in him. He calmly gazed
back, seeming not to notice the long-barreled rifle that
hung in the crook of his arm. His light-colored eyes were
frank and open, and a pleasant half-smile of anticipation
lay on his lips. One of his hands went into a small pouch
fastened over his shoulder. He brought out a silver coin.

The old woman bobbed her head at the white man
who spoke her language so well. With a peso she could
buy enough cornmeal or flour in Santa Fe to cook several
loaves of bread. "That is a fair price," she said.

She held out the loaf of bread on the wooden paddle.
"Do you have a knife to cut it with?"

"Certainly, Mother." Jacob slid his long skinning knife
from its scabbard.

Steadying the end of the wood slat with his hand, he
divided the loaf with one sweep of his sharp blade. He
returned the knife to its scabbard, then reached and took
one of the pieces of bread.

The old woman noticed that the division had been
quite even, and that the white man had chosen the section that may have been slightly smaller.

"You are an honest man," she said.

Jacob grinned at her and took a large bite of the warm
bread. The crust broke between his teeth, and the soft
bread within lay deliciously on his tongue. His grin broadened. He shut his eyes and started to chew, very slowly
and leisurely.

The old Indian woman remained, peering through the falling snow and watching the satisfied expression on the man's face as he devoured the half loaf. He finished and looked directly at her.

"Mother, that was most enjoyable. The men in your family must be well fed. They could grow fat just on your bread."

"They do not complain," she replied. A pleased smile creased her wrinkled features.

"That I believe," said Jacob. "I must be going. Goodbye, Mother."

He climbed astride his pony, guiding his animals into the snow and south toward Santa Fe.

CHAPTER 3

The day turned to dusk. On the gray snowscape, objects were blurred and distances distorted. The nipping wind had sharp teeth, and Jacob cinched his coat in more tightly.

He should have found shelter and a warm bed at Taos Pueblo. However, that opportunity was now past, and he would not turn back. He kicked his horse lightly in the ribs with his heels. The willing animal lengthened its stride, towing the three packhorses across a flat stretch of land studded with scattered clumps of juniper.

Ahead at the border of a dark wood, there was a tiny flicker of light. Jacob recognized the short burst of sparks rising from a chimney as someone poked the fire or tossed on a log. He headed straight toward the spot.

The squat outline of a small adobe cabin with a flat roof took form. Shutters were drawn closed over the windows. A heavy plank door barred the entrance. Jacob smelled smoke and felt warmer just thinking of the fire.

A cramped rail corral lay off to the right of the house. From within the enclosure a bony horse watched Jacob. He saw no hay or other feed for the gaunt animal.

Jacob rode up to the front step of the house. He hung his rifle on the saddle horn and climbed down. At his knock he sensed the people inside becoming instantly quiet and alert.

"My name is Tamarron," Jacob called in Spanish. "I want to talk to the man of the house."

There was no response, only a waiting silence from within. Jacob understood the wariness of the occupants, for strangers at night could mean attack and death.

"I mean you no harm," Jacob spoke through the door. "I wish only to buy some food and a place to sleep tonight. I will pay two pesos and leave early in the morning."

Slowly the door opened, showing yellow light from the fireplace. The bearded face of a Mexican peered past the doorjamb. He held an old blunderbuss, and he swung it to point straight at the man on the stoop.

Jacob slowly reached out, caught the end of the barrel, and deliberately started to push the heavy weapon aside. The blunderbuss had no range, but up close like this, it could blast a cave in the chest of a man.

The man's arm stiffened against the thrust of Jacob's hand.

"I'm a friend," Jacob said.

"Then you shall be treated as a friend," replied the man. He moved the gun to the side. "Come inside."

"My horses?" asked Jacob.

"Let us talk. Then we shall decide about your *caballos*." The Mexican motioned for Jacob to enter.

He is a brave man, thought Jacob as he stepped through the doorway. He jerked off his fur hat and shook the snow from it, his eyes examining the short, squarely built Mexican.

"My name is Jacob Tamarron, and I'm on my way to Santa Fe."

"I am Joaquin Otego," said the man.

Jacob nodded and glanced around the one large room that made up the man's home. A dark-skinned woman, almost pretty, held a boy of four or five years pressed close to her. From her round face and small hands and feet, Jacob judged her to be a Pueblo Indian.

All the sharp, black eyes of the family watched Jacob as he untied his fur coat. He pointed at the leaping flames in the fireplace. "May I warm myself?"

"Yes," replied Otego, still evaluating Jacob with narrowed, cautious eyes. He cast a questioning look at the woman.

Jacob pivoted to put his rear to the fire. As he turned, he saw some communication pass between the Mexican and his wife.

"You said two pesos?" asked the man.

"Exactly so."

"You may stay the night. Our food is very simple. And I have no feed for your horses."

"Then they will have to do without one more day," Jacob said, glad that the man had made a quick decision to allow him to stay. A night under a roof with friendly people would be a pleasant change. "I'll turn them into your corral."

"I will help you. Mariana, prepare Señor Tamarron some food."

The horses were led into the corral and unloaded. In the growing darkness the animals stood slackly in the snow, eyes sad and ribs showing through the long winter hair covering their bodies.

"There are bandits roaming the valley," said Otego. "You must bring your furs inside the house to keep them safe."

"I appreciate your advice," said Jacob. He hoisted a heavy pack and, taking his rifle, carried it to the house.

The remaining bales of pelts and the saddle were soon stowed against a wall of the room. Jacob removed his long fur coat, unbuckled his holstered pistol and knife, and placed them all on the top of his mound of possessions.

He ate a great quantity of boiled brown beans in rich soup, winter squash, and two large tortillas. Simple fare but heavily seasoned with red pepper, butter, and garlic.

Very delightful after weeks of food seasoned with nothing other than a dash of salt.

The woman noticed Jacob had finished. She went to a
wooden cupboard and brought him a wedge of dried
apple pie.

Jacob cut the pie into small pieces and ate it very
slowly, savoring every crumb. He always had a fondness
for sweets. He finished and smiled his thanks to the
woman. "The food was delicious." He laid two silver
pesos on the table.

Through the evening in front of the fire, Jacob talked
with Otego. They discussed the harsh winter, the growing population in the Rio Grande valley, the scarcity of
open land that a man could claim, and many other things.

The fire was fueled several times, then finally allowed
to burn down. The boy went sleepily to his cot. Otego
and his wife retired to a double-framed bed behind a
blanket partition she had hung.

Jacob had been given three sheepskins for a mattress.
He spread them near the fireplace and placed his buffalo
robe on top of the soft hides.

From long habit, he laid his rifle and pistol on the floor
within easy reach. He rested, listening to the dissonant
sound of the wind scurrying around the corners of the
house and complaining of the cold outside.

The boy tossed under his bed covers and broke into a
rapid babble of childish dream talk. Then he fell silent.
The only sound inside the snug little home was the char-
coal snapping now and then as it cooled in the fireplace.

"Señor Tamarron, wake! Wake!" The woman had Jacob by the shoulder and was shaking him violently.
"*Banditos* outside! Hurry and help Joaquin!"

Jacob surged to his feet, snatching up his rifle and
pistol. He has slept so soundly that Joaquin had crossed
the room and opened the door without being heard.
That's what came of sleeping in a house. You grew so
used to the noise of other people that you became careless.

Jacob paused at the open door and warily peered outside. Joaquin was near the corral. A large Mexican stood close to him and held a pistol pointed into his face. A second Mexican, young, hardly a man, was inside the enclosure. He had a lariat, the loop spread and his arm cocked to throw. He approached Jacob's riding horse.

Two strange mounts stood in the snow just to the right of the corral. That satisfied Jacob that there were only the pair of bandits. He shoved the pistol in his belt and cocked the rifle. He moved swiftly outside.

The big Mexican spoke to Joaquin. "You have four good horses, hombre. They are skinny, but all horses are skinny this time of year. We will leave you the broken old nag. We will look inside the house and see what else you have that is worth taking." He laughed slyly. "Is your woman pretty?"

The big man caught Jacob's movement and spun toward him. His pistol whirled to the right in Jacob's direction.

Jacob raised his rifle and quickly fired. The bullet broke the bandit's arm and plowed onward, shattering a rib and stopping in the center of his chest. The man fell to the side, burying his face in the snow.

Jacob let the rifle fall into his left hand and pulled his pistol with a flick of his fingers.

At the crash of the shot the bandit in the corral spun around, dropping his lariat and reaching for his pistol. He halted his draw, his hand not yet touching the butt of the gun, for he was looking directly down the open end of the barrel of Jacob's revolver.

"Go ahead," challenged Jacob. "See if you're fast enough to pull that gun before I can kill you."

"No, señor, I do not wish to try that." There was a quiver in his voice, and the whites of his eyes showed.

"But I want you to. Grab for it like a brave *bandito*!" Jacob's voice was flinty.

"No. I want only to go. I promise never to bother you again."

Jacob laughed at the young man who would be a horse thief. Then he sobered. It was either shoot the damn fellow or let him go. He certainly didn't want to waste effort taking him to the officials in Santa Fe. Long-term prisoners weren't kept there but instead were sent the long distance south to Saltillo. That wouldn't happen to someone so young. Most probably he would serve a short sentence in the local *calabozo* and then be released. The officials wouldn't think it much of a crime to try to steal an American trapper's horse.

Jacob's anger was cooling. He could not kill one so young. "Leave. Do it now, before I change my mind. If I ever see you again, I'll surely shoot you."

The youth sprang in the direction of his horse. He didn't believe what the gringo trapper had said. It was a trick. He kept his eyes riveted on the American.

"No!" shouted Joaquin. "Kill him." He had grabbed up the dead man's revolver. He waved it in the air to emphasize his cry.

The outlaw ran faster. He leaped upon the back of his *caballo* and spurred it savagely. The youth jerked a riding crop from the pommel of the saddle and furiously lashed his horse. The straining animal flung snow from under its driving hooves as it sped away.

"No! Don't let him escape," screamed Otego. He pointed the pistol at the back of the racing figure and fired.

The bandit threw wide both arms. He held his seat for three strides, gradually leaning forward until his face lay in the mane of his mount. He slid sideways from the saddle, rolling and tumbling on the snowy earth.

Otego spoke to Tamarron in a low, apologetic voice. "You scared him and he ran. He could never let us live and tell of his cowardice. He would have returned with other *banditos* and harmed my family. I had to kill him."

"Maybe so, but I don't feel good about the shooting." Jacob swiftly strode off toward the house. A moment later he reemerged with his saddle and a bale of furs.

Otego hastened to help Jacob load the packhorses. When they had finished, Otego spoke to Jacob in a low voice. "Señor Tamarron, may I have one of their horses? Mine is of no use."

"Take them both. And all of their money, if they have any. I want nothing that belonged to them."

Jacob climbed astride his pony. He glanced at the woman and little boy in the doorway. Far removed from the safety of Santa Fe, the small family was striving to survive. Realizing that, some of his distaste for the young bandit's death was washed away. In reality Otego probably had greater reason to kill than Jacob. Otego had a wife and son to protect. Jacob had killed for a horse.

Tamarron traveled along the top of the winding lava canyon of the Rio Grande. By noon the storm clouds had risen far into the sky. The sun shone, pale as a daytime moon, down through the high, thin mist.

In the afternoon the last traces of the storm ran away across the heavens, leaving behind a blue-domed world swept clean by the arctic wind. The wonderful sun burned down, and Jacob felt revived, growing stronger, like a bug or a crawling thing after a frost.

All around him the warm rays of the sun melted the snow and sucked up the moisture. Already the white covering had turned shallow, and there were bare spots on the south-facing slopes.

Jacob veered from the great chasm of the Rio Grande and took a course southeast. He reached the valley of the Rio Tesuque. On the riffles, the river ice was thawed, and the water ran black and swift.

Jacob crested the last range of hills and gazed down on the two-hundred-and-fifty-year-old Mexican city of Santa Fe. The town consisted of a gathering of brown-and-white adobe buildings four streets wide that strung for a mile and a quarter along both sides of the Santa Fe River. The town had a population of approximately eight thousand.

The tall, high-steepled church, La Parroquia, east of the broad central plaza, dominated all structures, even the long, single-storied Palace of the Governors. Dwarfed by the distance, the tiny figures of men, horses, and oxen could be seen moving on San Francisco Street, the main thoroughfare. Wood smoke rose from hundreds of chimneys, then bent and went off with the wind.

Jacob sat his horse in the sunshine and looked at the town, so isolated from other sites of civilization. He would begin his search there. He would be a persistent man in this endeavor. If he should be unsuccessful in Santa Fe after a fair attempt, he would ride to Saint Joseph or Independence.

Jacob felt the warmth in the low river valley. The snow from the last storm was already retreating up the hillsides. His fur hat and long fur coat were rolled up into a bundle and stowed in one of the packs. He donned his battered cloth hat and hurried down toward the town with his horses. He believed the forest and mountains were forever gone behind him.

Tamarron rode slowly along San Francisco Street, a narrow avenue hemmed in by adobe buildings. Most of the structures were jammed tightly against their neighbors, sharing a common wall. The side streets were even more restricted, and there were almost no alleys.

A woodcutter leading a long string of burros passed Jacob and continued on in the direction of the wooded hills. A meat wagon, with two freshly slaughtered sheep hanging on hooks, was halted in front of a residence. The butcher and a housewife were haggling over the price of a slab of red meat.

At the hitch rails of the stores, offices, and drinking and eating establishments, a dozen or so horses stood on the muddy street, heads down, half asleep in the mild winter sun. On the left side, leaning against the front of a dry-goods store, were two vaqueros, Mexican cowboys, in tightly fitted leather pants, intricately decorated jackets, leather boots, and large-brimmed hats with high, peaked crowns.

Holding possession of a large sunny section of ground near a two-story cantina on the edge of the plaza, eight American trappers lazed about. With their long, shaggy hair, beards, and fringed buckskin outfits, the mountain men looked like half-tamed wolves. No rifles or pistols were in sight, but each man carried a long-bladed skinning knife on his belt.

Other trappers had already arrived in Santa Fe before Jacob. For the men to be here while the pelts of the animals were still prime on the snow-covered mountains meant that they had encountered trouble—Indian attacks, thieves, or poor trapping.

A Mexican woman, holding the tail of her dress up to keep it out of the mud, crossed the street ahead of Jacob. She ignored him. Three boys ran by kicking a muddy ball.

Jacob aimed his pony toward the trappers. They would know the price of pelts and which buyer was paying the highest dollar. If they had been in Santa Fe a few days, they could tell him the latest news of the outside world. After five months of being isolated in the mountains, he wanted to quickly gather information about Texas, the eastern states, and Mexico.

One of the trappers, a skinny man, spoke to a large fellow near him and pointed at Tamarron. They both moved a few paces away from the wall of the cantina.

The smaller man shouted out a greeting. "Jacob Tamarron, you damn rascal, what are you doing in Santa Fe so early?"

"Hello, Tim," Jacob called back. He smiled broadly. It felt good to meet an old acquaintance. He slid from his horse, dropping the reins to ground-tie the animal, and came to meet the two men.

"Where's Daniel?" asked Tim.

"The Arapaho killed him a few days back," replied Jacob. He felt his sorrow anew.

"That's too bad, Jacob. A man doesn't often find a partner good as Daniel. But he lived longer than most do."

Tim gestured at the man beside him. "I'd like you to meet Deek Craner. I knew him up in the Teton country. Him and me partnered up together this past winter."

"Hello, Deek," Jacob said, and shook hands with both men. "How long have you fellows been in Santa Fe?"

"We came down about four days ago when the weather turned warm," replied Tim.

"How's fur prices?" asked Jacob.

"Beaver is fetching only a dollar a pound and not worth skinning. It's not like the old days when a plew brought three to four dollars a pound. Silk's almost completely replaced beaver for men's hats and has killed the market. But fur that's suited for the coats of Eastern ladies and gents is bringing a goodly price. The hell of it is, those kinds of animals are a damn sight smarter, and harder to trap than beaver."

Deek nodded agreement with his comrade's words. "And a man has to run a twenty-mile trap line to catch enough critters to make a couple of small-sized bales of pelts."

"That's why few young fellows are trapping today," said Jacob, glancing around at the group of Americans. He saw only two men who didn't have gray in their beards. "Who's buying skins?"

Tim answered. "There are two buyers in town. I suspect there'll be more later. But right now there's a representative of the Tolleson brothers of St. Joe, and another man named Randolph from Cincinnati. They do a little bidding against each other, and that helps keep the price at a reasonable level."

"Good, where can I find them?"

"Randolph has an office on the plaza across from the Governor's Palace," said Tim. "The Tolleson man has a room at La Fonda. But he's a gambling man and most often can be found at one of the card parlors."

"What's the charge for Mexican customs tax?"

"Two bits a pelt," Tim answered.

"Damnation, that's high. Up a nickel from last year," Jacob said.

"Yep. And Governor Armijo and his soldiers are tough about collecting it. Better check in at the Custom House first thing and get your *guia* stamp."

"Well, two bits' tax or not, I'm going to sell my furs," said Jacob. "I'll buy you and Deek a drink later on this evening."

"That's a fine offer," said Tim. "We'll be around somewhere close."

As Tamarron turned to leave, he heard one of the trappers call out along the street in a rough, loudmouthed voice, "Woman, come and give a lonely American some lovin'."

CHAPTER 4

The pair of gray riding horses traveled at an easy gallop, carrying Petra and Conrado Solis along San Francisco Street. The brother and sister rode easily, their bodies swaying smoothly to the stride of the mounts and the big rowels of their spurs reflecting bright silver sun arrows.

Petra swung her gaze out over the town. She enjoyed riding through Santa Fe. When dressed much like a man, as she was now, and on horseback, she didn't feel so strongly the difference that separated her from other women.

Petra gave only a short glance at the group of buckskin-clad mountain men loitering by the cantina. It was best to ignore the rowdy Americans. She drew her horse to a halt beside Conrado in front of the Estudillo Mercado on the opposite side of the street.

Refugio Estudillo, owner of the large general store, was watching through the window. He saw the Solis man and woman dismount and tie their horses to the hitching post. The Solis family held an old Spanish land grant of more than three hundred thousand acres in the Pecos

River valley. The family was one of his best customers. He hurried toward the store entrance to greet them.

"Good day, Petra, and to you, Conrado," Refugio said in greeting.

"Good day," Petra replied. "How are Dona and the children?"

Refugio looked at the Solis woman standing straight and slim beside her brother. They were dressed like caballeros, in leather pants and decorated jackets, hers a lively maroon and his a somber black. Conrado wore a broad-brimmed felt hat. Petra was bareheaded, her black hair woven into a large braid that hung down her back. She carried a thin-bladed stiletto in a sheath on her belt. She would have made an outstanding caballero had she been a man, thought Refugio.

"All are well, and the children are growing rapidly, Petra. How are Señor and Señora Solis?"

"They are anxious to return to the rancho and see about the sheep and cattle. We've sent a crew of men with shovels to the mountain pass to dig out the snow-drifts and open the trail over the summit. They should be finished by Monday, and then we'll leave for the Rio Pecos."

"Dona and I shall be sorry to lose your pleasant company," Refugio said.

"And we yours," Petra replied. She spoke to Conrado. "I will see if my dress for the *baile* is finished, and make the purchase mama requested. I'll return here in a quarter hour or so."

"Very well, Petra. While you're doing that I will order our supplies," said Conrado.

Petra turned and walked across the street. At the edge of her vision she saw the Americans halt their conversation and watch her as she stepped up on the stoop and entered the dressmaker's shop.

The seamstress came forward quickly with the dress she had been working on for two days and held it up proudly for Petra to see. "Señorita Solis, it has turned out beautifully. You selected just the perfect cloth and color."

Petra reached out and fingered the soft yellow silk that had come the long distance from China. She had given one steer just for the material, and then three sheep to the dressmaker. A very high price for one dress. But her herds of animals were growing, and she could afford it.

She lifted the dress gently and, stepping before a long mirror, held the garment up against her body. "Yes, it is beautiful. Please wrap it." She did not look at her face.

Petra left the dressmaker's shop with her bundle and turned up the street. She would have to pass through the lazing band of Americans. However, that did not worry her. Though the trappers would watch the women of the town with sharp eyes and sometimes whisper words deep in their beards, they really never bothered them. Except the ones that were for sale in the cantina.

To Petra's surprise, one of the Americans, a huge young man, separated himself from the group and marched a few steps to intercept her. He spread wide his long arms, completely blocking her path. "Woman, come and give a lonely American some lovin'," he said in a loud voice.

Petra stepped to the right to go around the trapper. He moved in the same direction and stopped her passage again.

"Please allow me to pass," she said in cold, precise English.

"What's the matter? Ain't us Americans good enough for you Mexican ladies?" growled the man.

"Just let me by." Petra made a motion to go to the left. But the trapper barred her path.

"Damn you! Get out of my way!" Petra said, her voice slashing the air.

"Don't talk to me like that, you ugly bitch," snarled the American. "I'm doing you a favor."

Petra caught her breath at the horrible insult. Her hand closed around the hilt of the stiletto in her belt.

*   *   *

In astonishment, Tamarron watched the trapper block the Mexican woman's course along the public street. He listened to the argument for a moment, not believing what he was witnessing.

"What in the hell is wrong with that fellow?" Jacob asked Tim.

"This is Unger's first winter in the mountains. He and his partner were hit by Cheyenne. His partner stopped some arrows. But Unger killed two braves with his knife, and now he thinks he's a real bear of a man."

"Why hasn't somebody taught him some manners?"

" 'Cause he's strong as an ox and not smart enough to be afraid of anything."

Jacob heard the man's insulting words—"You ugly bitch"—and saw the woman's eyes flare black flame. Her hand jumped to her knife. God! Jacob liked her bravery. A sudden thrill ran through him at just watching her. He shoved aside two trappers and strode forward past Unger.

The woman hastily backed up a step at Jacob's swift advance. She half drew her stiletto.

Tamarron stopped beside her and pivoted to face Unger.

"Let the lady pass, Unger. But first apologize to her." Tamarron's voice was like rocks breaking.

"Apologize, hell! And to a woman so ugly, I'd have to put my hat over her face to get close enough to make love to her." Unger threw back his head and laughed.

"Do it now, Unger, or I'll make you one sorry bastard," warned Tamarron.

"Why, you gray-bearded old fart, I'll cut you into ribbons." Unger's face lost its mirth, and his eyes flattened and glinted cruelly. He slid his knife from its sheath.

Unger heard the sharp, amazed voices of the trappers at his rear. He didn't understand their concern. He would cut the old man just enough to show him who was cock of the walk.

He recognized the voice of the trapper called Tim speaking above the general clamor of words. "Unger, you just signed your own death warrant. That's Jacob Tamarron. He's killed more men with a knife than your small brain can count."

Petra understood the English, and she looked at the man called Jacob Tamarron. She sensed him drawing in, coiling like a great steel spring. His beard bristled as the muscles along his jaw became tense and ridged.

A low chuckle, more like the low growl of a lion, escaped from Tamarron. A crooked smile stretched across his mouth. An eagerness for battle rose hot and somehow pleasant in him. He'd come down from the mountains looking for a different kind of life, but he knew he was ultimately a warrior and would always be ready to settle his argument with violence.

"I'll give you one last chance, Unger, because you're young and ignorant. Put your knife away and apologize to the lady."

"Hell, no, I say. Hell, no!" Unger extended his extremely long arm with the knife clutched in his hand. "I've got five, maybe six inches reach on you. I'm not afraid."

"If I have to pull my knife, I'll make your arms a lot shorter," Tamarron said, his eyes boring into Unger. "You'd already have been dead for what you said if we weren't in this Mexican town. I don't want to spend time in their filthy *calabozo*."

"Unger, this is Hadden," called a man directly behind the young trapper. "You can't beat Tamarron. I've seen him fight. Put the blade away and do as he says. We don't want trouble with the governor's soldiers."

Another voice chimed in. "Here comes a Mexican now. He's dressed like her. Probably kinfolk. He'll fight, for sure. Damn it, Unger, give it up. The whole town will come down on us."

Conrado had seen the trapper preventing Petra from going along the street. Then the other American had gone up close to her. From his angle of view Conrado couldn't be sure what the second man was doing. He could only hear the mutter of the trappers' words. He broke into a run across the street.

"Unger, damn you, apologize before we all have to fight our way out of this town. That means we'll lose everything we're not carrying." Hadden's voice was like flint.

Unger hesitated, listening to the angry exclamations of the pack of trappers at his rear. He sheathed his knife. "Goddamn," he said.

Jacob saw the cunning slither over Unger's face. He was figuring out a plan for revenge, at a time when he would not be expected, in the dark when an enemy couldn't be seen.

"I apologize," Unger said with a growl. He spun around and bulled his way through the group of trappers. He stopped in front of Tim. "I'll remember what you said about me. You'll pay big for that."

"Unger, I wouldn't fight you with a knife like Tamarron would," Tim said coldly. "If you come after me, well, I'll just stand off with my rifle and shoot the hell out of you. I've kept this skinny old body alive for twice your age. I suspect I can keep going for a while longer."

Deek spoke to Unger. "And if by chance Tim got killed somehow, I'd take that personal. I'd find you and blow a .50-caliber hole through you sure as hell."

Both partners grinned at Unger, secure in the knowledge of their skill with a rifle and the strength of their friendship. Unger stormed away pounding his feet.

Petra looked at the American who had come to her aid unasked. He was gazing at her in an intent, measuring way. She was startled by his light gray eyes, almost white, as if they had been bleached by a thousand suns. So very strange and different from the black eyes of her people.

She turned squarely to face him and let him see plainly the horrible scar on her face. Let him see how ugly she truly was; so ugly, as the other American had said, that a man would have to put his hat over her face to make love to her.

His expression of calm appraisement did not change. It was so unlike the many times the interest of other men had faltered when they looked fully at her. Always they were quick to hasten away. She felt her heart lift at the steadiness of those grayish eyes and the interest still showing in them.

"I am Jacob Tamarron," said the American.

"Yes, I know. I am Petra Solis. Thank you for your help." She extended her hand.

He clasped her hand. He didn't shake it as she had seen men do. Instead he simply held her hand firmly in his grasp, the calluses on his hand pressing against her palm.

"He was a fool," said Jacob, motioning in the direction in which Unger had gone. "Please don't judge all of us by his actions."

Petra thought she could detect his heartbeat in the warm blood pumping through his hand. Foolish thought. She smelled the wood smoke on him, and the odor of horses. His buckskin clothing was dirty with ashes and soil, and there were big brown splotches that she was certain were from dried blood. She smelled the male scent of his unwashed body. It was not unpleasant.

"I do not think you are like him," Petra said. She extracted her hand. "This is my brother, Conrado."

"Hello," said Tamarron, and held out his hand.

Conrado Solis was slow in reacting to Jacob's overture. Jacob noted the grudging response and the weak, short shake. Mexican men held no liking for the gringo that came unasked into their land and lay with some of their women.

"Yes, I, too, thank you for helping Petra," Conrado said. "There easily could have been a fight."

And you probably would have died, thought Tamarron, measuring the young man.

"It's over," said Jacob.

"Yes, over for now. Come, Petra, let us go. We have much to do before we leave for the rancho."

Petra turned away with her brother, then slowed in the middle of the street and partially turned to look back. She showed only the unmarred side of her face, as she'd become accustomed to doing, and watched from the edge of her vision. Jacob Tamarron still stared after her. She smiled a short, quick smile at him, the first time she'd done that in a very long time to a man who wasn't a member of her family.

The American trapper did not return the smile. Unless, yes, she thought there was a slight lifting of his head and those gray-white eyes were opened more widely and quite visible.

Jacob closely observed the woman as she moved away, evaluating the strength of her body, the swell of her hips under the leather pants, the narrowness of her waist, and her straight back. When she turned and smiled, only the undamaged portion of her face was to him, and her true beauty showed.

He smiled beneath his beard. His heart was tapping high in his chest and his breath was blowing quick and shallow. The Solis woman could give a man fine children.

He spun around and, paying no attention to the group of trappers frankly eyeing him, grabbed up the reins of his ponies and headed off along the street.

Jacob entered the broad, main plaza of Santa Fe. On the north side lay the Palace of the Governors, together with the military headquarters, national jail, customhouse, and warehouse of the army garrison.

Some four hundred feet directly opposite across the plaza were dwellings and a church, smaller than La Parroquia and not yet finished. On the other sides were stores and additional residences. Many of the houses were quite large, obviously the homes of the town's wealthier families.

People strolled unhurriedly beneath the shedlike roofs

that extended out from every building. Others stood in groups talking in a neighborly way in the sunshine. A dozen children ran and played among the trees bordering the square. Their happy cries rose above all the other sounds.

In front of a gambling parlor advertising dice, faro, and monte, a young juggler was trying to draw a crowd with his amateurish tossing of four balls. Men came and went through the door of the building without giving him a second look. Near the southeast corner of the square in front of La Fonda, a ragged beggar called out to pass-ersby in a wheedling voice pleading for pennies.

The sound of a guitar skillfully played came from a cantina. Jacob had heard no music for months. He slowed and listened to the pleasant tune until it ended.

He entered the customhouse and had his furs counted and the number recorded. A second copy of the paper was drawn up by hand, stamped with the government seal, and given to him with the *guia*, a clearance to sell in Santa Fe.

Jacob paid the tariff and left. He moved around the plaza looking for the office of the fur buyer.

Randolph knew the quality of fur and was a tough bargainer. Tamarron dickered patiently with him in a low voice.

He extracted only one pelt at a time from the bale. This he placed on the countertop in front of the buyer. They discussed the softness, density, and length of the hair of each skin, and dickered until they agreed upon a price. Then Randolph made a tally on a sheet of paper, and Tamarron brought out the next pelt.

Jacob had learned years ago that the fur buyer must never see more than one pelt at a time. Numerous pelts meant low prices.

The last skin in the bale was sold, and Randolph reached for the tally sheet.

"Wait," said Tamarron. "I have a few more pelts."

"Then bring them in," directed Randolph, and laid down the paper and pencil.

Jacob went outside and returned with a second batch of pelts.

The sale went much faster because a standard price was evolving for skins of a particular quality and species. When the last one had been tallied, Randolph glanced at Tamarron.

"Is that the last of them?"

"Not quite," replied Tamarron. "There is one more bundle."

Randolph sat back in his chair and grinned. "Are you sure it's the last of them?"

The final dry skin was sold. The raw wolf pelts were sold for half price. Randolph made his computation. "The total is two thousand and fifteen dollars. Not bad for a winter's work."

Tamarron was pleased with the price, but the fur represented the work of two men not one. "I've made twice that much money in the beaver days."

"That was before I started buying fur," said Randolph. He brought out a heavy leather bag and began to count gold pieces out on the countertop.

CHAPTER 5

Jacob entered the big general store of Andrew Dexter. He stopped and breathed the scores of odors rushing to escape out the open door. He teased his nose with the high aroma of cinnamon, pepper, dried apples, peaches, raisins, and cheese. A smile of anticipation crossed his face. There were many kinds of foods he wanted to sample.

Nodding a greeting to the clerk at the front counter, Tamarron walked toward the back of the building. He passed down a long aisle flanked with shelving that reached to the ceiling and was crammed with a hundred things for sale. He took a dried peach half from a cloth bag full of them and began to chew on it.

Against the rear wall of the establishment, a huge iron vault squatted on a thick stone foundation. Nearby, Andrew Dexter sat behind a wooden desk. He saw Tamarron and, with a smile, got up and came forward.

"Good to see you again, Jacob," said the storekeeper, and held out his hand. "How long have you been in Santa Fe?"

"Hello, Andy," said Jacob, shaking the offered hand.

"I came in a couple of hours ago." Jacob liked the storekeeper. He held a choice location on the plaza and had a thriving business. The trappers swore by his honesty. Some trappers frugally saved part of their hard-earned fur money, and most of them left it with Dexter for safekeeping. The merchant was also a moneylender. He would, for a fee, manage the trappers' savings, lending it out at interest.

"Come and sit a spell," Dexter said, and motioned to a chair. He recalled the day four years earlier when Tamarron had deposited a thousand dollars with him. Each year thereafter, the trapper had brought additional money.

"What's happening, Andrew? Bring me up-to-date on the news. How's the banking business?"

"The interest rate is eight percent. I think soon I'll be able to raise it to nine. Santa Fe is growing slowly but steadily, and there's a demand for cash money."

"What about land values?" asked Jacob.

"Since the governor raised taxes on all property last year, the price of land has fallen some. Why do you ask?"

"This is my last year for trapping, and I'll be looking around for something to work at. Americans can't settle on land and claim it in Mexico like they can in the States, so I may look for a small ranch to buy."

Tamarron saw a doubtful expression pass over the merchant's countenance. "These are uncertain times to be buying land. Also there're at least four hundred thousand cattle and sheep grazing in the Rio Grande Valley right now. There's not enough of a market in Santa Fe for all these animals; and other markets for our wool and hides, either north in the States or south to Mexico, are so far away that transportation costs eat up nearly all the profit. Hard money is scarce, and most trading is by barter. The American traders coming down the Santa Fe Trail from Independence and you trappers are about the only source of gold. None comes from Mexico City, that's for certain."

"I was thinking about looking on the other side of the mountains on the Rio Pecos. I was through that country two years ago, and there were a few ranchos on big Spanish land grants. The grass looked good, tall, and thick."

"Those folks on the Pecos may have an advantage over the Rio Grande ranchos. They can take their hides and wool into Mexico or to Texas without paying Governor Armijo's tax. But even those ranchers are surviving mostly by bartering their products for supplies to operate their ranchos."

"The Mescalero Apache claim the land on both sides of the Rio Pecos. Have they caused any trouble lately?"

"Five men were caught and killed by Indians last fall. And bandits often make hit-and-run raids. But the Mexican families are a brave and hardy lot and are still holding on to most of their animals. Their haciendas are fortresses, but they need more fighting men to be really safe from attack."

"Some day that Rio Pecos Valley will be running a quarter million cows," Jacob said. He removed his gold from the pouch slung over his shoulder and stacked it on the table. "I'd like to put this two thousand dollars in your vault."

"Do you want it loaned out at interest?"

"No. In fact, I'd like to have all my money on the cash side of your ledger."

"I can do that. I'll shift your loans to some new money I've taken from other trappers during the last few days."

"Andy, I'd prefer gold. Do you have enough hard money to cover all I've got with you?"

Dexter pulled a large flat book from his desk and scanned down a series of entries. "You have seven thousand eight hundred dollars, plus two hundred and ninety in interest. I do have that much gold. It'll run me close for a few days, but I will lay your money in gold on the cash side of the vault. I'll start charging you my usual fee for holding it."

"That's fair," Tamarron said. "Keep it all handy. I

may want it on short notice." Jacob climbed to his feet. "Andy, I'm always pleased to do business with you, but now I've got to go. My horses have had rough treatment lately and need feed and a good stall to rest in."

Dexter watched Tamarron move with long, gliding strides along the aisle. The trapper was a strong fighter and a skilled hunter, but Dexter didn't think a ranch would hold him through even one rotation of the seasons.

Tamarron led his horses to a stable just off the square and ordered a gallon of grain for each, and all the hay they could eat. When the stable man began to feed the animals, Jacob left, carrying his firearms and duffel.

He headed for La Fonda, cutting across a block of drab adobe houses, the walls and the mica-lime white-wash stained and eròded by the rains and snows and winds of the winter. He passed animal yards, dry irrigation ditches, and vegetable gardens brown and winter-barren, and came out on the plaza near La Fonda.

The beggar was gone from in front of the hotel. The juggler had moved his act to the opposite side of the square. He still drew no attention from the men and women on the street.

Tamarron shoved aside the thick wooden door of La Fonda and entered. He always enjoyed staying in the comfort of the aged building. It had been constructed many years in the past and had seen the coming and going of Spanish and Mexican governors, Catholic priests, Indian chiefs, American traders of all sorts, and thousands of other travelers.

The lobby was high-ceilinged with thick wooden beams supporting the roof. The earthen floor was covered by *gerga*, a heavy, tightly woven cloth. A giant fireplace was full of crackling flames from burning pine logs.

Two Mexicans and a man who could have been an American sat before the fire in big chairs draped with Indian blankets. They glanced at Jacob as he passed, then went back to their discussion in rapid Spanish.

Jacob registered and received his key and directions to

his room. He ordered a hot tub of water to be made ready in the bath located at the back of the hotel. Carrying his belongings, he walked down a long, dim hallway full of the musty smell of old adobe.

The hotel room was larger than the whole cabin that Daniel and he had lived in. A wide bed, with a feather tick, clean cotton sheets, and wool blankets, occupied much of the space. There was a pile of wood near a fireplace in one corner of the room. A coal-oil lamp sat on a small table. One straight-backed chair completed the furnishings. The room was more than ample for Jacob.

He laid his rifle and pistol on the table and piled the remainder of his gear on the floor. There was a chill in the room, so Jacob lit a fire. He lay down on the bed. There would be time for a short nap while the bathwater was being heated.

"I want a tub filled to here with hot water," Jacob touched his chin as he spoke to the Mexican boy in the bathhouse. "Also have an extra bucket of water heating and ready when I call for it."

"Sí, señor. It will be done exactly as you wish," the boy said. "I will fill the tub now." He began to carry water and pour it into a tub in one of the cubicles of the bathhouse.

Jacob eased himself into the warm water of the deep tub. The liquid encased him to the very point he'd indicated to the Mexican. He sighed at the pleasurable feel of the water on his skin. He dipped his hand in a bowl of soft soap and began to lather himself.

When the liquid started to cool, he ordered the hot bucket of water and reheated the tub. What was five cents when a man felt so damn good?

The water lost its heat again, so he climbed out, dried himself, and donned his fresh set of buckskins. He tossed his dirty clothing to the attendant.

"Burn these," Jacob said.

*   *   *

The barber waited as the trapper inspected himself in the big mirror hanging on the wall. The shaggy-haired man seemed to be taking special pains to examine himself.

Jacob twisted his head from side to side, peering at the white in his beard. He untied his brown hair and extended a lock to look at it. Five months had passed since he'd last seen his reflection. The amount of additional gray surprised him. He would shorten his hair, but there would still be many streaks of gray left. The beard would certainly have to go.

He stepped nearer to the mirror. Every cold wind and all the burning sun he had ever encountered over the years were etched in lines on the brown skin of his face. Those years had melted away like snowflakes on the palm of his hand. He grinned ruefully. He was no longer a young man.

"Shave off the beard and cut half a foot off the hair," Jacob instructed the barber, and seated himself in the padded chair.

"I will give you a fine haircut," promised the barber. "You shall be very handsome. All the women will love you."

Tamarron relaxed as the barber made a soapy lather with a brush in a shaving cup. I only need one woman, Jacob thought. Just one good woman.

The boot maker was a lean, angular American. He placed his whole supply of seven pairs of boots before Jacob. "If one of these don't fit you, I can make you a pair to order in a day."

"Let me try them on," Tamarron said.

He found a pair that satisfied him, a tall boot made of soft leather with good solid heels.

Carrying the boots under one arm, Jacob walked past several stores and dwellings until he spied a tailor's shop. Soundlessly, on moccasined feet, he entered. The man working at the sewing table was unaware of his presence.

The tailor was a strong-looking man with a freckled face and big hands. But his fingers were nimble and accurate. Jacob watched him cut and snip to shape a piece of cloth into a sleeve. Then the tailor's needle flashed and winked as he swiftly sewed with precise stitches.

Jacob was not surprised that the tailor, just as the cobbler, was an American. An American also owned the only distillery in the town. The blacksmith, gunsmith, and harness maker were gringos. The Mexicans were good cattle and sheep men. They were excellent horsemen. But most of them seemed to have a lack of interest in certain types of business ventures.

"How about a suit?" Jacob said.

The man jerked, startled at the sound of a voice so close. Then he smiled and stood up.

"I'd be glad to make you some clothing," he said. "Cloth's over there." He pointed at nearly a score of bolts of fabric on a long table. A wide assortment of hats were on an adjoining display rack. "Do you want leather, cotton, or wool?"

"Let's take a look," Jacob said.

He examined the fabrics at length. Finally he identified what he wanted.

"Make me a suit of this gray wool. And then an extra pair of pants of the same material and a pair out of leather. I want two white cotton shirts and two of this heavier blue cotton."

"When do you want the clothing?" asked the tailor.

"The suit and one shirt by noon tomorrow. I've got something that I want to start right away."

"That's quite a short time for all the cutting and sewing that has to be done," said the man in surprise. "But by working part of the night and then starting early tomorrow, I can have the one outfit by noon. Let me take your measurements."

With a practiced hand the tailor took Jacob's dimensions and wrote them down. "That'll be ten dollars in advance, the balance when you pick up the clothing."

"First I need a hat," replied Jacob. He chose a broad-brimmed, felt one with a flat crown. "Hold this for me

until tomorrow." He extended a gold coin from his pouch
and paid the tailor.

The sun had fallen from the sky and lay smoldering on
the horizon when Tamarron came out onto the plaza.
Rays of sunlight slanted in at a low angle, striking the
walls of the plaza buildings, and the adobe glowed with a
soft orange radiance.

Even as Jacob watched, the sunlight weakened, and
shadows filled the plaza. The laughter of the children
faded away to nothing. The people left the darkening
streets, vanishing into the homes and cantinas.

Lights came to life within the buildings and shined
through small glass windowpanes, or the thin sheets of
crystal gypsum that served as glass in most instances.

Jacob stood in a splash of light that shined out from
one of the houses. Somehow, by being in the light, he
felt uncomfortable, as if he were spying on the people
that had created it. A heavy shutter swung shut with a
thump, and the light vanished.

Jacob and a few other men, mostly mountain men,
continued to wander the square in the twilight. Now and
then a mixture of voices of a man, a woman, and children, a family recounting the happenings of the day,
slipped out between the shutters. Jacob felt a pang of
loneliness.

Three bold walkers, street whores, brightly rouged,
brazenly strutted close and with teasing smiles spoke to
the strolling men. Two couples struck a bargain and went
off arm in arm. The last woman approached Tamarron,
but he shook his head in the negative and she turned
aside with a sour expression.

The dusk became darkness under the covered walk-
ways, and Tamarron at last decided to have his evening
meal. He halted and turned around, retracing his steps to
a restaurant he had passed earlier.

A large man that had been following Jacob in the
gloom stopped abruptly. Jacob watched the man peering
through the murk at him. After a moment the man began

to retreat, soundlessly walking backward. Then he spun
around and went off hastily.

Tamarron recognized Unger and cursed softly. The
man was not going to let the argument die. Men seeking
revenge were the most dangerous of all enemies. Jacob
touched the handle of his knife. Eventually he would
probably have to kill Unger.

Tamarron sat in the rear of the restaurant and ate his
meal of beef stew, bean soup, soft cheese, a stack of
blue-corn tortillas, and sweet custard. He ordered a cup
of coffee and a second sweet custard, then leaned back to
finish his meal leisurely.

He listened to the hum of conversation from the crowd
of diners. Two trappers in buckskin were eating near the
door. Three Americans in town clothes talked in low,
confidential voices and didn't seem to be thinking of the
food before them. Jacob heard the word *Texas* once, and
a little later the word *war*.

He wondered what special meaning the men's conversation might have. Texas had fought itself free from
Mexico ten years ago. It had finally become a state just
the past summer. Surely Mexico wouldn't try to retake
Texas from the United States.

The remaining tables held Mexican citizens talking in
pleasant tones. Jacob's mind shifted to that lingo. From a
nearby table he heard the people discussing the coming
of an early spring and the traces of green grass already
sprouting from the earth on the south-sloping hillsides
near the Rio Grande. These folk weren't thinking of war.

Tamarron rose and left to find Tim and Deek, and to
make good his promise to buy them drinks.

CHAPTER 6

Rio Pecos Valley, Mexican Territory, March 3, 1846

The band of six scalp hunters mounted on strong, long-legged mustangs, crossed the range of yellow sand hills, and halted behind the caliche bluff above the Rio Pecos. The men had been riding sixteen days since leaving Austin, Texas, pressing swiftly onward from morning's first light until the next darkness overran them. Three times they'd stopped and ambushed small Indian camps. They had taken thirty-three scalps.

Kirker swung his tall, wiry frame down from his mount. He stretched once, then shook himself like a wolf flinging off water. The kinks, bent into his muscles from riding fifty miles since daylight, fell away from his tough body. He looked at his riders.

The men stared back at him from lean, hard faces shaded beneath broad-brimmed hats. Each member of his gang wore two Colt cap-and-ball, five-shot revolvers. On their ponies they carried a pair of the latest model rifles, breech-loading .54-caliber weapons. All were expert gunmen. They were the finest bunch of fighters Kirker had ever assembled. He believed they could whip a war party of fifty Indians, Comanche or Apache.

"Connard, you care for the horses," Kirker said in a gravelly voice. He pointed a finger at the saddled horses, the three extra riding horses, and the two pack animals. "Keep them out of sight and quiet until the rifle work is done."

"Hell, Kirker, I want to get in on some of the shooting," Connard growled. "It should be some damn fine target practice from up here."

"You're a good rifle shot, but you're the worst of the lot of us. Somebody has to tend the animals. That's you. So enough said. Understand me? You'll get some pistol shooting."

"All right," Connard said, grumbling.

"Settle down and rest," Kirker said to the men. "Don't make noise. I'll check and see how things lay. Rauch, come with me."

The two men went quietly across the swale toward the caliche hill separating them from a view of the Rio Pecos. When the ground angled upward, they dropped down to their knees and crawled up to the crest of the ridge to peer over cautiously.

The two-mile-wide valley of the Rio Pecos spread itself before the men. The current of the river, lying some three hundred yards distant and a hundred feet lower in elevation, sped south in a yellow, muddy flood. With a wet, drumlike rumble, the rushing torrent of water poured around the tight bends and curves. On the outside of the turns, the full force of the straining current struck the side of the river channel, and the frothy waves cut and tore at the high banks. The stream had escaped the confinement of its banks in several places, and ran in yellow fingers among the boles of the giant cottonwood and walnut trees lining the channel.

"The snow in the mountains is melting fast," Kirker said. "The river's risen three feet since we saw it at dawn this morning. And it'll get worse too." He pointed down at the bend of the river that curved away from them. "There's the Indian camp we came to find."

Rauch had also spotted four tepees in an open stand of

large trees. The skin lodges were heavily stained with the soot of many fires. Up near the smoke holes they were nearly black. Winter storms had damaged the pyramidlike structures, and the patches that had been used to close the rents and tears showed like white scars.

"This time we got here before they left for their summer camp in the mountains," Rauch said.

Kirker scanned the encampment and did not reply. A group of squaws knelt around a buffalo hide stretched on the ground and worked on it with sharp flint scrapers. The women wouldn't live long enough to finish the hide.

Another woman was gathering wood downstream from the camp. She finished breaking some dead limbs into shorter lengths and loaded her arms with a heavy pile. As she passed a group of children romping and playing dangerously near the speeding floodwaters of the Pecos, she shouted out sharply to them. In laughing obedience the youngsters scurried back from the riverbank and, hollering at each other, ran off among the trees.

"The bucks aren't here, only squaws and kids," Rauch said.

"Most likely out hunting," Kirker said. He measured the sun, which lay half a hand-width above the Capitan Mountains sixty miles to the west. "It'll be dark in less than two hours, so the bucks will soon return. They won't leave the women alone, with the spring weather good and men traveling."

"Like us," agreed Rauch.

"We'll get into position for the ambush. Let's go."

Kirker and Rauch dropped down from the crown of the hill and returned to the other men. They all climbed erect and looked at Kirker, awaiting his orders.

"Only squaws and kids there now," said Kirker. "But that's okay, for the bucks will surely come. Check the loads in all of your guns. Be sure all the balls are tight on the powder in every chamber. I don't want any misfires. Bring both your rifles—the shooting will be fast, with no time to reload!"

The men inspected the charges in their long guns.

They slid ramrods down the barrels of the pistols to tamp the round lead balls down firmly, then closely scrutinized the caps.

While the men completed their preparations for the coming ambush, Kirker spoke to Connard. "Bring the riding horses up quick when the rifle shooting stops. Some of those Comanche may try to run for it. We'll need horses for sure to catch them. Until then, keep the horses out of gunshot. I don't want any hurt."

"Right," Connard said.

"Follow me," Kirker said to the other men. "Fan out to lay along the top of the ridge. Don't let yourself be seen from below."

The sun began to turn red as it floated lower to rest on the crown of the far-off Capitan Mountains. The yellow sand hills turned crimson, like waves on a pool of blood. The flooding Rio Pecos rose another half foot.

Kirker lay basking in the sun and did not stir. He was a patient man, and the outcome of the battle wasn't something to worry about. The Indians would be easy to kill. In a month he'd be in Chihuahua selling a sack of scalps to Governor Antonio Canales. The savage raids of the Apache and Comanche into the northern Mexican Province had so angered the governor that he'd placed a bounty of one hundred dollars on every Indian man, and fifty dollars on each Indian woman and child. The long-haired scalps proved their deaths. Kirker and his gang would make six, maybe seven, thousand dollars in only a few months. Kirker's cut would be one third.

The men had spent the winter in Austin, the capital of the new state of Texas. When the days had turned warm, he had gathered his band to ride. The white men journeyed swiftly, attacking the Comanche on the plains and along the Pecos. They would continue south and kill the Apache on the lower Rio Grande and in northern Mexico.

Kirker rolled onto his back and stretched. Events much more important than killing Indians were brewing. Throughout Texas there was heated talk of war to force a settlement of the western boundary between Mexico and Texas. Simon Caverhill, a Texas State senator, was the loudest proponent of the need to fight.

Caverhill had made several speeches in the Texas Senate, pressing for a vote of war against Mexico. Once he'd managed to speak before a joint session of senators and representatives. Always his proposal had been voted down.

After the last stormy defeat Caverhill sought out Kirker and had given him a secret mission. The senator gave the scalp hunter five hundred dollars to carry out the task.

Kirker touched his money belt, which contained the thick wad of U.S. currency. He hadn't told his men of Caverhill's payment, nor of the mission.

Kirker had led his men farther north than ever before, almost to the headwaters of the Rio Pecos. As they had traveled searching for Indians to kill, he'd located the Mexican ranchos and had stolen in close to examine the strength of their defenses. He'd made a rough count of the sheep, cattle, and horses. When he returned to Austin, there would be plenty to report to the senator.

Kirker turned to look at Rauch. The man was watching him from squinty eyes.

"Kirker, how did you come straight to this place after wandering hundreds of miles over the country?" Rauch asked. "It's been three years since we last saw this Indian camp."

Kirker knew Rauch's question was only a ruse to cover the real thoughts in his mind as he had secretly observed the gang leader. Rauch wanted him dead so he could become leader of the band. Kirker would not let that happen. He'd kill Rauch before they returned to Austin. In the meantime he needed Rauch's skill with guns.

Nevertheless Kirker thought about Rauch's query. For days, under thick winter storm clouds that had hidden the sun, he'd led the men across the flat, unmarked Llano Estacado. Then the band had roamed in a circuitous route over the Rio Pecos Valley. Yet unerringly, after six hundred miles, Kirker came to this one small caliche hill. Without fail he could return to every distant spot he had known during all the years of his life.

Once Kirker had tried to analyze the instincts that guided him. But as he cast about through his mind searching for the unique sense, he felt the skill slipping away. The desire to understand the gift—indeed, the mere quest for it—could mean its destruction. He'd immediately ceased his mental probing. It was enough to possess the knack.

Kirker turned away from his enemy and stared down into the valley. Six Indian men on horseback were emerging from behind a small hill a quarter of a mile up the river.

Kirker called out quickly to his men. "Get down and keep low. The Indian bucks are coming. Like always, when they get in range, we'll kill all of them with our rifles. Then, on horseback, we'll ride down the women and kids."

"Some of the young squaws might be pretty," said Rauch. "It'd be a damn shameful waste to kill them."

"I think so, too, Kirker," chimed in Borkan, who lay near Rauch. He rolled back from the top of the hill and sat up. "What do you two think?" he asked Flaccus and Wiestling.

The two bandits grunted in agreement. All the men watched Kirker expectantly.

"All right. Save a couple of the prettiest. But don't let that get in the way of catching every one of them and their kids. Now, stand ready with your rifles."

The Indians rode into a grove of cottonwoods and out of sight. They reappeared a few seconds later, much closer. Kirker saw their long war lances tied on the sides of their mounts and sticking up at steep angles in the air. Two braves had bows and arrows, and three held rifles across the saddles in front of them.

"They've killed some buffalo," Rauch whispered. "I can see the big haunches tied over the backs of those two packhorses."

"Plenty of buffalo back to the east," Borkan said.

"No talk," snapped Kirker. "Listen for my word to begin shooting."

One of the women spotted the approaching horsemen. She shouted out a happy greeting. The remaining women and children spun around to see what she saw. Then the whole group started to call, the children running forward in young, loose-legged strides.

The riders stopped in the center of the cluster of tepees. Five slid from the backs of their cayuses. The last man started to dismount, then caught himself, and his eyes jumped to the rim of the caliche hill. He ignored one of the women speaking to him and stared hard, directly at Kirker's hiding place. His rifle began to lift.

Kirker saw the gun moving and the man's chest swelling with a large draft of air, like a man who is preparing to shout a mighty blast.

"The smart son of a bitch knows we're here," Kirker cursed. "I'll kill him. You fellows shoot the others. Shoot!"

Kirker hefted the rifle to his shoulder. At a range of slightly more than two hundred yards, putting a bullet into the center of the man's chest wouldn't be a difficult feat. Kirker fired.

The Indian dodged to the side with amazing swiftness. Kirker knew the man had moved before he could have heard the gunshot. He must have seen the gunpowder smoke spouting from the rifle barrel, and as difficult as that was to believe, reacted to that sign of danger before the bullet could reach him.

But even as quickly as the Indian had moved, he was not swift enough to entirely escape the ball of lead hurtling at him. Kirker saw the bullet strike the Indian, spinning him violently to the side. The shot meant for the heart had hit the arm up high near the shoulder. The man caught his fall and pulled himself erect, instantly flinging himself forward along the neck of his cayuse. He almost vanished from view behind the body of his mount, only an arm showing over the neck of the animal, and a heel over its back.

The man was yelling orders at the women and children. They began to run in frantic haste, scattering up and down the riverside.

Beside Kirker, the snarling crack of his men's heavily charged rifles was deafening. In the Indian camp two braves were hit with deadly blows and fell to the ground. Another was knocked tumbling. He leapt up immediately and dashed for a clump of trees. A bullet broke his spine, and he went down in a tangle of legs and arms.

The man Kirker had shot had given a command to his pony, and the animal sprang into a full run down the riverbank. Kirker grabbed up his second rifle, caught the neck of the pony in the sights, and tracked the target. The .54-caliber slug would easily penetrate the neck of the animal and kill the brave.

The rifle cracked. The top part of the cayuse's neck exploded in a puff of hair and flesh.

The fatally wounded beast swerved to the side, away from the horrible blow of the bullet. It continued its wild run. In its pain the dying horse didn't see the riverbank.

The cayuse and the clinging rider plunged over the brink and vanished into the mad, swirling flow of the rushing river. Neither man nor animal reappeared on the foaming surface. The yellow torrent poured onward, hiding the things it had swallowed.

"Goddamn," Kirker cursed. "I just lost a hundred dollars." He swung his attention back to the Indian camp. Eight bodies lay in crumpled mounds on the ground. Both ways along the river, women and children were running in frenzied flight.

"Mount up," Kirker shouted.

The men ran to meet Connard who, mounted, was spurring his horse up the slope and dragging the saddled horses after him. All the men jerked themselves astride. They charged down from the caliche hill and onto the river bottom.

As Kirker gouged his horse ahead, an old woman jumped up from some bushes. He killed her with a shot from his pistol. A boy of seven or eight tore off at an angle, bounded over the trunk of a fallen tree, and then straightened out in a flat-out, dead-steaking run. The little brown bastard sure could travel, thought Kirker.

Lashing his horse, Kirker drew close to the boy. He slashed down with the heavy iron barrel of his revolver, clubbing the child to the earth. Kirker dragged his mount to a halt, whirled it around, and ran it back to the small, still body of the boy.

The firing dwindled and stopped as Kirker stepped from his mount. He deftly cut a circle around the top of the boy's head and ripped away a large segment of scalp and hair.

He halted at two other bodies as he returned to the camp, each time cutting away the victim's scalp.

Connard, carrying a handful of bloody scalps, came to meet Kirker. "Mighty fine target practice," he said with a laugh.

"Stretch and dry these with those you have," directed Kirker, and handed Connard the scalps he carried. "Did anyone get away that you saw?"

"No," Connard said, separating the scalps to see how many had been given to him. "That makes twenty of them," Connard added in a pleased tone. "That's every Indian we saw, counting the two girls Rauch and Wiestling caught."

"Good," Kirker replied. He walked to the men gathered around the two frightened girls huddled on the ground near the river.

"Now, ain't they pretty?" Rauch said. He reached down, clamped a brutal hold on the hair of the two young women, and roughly raised their faces so the men could see them.

"Yes," agreed Kirker, "but there had better not be any fighting over them or I'll take a hand to stop it," he warned. "Rauch, you asked to save the women, so now you see that their scalps are lifted and drying right along side all the others come morning."

Kirker took the prettiest girl by the shoulder, raised her to her feet, and led her into one of the lodges. He slapped her into obedience and took her on a pile of furs.

When he had finished, he brought her back outside and flung her at Rauch.

The bandit chief almost laughed when he saw the hate in Rauch's eyes. I am the leader of these men, thought Kirker. I will always have first choice of horses and women.

Taking an arm load of furs from the lodge, he climbed up to the top of the caliche hill. He sat listening to the voices of his men, muted in the distance, and watched the last trace of sunlight die away to nothing. He lay down on the soft furs and drifted off to sleep. It had been a very profitable day.

CHAPTER 7

Tamarron drank his first beer with Tim and Deek in the big cantina on the edge of the plaza. The brew had a delicious, tangy flavor and was icy cold from being immersed in a tub of snow brought down from the mountain above town. He took another long pull from his mug and let the savory liquid trickle delightfully down his throat.

"The first one is always the best," Tim said, and wiped his lips with the back of his hand. "But we may not be drinking many more beers in Santa Fe."

Tim paused, reflecting within himself, and then continued to speak in a matter-of-fact tone. "There'll soon be a war with Mexico."

"I heard some fellows talking about war earlier today," Jacob said. "But why do you say it?"

"I'll tell you why I believe so. Late last summer I was in Austin for a couple of months. Well, the talk was everywhere that Governor Pinckney Henderson wants to finally fix all the boundaries of Texas. They're already established on the north, east, and south. But the Texans claim a hell of a lot of land to the west that is still in the

control of Mexico. The governor says the west border of
Texas is all the way over here to the Rio Grande. Santa
Fe is in Texas, didn't you know that? Now, that could be
funny, except the man's serious. If Mexico doesn't start a
war to take back Texas, then Texas will start one to try
to take New Mexico," Tim said, his voice rising gradually
as he spoke.

Deek poked him sharply in the ribs. "Quiet down,
Tim. There's a lot of tough Mexicans in here. And be-
sides, Armijo might think we're plotting a revolution.
He's a mean son of a bitch, and would have us arrested
and shot."

Tamarron glanced around the cantina. A group of
seven American trappers were drinking and talking noisily
at a table near the wall. Scattered around were tables of
Mexicans, vaqueros, and townspeople, all in full-mouthed
debate on various topics. The quietest bunch of men
were the card players at the monte tables in the rear. No
one could have heard Tim's remarks above the loud
jumble of all the voices. However, all gringos had to be
careful, for Armijo was not a trusting man and had spies
in many places.

The door of the cantina was shoved open, and a small,
mud-splattered man wearing the blue-and-red uniform of
the Mexican Cavalry came inside. He staggered with
weariness and clutched the leather pouch hanging on his
shoulder as he made a course toward the bar. He ordered a beer and drank half of it in one swig.

Tamarron saw the man shiver as the strong, cold bev-
erage hit his gullet. He leaned against the bar for a
moment. Then he straightened and, with a second greedy
swallow, finished the beer.

The small man looked at the keg of beer behind the
bar in a hungry, wistful manner. He sighed and turned
away, making his way across the cantina and out the
door.

Tamarron noted the strained, exhausted face of the
man as he passed and went outside. "He's ridden far and
fast," he said to his two comrades. "All the roads are

closed to the north because of deep snow. Even the trail
east to Las Vegas isn't open yet. He could have only
come from the south."

"The nearest Mexican army garrisons are at Matamoros and Saltillo," Tim said. "I'm betting he came from
one of them."

"He has dispatches for the governor," Jacob said. "I'm
going to see if I can find out what the news might be."

"Me, too," Tim said.

Tamarron, with Tim and Deek following close at his
back, quickly left the cantina. They stopped in the darkness by the wall of the building.

In the center of the street, the dispatch rider was
leading a mud-covered horse. The worn-out animal did
not want to move, and the man cursed it and jerked the
reins cruelly.

"He's ruined that pony," Deek said. "I'm sure there
are other crippled horses along his trail. Now, a man
doesn't do that unless there's some damn important message that has to be carried fast."

"Quiet," Jacob said. "The moon is bright, and if all
three of us follow, we'll be seen. You two stay here."

"All right," said Tim. "We'll go back and have some
more brew. But you come back and tell us what you
see."

The dispatch rider went straight across the plaza to the
palace. Jacob stealthily trailed him, holding far to the
rear in the darkness.

The armed sentry that was stationed in front of the
Governor's residence intercepted the messenger, and they
talked together in low voices. They went hurriedly to the
front entry and knocked on the door.

Jacob, standing among the trees on the edge of the
plaza, caught a brief glimpse of the broad figure of Governor Armijo in the lit doorway. Armijo took the dispatch pouch and dismissed the rider and guard.

The rider stumbled tiredly off with his horse toward
the army stables. The sentry returned to his post on the
walkway leading out to the plaza.

The door of the Governor's residence was jerked open. "Private, tell Captain Archuleta to report to me at once," the governor shouted out.

"Yes, sir," the guard called back, and left at a trot through the night shadows in the direction of the officers' quarters.

A moment later Jacob saw the tall figure of Captain Archuleta, commander of the Mexican Army garrison at Santa Fe, striding swiftly along the border of the square. The captain was admitted by the governor, and the door closed.

An hour passed before the captain left. He went directly to the army barracks on the opposite side of the officers' quarters. Five minutes later a second soldier with a musket joined the first guard on duty at the Governor's residence.

Jacob stole away. Threatening news had reached the governor, news that required the doubling of his personal guards. That meant a major Indian uprising, or worse, war with the United States.

Tamarron methodically fitted the golden coins into the several pockets of his wide money belt. Andrew Dexter observed him quietly, controlling his curiosity as to why the mountain man had come at the first opening of the store and asked that his money be taken from the vault.

Jacob fastened the heavy belt, weighing nearly twenty pounds, around his waist and let the buckskin blouse fall down over it. In dangerous times one had to protect one's wealth, he thought.

He spoke to Dexter. "Last night an army rider brought a message to Governor Armijo. Captain Archuleta was called, and the two men talked for a long time. The guard on the governor is now two armed sentries."

Dexter's attention focused on Tamarron. "How do you know all this?"

"I saw the rider come in on a horse that'd been ridden nearly to death. Before the man delivered the message, he stopped off and had a beer in one of the cantinas. I followed him when he left. He went to the governor's home in the palace."

"So you spied on the governor?"

"I surely did," Jacob said with a wry grin. "I've been out of touch with what's going on for months. I want to fix that situation fast."

Dexter looked through the open door and out over the plaza. The palace, the quarters of the army garrison, and the prison could be seen plainly.

"So you came to get your gold in case Mexico is at war with the United States, eh, Jacob? Well, that's not such a bad plan. If war does come, the governor will surely confiscate all the possessions of the Americans in Santa Fe. That would include the money you trappers have deposited with me."

Dexter swung his view to Tamarron. "However, I don't think the governor will take my personal goods. I'm a Mexican citizen and married to a Mexican woman, the daughter of an important family in Santa Fe. But Armijo will spy on me, so I'll have to be careful in my actions. Thanks for telling me about the dispatch."

Jacob had been carefully watching the American trader. Dexter hadn't mentioned Indians as a possible source of any trouble but rather had spoken only of the possibility of war with the States. "Dexter, you knew of the dispatch before I told you," Jacob said.

The businessman did not respond to Jacob's claim; instead he thoughtfully rubbed his chin and stared with a troubled face out over the plaza.

"Tell me what you know," Jacob said, pressing Dexter.

"You were willing to share your news with me, so I can do no less. Already several Mexicans and Americans are aware of the contents of that dispatch pouch. Soon the whole town will know. The messenger brought information that General Zachary Taylor has three thousand American soldiers in winter camp at Corpus Christi. He's been ordered to march the whole army, cavalry, artillery, and infantry to the Rio Grande opposite Matamoros."

"Mexico claims all that land between Corpus Christi and the Rio Grande," Tamarron said.

"So does Texas, and now it's one of the States of the Union. Therefore the United States must take a stand. Apparently they've decided to back the Texas claim to the region. I strongly believe President Polk wants more than just that area along the Rio Grande. He's land-hungry and is after all of New Mexico and California. There will be a war because Mexico can't allow an American army to remain there.

"Santa Fe is Mexico's northernmost city. It'll surely come under attack if war begins. A large American force could be coming down the Santa Fe Trail right now."

"What do you plan to do?" asked Jacob.

"This is my home," Dexter replied. "All I possess is locked up in this store, and the money I have is loaned out. If there is a war, I'll see it through right here in Santa Fe."

"Who do you think would win the war?"

"The Mexican soldiers here number about two hundred. Even with the three to four thousand volunteers Armijo could muster up from the region, they could never hold New Mexico against a determined American army. What are your plans?"

"For now I'm going to remain here. I want to see what the next few days brings. And, anyway, I can be gone in ten minutes after I make up my mind to leave. If I don't see you again, best of luck to you."

Tamarron went directly to the livery and saddled his horse. He rode east into the hills. He did not return for better than two hours.

Petra danced with her father in the large ballroom of the Palace of the Governors. The musicians, two violinists, two guitarists, and a flutist, played a lively tune for the forty or more dancing couples. The women, in long, full gowns of silk or satin decorated with ribbons and bows, swung elegantly on the arms of their partners. She thought the men in their heeled boots and embroidered, tight-fitting trousers and jackets were splendid and courtly.

Petra smiled at her father. He was an excellent dancer, always knowing exactly the next movement, always in perfect rhythm to the music. He danced with her twice.

Conrado came to her and whirled her about the floor in a gay dance to a spritely piece of music. He knew how much Petra enjoyed the music and dancing. She loved him for his kindness. Then the music ended and he was gone. A few moments later, with a new melody filling the ballroom, Conrado was spinning his pretty, laughing wife through a lively series of dance steps.

An elderly friend of Petra's father danced with her. She knew the man did so in politeness to the Solis family. Still, it was a kind gesture and she had accepted the invitation to dance.

The musical instruments finished their lovely melody and the man left Petra. She took her cape and went outside to the lantern-lit walkway leading to the plaza. She breathed deeply of the crisp March air and brushed the hair from her warm brow. The *baile* was over for her. She would leave the Palace of the Governors and return home, to sit in the seclusion of the patio and listen to the distant music late into the night.

Ten lanterns hung from the rafters to illuminate the fandango in the big cantina on the plaza. The cantina floor was strewn with clean straw to keep down the dust and to smooth and enhance the spin and whirl of the dancers' feet. Jacob swung a dusky-skinned woman in a fast, floor-stomping dance that heated his blood. A throng of other dancers swirled and promenaded with him around the dance floor.

A wizened little Mexican played a fiddle with a swift, bobbing saw of his bow. A handsome man with a face showing intense concentration skillfully played a guitar. A little Indian drum with a mellow, pleasant tone was being thumped in perfect rhythm by a fat man with a never-ending smile.

The tables of the cantina had been moved back against the wall to provide room for the dance. Spectators and couples waiting for space on the floor stood jammed in the corners and doorways. Men waiting to buy drinks for their women and themselves crowded two deep at the bar.

The tune ended. The fast step of the dancers came to a halt. The wide, happy smiles of the dancers dimmed a little as the intoxication of the music faded.

The woman with Jacob rolled her eyes conquettishly at him, and her teeth flashed white in a face powdered pale lavender. She pressed willingly against him.

A few more dances and a drink or two and she would be Jacob's for the taking. He winked at the wench, pulled her to him, and kissed her on the cheek. He smelled the pleasant aroma of her scented powder.

Tamarron backed away a step and wiped the moisture on his forehead. The wool suit and the dancing had made him hot.

The woman removed a corn husk from a small pouch fastened to her waist. Into the husk she poured finely ground tobacco. With a deft twist of her fingers she rolled wrapper and tobacco into a *seegarito*. Laughing, she leaned over and placed the end of the *seegarito* against the glowing end of a man's cigar. She puffed the tobacco into fire and inhaled a deep breath of the smoke. She smiled prettily at the man in thanks for the light.

The woman's action sent a tinge of distaste through Jacob. He was wasting his time with such a woman. He turned away and wound a path toward the door. Behind him the woman called out, but he did not look back or slow.

Tamarron walked out into the darkness. Behind him, the music began again. He moved farther away in the deep murk that lay thick on the plaza.

The faint strains of music came drifting across from the opposite side of the plaza. The governor was holding the spring *baile*, the last party before the rich caballeros and their families left Santa Fe to return to their distant ranchos located along the Rio Grande and across the mountains in the far-flung valley of the Rio Pecos.

Tamarron's head lifted. Would the brave woman with the knife be there? She would fit into that class of people, for she'd been well dressed and obviously educated. He moved in the direction of the distant music.

A woman came from the Palace of the Governors as Jacob drew close. Her yellow dress, wide-skirted and billowing with her step, shone dark gold in the glow of the lanterns lighting the walkway. Her long black hair, loosely pulled back, hung down her back in a flowing stream of midnight. She was the very woman he had hoped to see.

Jacob hastened forward, wanting to reach her before she left the light. To approach her in the dark might frighten her. Then he grinned; she did not frighten easily.

Petra stopped quickly as a man came hurrying out of the night and halted in front of her.

He was dressed in a gray suit and was bareheaded. He smiled at her. His face appeared somehow strange in the lantern light. Then she realized it was the color of his skin that made his appearance odd. His forehead and the skin around his eyes were dark and weathered, while his cheeks, chin, and neck were very white. That complexion would result from a man removing a beard after many years. He was almost handsome.

The man came closer, and the flames of the lanterns shined fully into his eyes. Petra saw the gray-white eyes of the trapper who had come to her aid when she'd been insulted in the street. He stopped barely an arm's length away.

Petra felt a sudden flush warm her body. He had come to find her. She knew it with certainty. By habit, her hand rose to hide the scar on her face. Even though she deliberately had shown her mutilated cheek before, now, for some unexplainable reason, she felt a great desire to present only the most perfect view possible to him.

Jacob reached out quickly and caught her hand. He

pulled it gently down. The fiber of her beauty was not marred by the scar.

"You never have to do that for me," Jacob said.

Petra remained perfectly still, the man called Jacob Tamarron continuing to hold her hand and staring at her, not saying a word.

Never had a man touched her in that fashion and with such a look in his eyes. His masculinity delighted and frightened her.

"Would you dance with me?" asked Jacob.

There was a tremulous, joyous light in Petra's face as she glanced around. "Yes, but it is impossible to dance here," she said.

"I didn't mean out here, but in there." Jacob gestured at the ballroom. "I want to hear the music plainly."

Petra hesitated. What would her mother and father think of her dancing with an unknown man, a gringo? And the other women, how they would shake their heads and talk behind their fans!

"Do you really want to?" she asked.

"Certainly."

"Then we shall." Petra was no longer a girl who had to have a chaperon and ask permission to speak to a man. She led the way back along the walk and in through the door.

She looked around and saw her parents talking at Governor Armijo's table. She would introduce Jacob before the music began.

Jacob followed closely behind Petra. The room was large and almost square. The earthen floor was covered with a tightly woven wool carpet. The doors and part of the walls were paneled in buffalo hides painted to resemble wood. Small tables and many straight-backed chairs were spaced along one end of the room. To the rear of that was a table full of bottles of wine and brandy from Pecos, and whiskey from Taos. Some of the bottles of wine were chilling in a wooden tub of ice.

The clothing of the many guests appeared expensive and in nearly all cases was of bright colors. Like the women at the fandango in the cantinas, these women painted their faces with powder of Mexican white lead, turning their skin an ashen violet, in which their eyes were dark caves of emotion. Only Petra wore none. All the women were bedecked in jewelry of some sort. Many had several large pieces on.

Petra and Jacob had almost crossed the floor when the violinist made a sweep with his bow across the strings of his instrument and a loud note sounded to call the dancers to the floor. Immediately all three musicians joined into the tune.

Jacob caught Petra by the arm and turned her to him. The music was a waltz, and he swung her into position.

Petra glanced over her shoulder at her parents. They had seen her with Jacob. Her father was pulling at his beard, and her mother's face was glacial and disapproving. She smiled at their bleak countenances and looked away. She began to move to the man's lead, picking up the tempo of the music, her step in synchrony with the beat of the melody.

By the time they had half circled the dance floor, Jacob and Petra were caught up in the music and the nearness of the other. He felt her soft breath, light as the fluff of milkweed on his cheek. He smelled her sweet women's perfume. She smiled at him, and the beauty of her smile caused him to smile happily in return.

CHAPTER 8

The musicians played many tunes, barely halting one before starting another. The last was the melody for the *cuna*, the dance of the cradle. Jacob pulled Petra in close, and they circled each others' waists with their arms, making the top of the cradle. They began to swing around and around, leaning back to form the top of the cradle, their lower bodies moving inward to close the bottom.

The dance ended. The musicians laid down their instruments and went to have a cold drink.

"Come with me," Petra said. "You must meet my parents." Her father had been watching his daughter and the American. He stood up as Petra and Jacob came close.

"Father, this is Jacob Tamarron. He assisted me when a man insulted me on the street. Mr. Tamarron, my father, Emmanuel Solis."

"Señor Solis," Jacob said, and offered his hand.

"Señor Tamarron, I wish to thank you for aiding my daughter. That was most kind of you. May I introduce my wife, Señora Solis."

"Señora," Jacob said, and bowed to the woman.

"Hello, Señor Tamarron. I understand you are a trapper, one of the men of the mountains." Her tone was cold.

"I have been in the past," replied Jacob. "I have also ranched, been a guide and a contract scout, as well as other things."

Manuel Armijo, dressed in a dark blue uniform with gold lace running down the outside of his trousers and a Mexican general's shoulder straps, left the adjoining table and came toward the Solis family. The governor carefully scrutinized the gringo. He thought he knew all the American businessmen in Santa Fe. But he had never seen this man before. Petra noted Armijo's approach and turned to greet him. "Good evening, Governor Armijo. May I introduce Jacob Tamarron. He is a friend of mine."

The governor extended his hand. "I am pleased to meet you, Señor Tamarron. Are you a visitor to our town, or have you come to trade?"

"At the moment I am a visitor," Jacob said.

"Señor Tamarron is a trapper," Señora Solis said.

Jacob saw the governor stiffen, and his face took on a look of reproach, as if he thought he had been tricked somehow. Jacob's smile broadened. Armijo did not think highly of American trappers.

Armijo pivoted away with barely a nod to Solis, ignoring Jacob entirely.

"Jacob, let us have some wine," said Petra, attempting to draw Tamarron's attention from the governor's affront. She motioned at the bottles cooling in the wooden tank of ice.

"I am thirsty," agreed Jacob. He bowed to Señora Solis and said good evening to Emmanuel Solis. He took Petra by the arm and they crossed the room to the wine table.

Petra and Jacob danced to every tune of the musicians. They especially like *la raspa*, with the heel thumping and laughing fast walk. At times Petra's happiness filled her eyes with moisture, creating a mystical, unreal haze to everything upon which she looked.

The night grew old. The crowd of dancers and onlookers thinned. Finally the musicians became weary and packed away their instruments.

Jacob walked Petra home through the cool March night. Without hesitation she graciously agreed to go riding with him the following morning. He watched her enter the large town house of the Solis family, and then he went off toward La Fonda.

Tamarron reflected upon the emotion so strong within him. He had known women for an hour, for a week, and a few times for all the cold months of a winter. He had especially enjoyed the women of the northern Crow Tribe. Then he had traveled south where the beaver pelts were of a lighter color and thus more valuable. There he had known Mexican women and the beautiful, tattooed Mojave girls along the Gila. Always he had thought of women as one of nature's more delightful afterthoughts. Now, tonight, he knew that the search for a good woman to take as a wife and give him strong children was the primary goal of a man's life.

Petra remained on the patio and listened as Jacob's footsteps faded away to silence. Then she listened to the stars murmuring their song to her. She smiled and hummed the star song back to them.

Tamarron arrived early at the Solis hacienda, for he was anxious to see the woman again. Earlier still, Petra had risen and her horse stood saddled and tied near the front entrance of the house. She came immediately from the patio and joined Jacob.

Petra's eyes touched Jacob for a fleeting moment, and then both stepped to their horses and mounted. Jacob's face had been unsmiling, as if momentous decisions were being considered. But his gray-white eyes had been gentle when they had rested on Petra.

He led them from the mist-filled valley of the Santa Fe

River and east toward Atalaya Mountain. No conversation passed between them. Jacob liked the fact that she didn't try to talk with him. No words were needed.

The horses huffed and drew deep drafts of air as they scrambled upward along ancient trails carved into the steep flank of Atalaya by deer and mountain sheep over thousands of years. Now and then a rock was loosened by the horses' hooves and went tumbling noisily down the slope.

Jacob halted in a forest of piñon high up near the snow line. He and Petra dismounted, moved close together, and stared to the west. Below them, the town was a string of miniature buildings along the river. The few whitewashed structures shone like pearls among the plain, earth-brown adobe homes.

Directly across the broad valley of the Rio Grande, the shadowy form of the great *caldera* on top of Jemez Mountain could be seen. In some long-ago, forgotten time a stupendous volcanic explosion had blown away the top of the mountain, leaving behind a gigantic sixteen-mile-wide crater. As Petra and Jacob watched, the morning sun, climbing its fiery arc, crested the backbone of the Sangre de Cristo Mountains behind them. The flaming rays struck fully upon Jemez Mountain and the snowy peak began to glow with brilliant incandescence.

As the new, bright light reflected back upon the dark side of Atalaya, Jacob turned and went to a large slab of rock lying neatly buried in pine needles. He lifted it aside with a mighty heave. From a cavity in the ground he took up a bulky money belt and a leather pouch of approximately equal weight.

He came to Petra and stopped in front of her. He held out both hands, one containing the money belt and the other the pouch.

"Petra Solis, I am Jacob Tamarron. I have gold coin from the many furs I have trapped, and nuggets that I found high on the mountains. All together they are worth eighteen thousand dollars. I own four horses and some guns. I'll give all this to you if you will become my wife."

Jacob saw the woman's eyes widen to broad circles. A blush slipped across her cheeks. A pulse began to beat in her throat like a tiny, trapped animal.

At that moment he was almost overwhelmed with the desire to drop the gold, take Petra in his arms, and hug her until she cried out. But instead he remained with his hands outstretched, holding the cold metal.

Petra realized the man had offered her everything he owned. The gold meant nothing to her. But there was clear yearning for her in his eyes. And that meant everything. What more could a woman ask? She felt her own desires welling up, warm and pleasant.

"You do not know me," Petra said. "We met only two days ago. A man and woman should become well acquainted before marriage is considered."

Jacob's eyes sharpened. Then they became hooded, hiding his feelings. He lowered the gold to his sides. He had made a foolish move. "I misjudged the situation. I thought our rightness for each other was as obvious to you as it was to me."

Petra heard the sadness in Jacob's voice. He had interpreted her words as a rejection of his proposal. This was no time to play the coy female role. Jacob was a man worthy of a straightforward, honest answer.

"Jacob, I, too, feel we are correct for each other, even though our lives have been so different. I will speak to my father and mother."

"Do you need their approval?"

"No. But I want their good wishes."

"Does that mean you will be my wife?"

"Yes. I want to be your wife very much." The directness of her reply shocked Petra. But how else could she respond to this man who had stirred her so much?

Jacob lifted his head and shouted out happily. The joyous cry sped across the mountainside. In places it was caught against steeply faced rock outcrops and echoed back to him. He heard the deep emotion in his voice. But never would he be ashamed at the depth of his feelings for this woman. He dropped the gold and encircled Petra tightly in his arms.

"He is not a man, but the mere shadow of a man." Emmanuel Solis's voice was heated. "He would not make a proper husband for you, Petra." He strode angrily across the *sala*, the large main room of the house, then came back to stand in front of his daughter.

"These American trappers come out of the deep mountains in the spring and disappear back into them in the fall. They're like wisps of smoke, gone in an instant. This Jacob Tamarron is no different from any of the others."

"Father, he *is* different," Petra cried. "And he has asked me to be his wife. I have agreed."

"You have rejected proposals from other men, men of our own kind. Do the same with this American."

"Those other men didn't want me for myself. Vincente Jurado was an old man who wished a young wife to nurse him. Anastacio Melgares desired to marry me so he would one day own part of Rancho El Vado. Jacob wants me. Do you understand, Father? He wants me as a true wife."

"How do you know he is not like Anastacio? Perhaps Rancho El Vado is his goal."

"He doesn't even know that I own part of the family land. He offered me eighteen thousand dollars in gold. With that much money he could buy land for a very large rancho of his own. Even with all our land we have less than four thousand pesos to spend."

"In truth, gold and silver are hard to acquire." Solis pulled at his beard and examined the determined face of his daughter. She stared defiantly back, and he knew that nothing he could say would change her mind.

She was the most resolute woman he had ever known. He had watched that resolve grow in Petra as she came to the realization that her lack of prettiness would prevent her from ever having a proper proposal of marriage. He remembered the very day when, while still in her youth and after her injury, Petra had appeared at the stables dressed as a vaquero. From that time so many years in the past, she had worked like any common rider herding cattle and sheep, branding and shearing. No snowstorm or burning sun had ever prevented her from being at his or Conrado's side in the meanest of work. In the evening, while the men rested, she still worked in the house doing women's chores.

Conrado had taken a wife and asked for land of his own. Solis agreed to the request. However, he also knew Petra had earned an equal share. So he had deeded son and daughter each a quarter interest in Rancho El Vado.

"Father, Jacob is said to be a strong fighting man and would make the rancho much safer for all the families."

"That is true. I believe he is a brave man and knows the ways of the Indians. There is something else. The Americans have been crowding west across the continent ever since they stepped foot upon the Atlantic Coast. Now they have taken Texas from us. I think the Americans will one day make war on us here in New Mexico. Our president in Mexico City doesn't see the danger clearly enough to send sufficient soldiers to defend us. And we certainly cannot defend ourselves. We would lose any conflict with the United States, and victors have the terrible custom of taking what they want from the defeated. An American in the family might stop some gringo from taking Rancho El Vado from us."

"Then I have your blessing to marry Jacob?"

"Yes, Daughter. I do wish you happiness. However, you must wait a proper period of time before the marriage. We can arrange it for next fall when we return to Santa Fe."

"No, Father! No! No! I have already waited far too long. It's been more than twenty years since I was old enough to wed. I will not delay. The notices to our family and friends must be sent immediately, and all arrangements completed within a few days. On Sunday I shall be married. Then Jacob and I shall go to the Rio Pecos as man and wife."

"So quick. So very quick. But I understand, Petra. It

shall be as you say. Your mother will be very disappointed with your selection of a husband, and also with the early date for the wedding."

Petra took her father by the arm. "Together we can convince her that Jacob is a fine man and would only add strength to the family."

Jacob knelt beside Petra in front of the priest and listened to the words of the matrimonial rites. The priest's voice was almost a monotone as he spoke the familiar words. However, Jacob would endure the ceremony, as well as the nuptial mass and the many scores of people crowding the chapel of La Parroquia, for Petra wanted the blessing of the church. Though he felt no need for religion or chapel, he thought it a good thing that Petra did.

Her shoulder brushed his as she moved slightly. At the soft contact with her, Jacob's blood began to rush with a joyous strum through his veins. A low, happy chuckle escaped him.

Petra turned her veiled face to look at him. He winked roguishly at her. Through the white lace that partially obscured her face he saw her lips curve up in a smile of promise. Even after she had turned back to the priest, Jacob could still see the crinkle of a smile in her cheeks.

The Rio Pecos hurled its cold, snow-melt water down from the high reaches of the Sangre de Cristo Mountains. Like a giant beast chained in the bottom of the deep gorge, the river growled angrily and beat itself into a white froth against the hard granite boulders choking its channel.

The roar of the tumbling water soared up out of the canyon and reached Jacob, who was riding his horse in the pine woods on the flank of Glorieta Mesa. He ignored the distant noise and watched the caravan of four covered wagons pass along the Santa Fe Trail below him.

The heavily laden vehicles, drawn by three teams of horses each, wound through the snowy forest lining the road that led eastward toward Rancho El Vado. Conrado and the Solis's three hired vaqueros drove the wagons. The women and children of the vaqueros and Conrado's wife and mother rode with the men. Now and then Jacob could hear their voices calling out. All the people seemed happy to be returning to the rancho.

Emmanuel Solis and Petra each led a string of several horses in the vanguard of the caravan. The many tromping hooves of the animals broke trail in the snow and made the labor easier for pulling the wagons.

It was the evening of the second day since the cavalcade had departed Santa Fe. Jacob had been riding constantly from daylight to dark, scouting for danger, investigating the woods and the ravines where enemies could hide. Often he climbed his horse far up the flank of Glorieta Mesa, and from that vantage point he scanned the terrain in all directions. He was especially wary to the east where the Comanche of the Llano Estacado and the Apache of the lower reaches of the Rio Pecos and Rio Grande could come riding for an early spring attack.

Tamarron found no sign of human life. Only the prints of deer and elk and the hungry lion and wolf marred the blanket of snow.

Glorieta Summit had been passed in the early morning, and the caravan had encountered the Rio Pecos, hurrying in from the north. The wagons turned to follow the river in a long descent to the southeast. On the steep, snowy downgrade, the brakes of the wagons wouldn't hold tight enough on the icy wheels to control the speed of the vehicles. To prevent the heavy wagons from overrunning the horses or plunging into the canyon, the men had chained one of the rear wheels of each vehicle so it would not turn.

The locked and dragging wheels often cut through the snow to the ground, and Tamarron could hear the sharp, complaining screech of the iron rim grinding on the granite rock that underlay the mesa.

The sun was mellow for March, and the air, warmed by the bright rays, flowed past Jacob in a slow, invisible stream up the mesa slope. The limbs of the pines swayed with a whispering rustle. Tamarron breathed deeply of the pungent scent of the pine resins cast upon the wind. His heart beat a gentle tempo. It was a fine thing to be gone from the town.

Jacob's horse tossed its head, and its big ivory teeth rattled against the iron bit of the bridle. The animal was anxious to be traveling. Tamarron reached out and playfully slapped the muscular neck of the cayuse.

It was an ugly horse with a large, bony head and legs that seemed too long for its body. Its eyes were quite big, with lots of white showing, giving the horse an appearance of always being frightened and ready to bolt away. But the cayuse was steady, quick to obey, and as agile as a mountain goat. It was the swiftess runner Jacob had ever seen.

"Old fellow, we have fallen on good times," Tamarron told the horse as he watched Petra, Emmanuel, and the wagons melting into a dark green stretch of woods below him.

The mustang twisted its head and locked one large eye on Tamarron. It snorted as if it understood what Jacob had said.

"I'm glad you agree," Jacob said. He touched the horse with his heels, and it moved off nimble-footed along the snow-covered slope of the mesa.

CHAPTER 9

The sun floated down behind the high, rocky back-bone of the Sangre de Cristo Mountains and the Rio Pecos Valley filled with gray shadow. Below Tamarron on the edge of the gorge, the caravan continued onward into the swiftly forming evening dusk.

The last of the lingering heat of the sun radiated away into the sky, and the wind blew cold. The snowbanks stopped melting.

On the Canyon rim above the Rio Pecos, the cavalcade of horses and wagons entered a snow-covered meadow. The wagons pulled together around a small square of space and halted.

The men and women instantly sprang to their tasks of preparing the camp before the darkness of the night overtook them. The horses were unhitched and the harnesses stripped off. One man took a rifle and climbed up on a rise of land for the first night watch. Another man with an ax over his shoulder, followed by two of the larger boys, walked to a tall dead pine and began to chop. The tree soon fell, and the man started to cut it into short lengths. The boys filled their arms with the dry wood and carried it toward the wagons.

Tamarron reined his mustang in the direction of the camp. The horse, sliding on the steepest spots and trotting where it could hold its feet, carried its rider down to the cluster of wagons.

The smell of frying meat and baking bread wafted to Jacob as he unsaddled. Petra waved a welcome to him from the fire where she was helping the women cook.

Conrado passed Jacob with a sullen face and did not speak. The man resented Jacob. Conrado had even grown quarrelsome with Petra and at times deliberately refused to respond to her attempts to talk with him. The fact that Conrado would not speak to Jacob did not bother him, but he was sorry for Petra, for he knew how much she loved her younger brother.

Jacob believed Emmanuel Solis had accepted him as Petra's husband and part of the clan. Señora Solis spoke to him when they encountered each other, but always in a reserved manner that didn't lead to more than a few words of conversation.

A snowball whizzed past Jacob's head. He ducked and dropped his saddle. He grabbed a handful of snow and whirled to meet his attacker. A son of one of the vaqueros was fast disappearing behind a wagon. Jacob lobbed the snowball, coming close but missing. The boy shouted gleefully and dived out of sight.

Smiling, Jacob tied his mount to the long picket rope fastened between two pines just outside the wagon square. He gave the animal a ration of grain and approached the fire.

Emmanuel called to Jacob, and Jacob joined the group of men sitting near one of the wagons. He found a chunk of wood, like the other men used to keep their rumps out of the snow, and seated himself.

Solis had been an officer in the revolutionary army that had wrested Mexico away from the harsh control of Spain. He was a man who believed in organization. He spoke at length with the other men about the events of the day and the plans of the morrow. The periods of duty for the night guards were assigned. Jacob liked the stern,

protective manner of the old man in regard to the safety
of the women and children.

Señora Solis called out that the food was ready. The
men separated and moved off to eat with their own wives
and children. Jacob seated himself beside Petra, and she
handed him a heaping plate of meat, beans, corn bread,
and a large piece of dried peach cobbler. She had discovered Jacob's fondness for sweets and had baked several
pastries to bring with them on the journey.

The man on guard duty was called in. Another of the
vaqueros picked up a rifle and went outside the wagons
to begin his night vigil.

The fires gradually burned down and the conversation
ebbed. One after another, the families drifted off to their
sleeping robes. Jacob looked at Petra. She nodded that
she, too, was ready for bed.

In a corner of the space enclosed by the wagons, they
spread a length of tarpaulin, and upon that unrolled thick
buffalo robes. Petra silently entered the bedding.

Jacob placed his weapons on the fur robe near his
hand. Then, for several minutes, he sat with the cover
pulled up over his lap and listened to the night sounds.
Once in a while he could hear the crunching footsteps of
the guard beyond the ring of wagons, for the slushy snow
had grown hard and brittle as the temperature had
dropped.

On the canyon rim above the Rio Pecos, a March wind
came in from some unknown dominion and chased itself
in powerful gusts, and it moaned, cut by the high cold
stars.

Jacob slid in between the buffalo robes and took Petra
in his arms. They lay in a small world of their own
making, two bodies wrapped in fur robes in the night. He
felt the wonder of being alive and strong and having a
woman all his own. All of his yesterdays faded and
became lost; tomorrow was dimly ahead and just the
present was real.

Jacob went to sleep warm and near his woman.

*   *   *

The caravan dropped below the snow line in the morning of the third day. Near noon they passed the ancient ruins of a moderately large pueblo that once perhaps had contained a hundred rooms.

Jacob was near Petra, and she called out to him. She swept her hand, pointing at the crumbling adobe wall. "Legend says that a town of industrious Indians called the Forked Lightning People once lived there. Then they vanished. The legend doesn't tell what happened to them." Jacob saw Petra's face become sad as she contemplated what great harm might have come and destroyed the Forked Lightning People.

In the afternoon the wagons reached a split in the road at the fork on the Pecos River below Punta de la Mesa San Jose. Jacob arrived first at the water's edge, waiting as the other men came to stand along the bank.

"It is good that we are not going to Las Vegas," said Tomas, one of the vaqueros. "The bottom of the crossing is at least eight feet under water." He gestured along the main road that led down to the swift current of the flooding Pecos. On the opposite side of the river the road crawled out of the water and led straight east.

Tamarron had ridden the Santa Fe Trail and knew that Las Vegas lay twenty-five miles northeast. Seven hundred miles farther to the northeast was Independence, Missouri, the beginning of the heavily used trade route. In another month long trains of huge, Pittsburgh-built cargo wagons carrying more than five thousand pounds of goods each would be creaking and bumping their way south to Santa Fe, and onward deep into Mexico to Matamoros, Saltillo, and Chihuahua.

The American traders would bring manufactured goods, calicos and linsey, tables and chairs, spices, medicines, tableware, oil lamps, ink and paints, and scores of other items. They would return with Mexican rugs, cloths, hides, furs, gold and silver. And, more than likely, they would come south with oxen and return home with Mexican mules.

"Let us be on our way," said Emmanuel. "If we press on, we can be at the hacienda in three more days."

The men hastened to their wagons and climbed up the wheels to the high seats. They picked up the reins and popped the long bullwhips over the heads of their teams of horses. Shortly the vehicles were strung out along a road that headed southeast over a land rich with grama and buffalo grass. To shorten its length the road held a straight course just west of the bends and windings of the deep yellow water of the Pecos.

On the morning of the fourth day Jacob saw a small band of sheep grazing along the Pecos. Larger bands were encountered as the wagons journeyed south. Not one herdsman guarded the sheep.

"All the land we've crossed today, and the sheep, belong to the Bautista family," Petra told Jacob. "They were preparing to leave Santa Fe shortly after we did. The King of Spain gave Luis Bautista the Los Trigos Land Grant in 1794. That was the same year the king gave Carlos Solis, my grandfather, the El Vado Land Grant. Both men had been officers in the king's army and had fought many battles for him. He rewarded them with the land in Mexico for their valiant service. They traveled from Spain to Mexico together. Our families have been friends all these many years."

"How many other land holdings are there on the Pecos?" asked Jacob.

"There are two other privately owned ranchos. They are south from ours along the river. Both of them are much more recent than my grandfather's, having been deeded since the revolution by the federal government that now rules Mexico."

Night overtook Tamarron and Petra and the others as they approached the junction of the Gallinas River with the Rio Pecos. Emmanuel called orders to the drivers, and they drove on into the night. Jacob rode close ahead of the lead wagon and called out warnings about the bad spots in the road. When the half-moon was the height of a tall man above the black horizon, the travelers came to the Hacienda de Luis Bautista at the merging place of the two rivers.

Roberto Bautista, son of the ranch owner, had wintered at the rancho with the peons. He made the travelers welcome. Anxious for news of the outside world, he talked late into the night with the Solis family.

On the fifth day of travel Jacob saw scattered sheep and some cattle bearing the Solis brand grazing on the new green grass of the meadows near the river. By the afternoon of the sixth day the number of animals had increased greatly and were always in view, not only by the river but also on the grass-covered hills as far to the west as one could see. As at the Bautista rancho, not one man was to be found tending the herds. Jacob thought the loss of animals from wolves, Indians, and the river's quicksand must be very large.

The road veered away from the river, and the horses quickened their pace. The drivers encouraged them with shouts and cracking whips. Now and then the metal end of a whip would drop to bite a lagging animal not pulling its full share. The caravan climbed a slight grade and came out onto a ten-acre stretch of bench land above the Pecos. The teams began to trot, the iron wheels of the wagons rattling and banging on the gravelly earth.

The flat shelf of land was an ancient terrace of the Pecos, created by the stream when it had been a youngster. Now the river flowed a hundred feet lower and in a broad valley half a mile to the east. Beyond the river the broad, flat surface of the Llano Estacado stretched away into hazy infinity. West of the bench land, the terrain rose upward in a series of tall, juniper-covered hills. Miles distant, the woods ended and the horizon was full of large, rocky mesas stepping ever higher as they approached the far-off Gallinas Mountains.

The Solis hacienda stood in the center of the flat bench land. Immediately north of the house was a quite large round stone corral. To the east at the base of the bench

land near the river was a smaller corral with walls made
of willow stems.

The hacienda was a sprawling, single-story structure
surrounded by a protective stone wall six feet high en-
closing two or more acres. The house itself was a huge
rectangle made of brown adobe, like the earth it rested
upon. A round tower ten feet in diameter and thirty feet
tall reared above everything. Jacob saw gun ports located
at equal intervals midway up the tower, and again near its
top. From the most elevated position a man with a rifle
could kill any enemy that tried to use the wall as a shield
while assaulting the hacienda.

Three Mexican men trotted through a gate in the compound wall. A dozen or more children, both boys and
girls of many ages, ran behind. They cried out a greeting
in a loud chorus. All the children scurried beside the
wagons that continued directly toward the gate to the
hacienda without slowing.

A little girl dashed in close to the front wheel of the
wagon on which Señora Solis rode. The girl turned up
her happy brown face to the woman. "What did you
bring me, Señora Solis? What did you bring me from
Santa Fe?"

"I will show you soon," Señora Solis called back.
"Run on ahead."

Petra veered aside and rode her horse near Jacob.
"This is the home of the Solis family," she said. "I was
born here."

"A well-designed and constructed little fort," Jacob
replied. "I see that it has its own water supply."

"The hacienda was built around a spring. It comes out
of the ground in the main patio, then flows out under the
wall in a channel too small for a man to crawl through.
Beyond the wall, the water irrigates the garden in the
summer season."

Tamarron saw the garden, a large one, full of dead
vegetation from the previous year's vegetables.

"How many families live here?" Jacob asked.

"There are six vaqueros with wives and children. With Father and Mother and Conrado and Julian, and counting you and me as one, there are nine families. And, of course, there are *las viejas*, the old ones who are the mothers of the vaqueros. The women's husbands have died and are buried in the cemetery behind the hacienda."

"Nine fighting men. If we knew danger was coming and had time for everyone to get inside the hacienda, we could hold off a sizable force. When was the last time you had trouble?"

"We lose sheep and cattle to Indians all the time. But they don't take many at a time. However, there was a bad time for Apache attacks five years ago. We had to leave the hacienda and drive much of the livestock north to Las Vegas. All summer we couldn't return home because of raids. Twenty-two years ago was the worst time of all. The Navajo Indians were making war. My grandfather was killed, and many other people wounded."

"Is that when you were hurt?" Jacob asked.

Petra nodded. "I was caught outside when the Navajo came screaming up from over there." She pointed to the edge of the bluff overlooking the Pecos. "El Vado means 'the ford.' The Navajo had crossed the ford of the river in the night. At daybreak they attacked. I was leaving with grandfather and riding to the north to check water holes. An arrow struck me in the face. The Indians cut me off from the house, so I whipped my horse around and rode into the woods. I hid there for two days. The Indians looked and looked for me, but I stayed hidden and they finally gave up and left. They had killed Grandfather."

Jacob pictured the frightened and wounded girl hiding from the Indians. How had she managed not to be discovered by such skilled trackers? One day he would ask her for more details. But the expression on Petra's face said that now was not the proper time.

"There are plenty of people to help unload the wagons, so come and let me show you the hacienda," said Petra.

Jacob heard the pride in Petra's voice and knew it was well earned. The house was a magnificent accomplishment in this remote place.

With Petra leading, they entered the cool, dim hacienda by a wide, covered passageway as deep as a room and barred with heavy wooden doors secured with massive iron locks. The walls were two feet thick and made of adobe, mud mixed with straw for strength. The ceiling beams were peeled pine poles, and over that peeled saplings had been laid in a herringbone pattern.

A score of doors and windows sheeted with gypsum or small panes of imported glass opened onto a large patio. Heavy, carved wooden shutters hung from iron hinges. Each wooden panel had a gun port cut through it. A roof, supported by wooden pillars, also handsomely carved and with scrolled *cochels*, extended four feet out over the patio.

To one side of the main patio was a smaller one. Petra explained that it was the oldest, having been part of the original construction. The large patio had come into being as the hacienda expanded to accommodate the growing population of the rancho.

There was a chapel with a bell from Mexico in a short belfrey at the corner of the old patio. It was a plain room with an altar. A crucifix of dark wood stood between two tall candlesticks. A statue of Christ, carved to show his agony, with drops of blood in relief and painted red at brow and hands and feet, was suspended above the altar.

She showed him the *sala*, the great room of the hacienda, which was large enough for a dance. The walls were whitewashed with gypsum plaster. Over the walls were hung cotton cloth to protect clothing from the easily removed whitewash. The furniture was made of wood covered with velvet and leather. Several candelabra and oil lamps sat about. A wide, deep fireplace was at each end of the room. Iron fire tools sat on the wide hearths, and big mirrors hung beside each fireplace.

Petra guided Jacob through a dark storeroom hung

with beef, mutton, and wild game. In another room there were dried fruits, vegetables, wheat, and corn in jars, and nuts in cloth bags.

The kitchen was broad and sported a long table. A fireplace for cooking, copper kettles, and an iron oven occupied one end of the room. At the opposite end a huge wooden cupboard held dozens of plates, dishes, cups, tumblers, and a pot for melting chocolate. The floor of the hallway to the kitchen was slightly concave, worn down by the treading of countless feet.

They peered into the living quarters of the vaqueros and peons, located around a patio in the northern part of the hacienda. Jacob noted loaded muskets hanging on racks, high up above the reach of children, in many of the rooms. He had seen similar ready armaments in the part of the house used by the Solis family. These people were prepared to defend their isolated home.

The entire house faced inward, and there were no windows in the outer walls. Thus they were solid against danger from Indians or *banditos*. The only openings were small strategically located gun ports with thick wooden covers that could be locked over them.

Outside the main house were chicken pens, a milk shed, a small corral, and the blacksmith area with its forge, anvil, and leather bellows.

Jacob and Petra halted their tour of the hacienda and returned to the wagons. Every man, woman, and child was working. Emmanuel and Señora Solis held positions between the vehicles and the buildings of the rancho. As the people came by carrying their load of food, medicines, tools, iron for the forge, building materials, and dozens of other things, Señor or Señora Solis directed them to the proper place for storage. Jacob saw that the aristocratic Solises had changed, becoming hardworking man and wife with a huge rancho to operate.

Petra climbed up into one of the wagons and removed a small package that was carefully wrapped in a thick blanket. "These are the four panes of glass for our new house," she told Jacob.

"It won't be long before we need them," Jacob replied. He watched Petra gingerly transport the precious sheets of fragile glass away for safekeeping.

He didn't go to help with the unloading, for it was nearly finished. Instead he watched the hustle and bustle of the people and recalled all the things he had seen during the tour of the house. A pleasant, comfortable feeling rose within him. Belonging to this tiny tribe of people might not be so bad. Yet the Rio Pecos country was a hostile, savage land.

CHAPTER 10

Jacob rode with Emmanuel, Conrado, and the vaqueros across the gray, grass-covered hills lying west of the Rio Pecos. They searched for cattle and sheep that had been driven and scattered by the fierce winds of winter. In the cold months, the animals ate snow for the water they needed to survive. When the snow melted the moisture had collected in shallow, temporary pools. Soon those ephemeral supplies would be gone. To prevent the death of much livestock from thirst, the men worked from daylight to dark driving the beasts to the river or permanent springs.

Often the riders slept on the range where darkness caught them. They would stake out their mounts on the ends of long lariats to graze. Then, wrapped in sleeping robes, they lay upon the hard ground. Jacob often thought of Petra in those gloomy hours.

Near the end of March the flooding waters of the Rio Pecos subsided. The riders crossed the hard rib of stone that made El Vado, the ford, and rode for several days gathering sheep and cattle on the flat land of the Llano Estacado, the Staked Plains.

Jacob saw small herds of buffalo and the big white wolves that always trailed and fed upon them. The truly large herds of thousands of buffalo were a hundred miles east. Now and then, bands of antelope appeared. Once a band of fifteen Indians sat for more than an hour on their mustangs beyond rifle range and watched him round up a flock of sheep and shove it toward the Pecos. The Indians vanished, riding to the east. Jacob saw the tracks of unshod mustangs again two days later and knew the Indians were spying on the Solises' riders.

One morning as the men saddled their mounts at the hacienda, Emmanuel came to Tamarron. "Come and ride with me for a couple of days, Jacob. There is something I want to show you."

"Sure, Emmanuel," replied Jacob. "I'll have Petra pack us some food."

"I have already had *mi esposa* make us ready," Emmanuel said. He lifted up a pack and tied it behind his saddle.

With a mellow rumble of hooves the two men left at a comfortable, rocking-chair gallop to the southeast. An hour later Emmanuel pulled rein and halted by a large boulder on the bank of the Pecos.

"See that big chipped mark on the rock, Jacob?" asked Emmanuel.

Jacob nodded. The mark was not new.

"My father and a Spanish government official put that sign there many years ago, in 1794. That boulder is the corner of the El Vado Land Grant that the king of Spain gave my father. The eastern boundary extends fifteen miles along the Rio Pecos. From here"—Emmanuel pointed to the west—"the boundary goes thirty-five miles in that direction, then fifteen miles to the north, then returns straight back to the Rio Pecos. The grant encompasses three hundred and eighteen thousand acres."

"That is a very large rancho," said Tamarron.

"It is indeed large. However, land on the Pecos is not nearly as valuable as on the Rio Grande. There's much more danger here from Indians and *banditos*. Because of that, all the area surrounding the grant is federal land, and open and free for our use. Actually we benefit from grazing our livestock on half a million acres or more. The Solis brand is on ninety thousand sheep and twelve hundred cattle. Now, let us ride the full length of the borders of the land, for I want you to know where they are located."

As the two men rode westward across gently rolling hills, Jacob carefully evaluated the characteristics of the land lying outside the El Vado Grant. He searched to find a suitable homeside for Petra and himself, with water, wood, and grass. Before the fall arrived, he wanted a house and corrals built. Then he would purchase a base breeding herd of sheep and cattle from Emmanuel. When he had accomplished that, he would know that the direction of the rest of his life was set.

A night camp was made in the evening on the shore of a shallow lake of twenty acres or so. Emmanuel told Jacob that the lake was called Laguna de los Terreros. They sat before a fire of crackling mesquite and ate leisurely.

"Jacob, I know you desire your own rancho," Emmanuel said. "That is a worthy ambition, and there's plenty of land for that. You are married to a Spanish woman, or I should say a Mexican woman, now that the revolution has happened. It would be easy for you to become a Mexican citizen. Then you could buy the land you want."

"I have thought of becoming a citizen," replied Jacob. "But I don't know if it's a good idea. We may go to war, Mexico and the United States. I could be of more use to the family as an American."

"I have also considered that possibility. I agree with what you say. Until that matter is resolved, you could simply devise a brand for yourself and graze your livestock on the open federal land. Or graze them on El Vado, for there's surely ample grass for more animals."

"Thank you for that generous offer," Jacob said. He

sensed the friendliness in the elder Solis. Recently even Conrado had spoken a few words to him. Jacob felt his growing involvement and attachment to the Solis family and the other inhabitants of the rancho.

He looked to the far north where the Sangre de Cristos Mountains rose as a dark blur on the evening horizon. The primeval mountains, often harsh and cold, but at times incredibly splendid, seemed now very far removed, and he heard no call from them.

The day was only a lighter shade of gray in the east when Jacob and the other men left the hacienda and assembled near the corral. Petra had followed him outside and now stood by the corner of the house. Jacob positioned himself so that he could see her dim form and at the same time listen to Emmanuel. Jacob was anxious for the work with the Solis riders to be finished so that he could go about his own business.

Emmanuel said, "The wool buyers from Chihuahua will be coming here with their wagons. An army patrol will escort them. All of this was arranged last autumn. That gives us two weeks to do our shearing. I have five skilled men coming from Las Vegas. They should arrive here today. You three"—Emmanuel gestured at the vaqueros—"will also shear. Even with eight of you working, we can only shear a small portion of all the sheep we have. But that will be enough to fill the wagons from Chihuahua. The wool buyers have also agreed to buy fifteen thousand sheep and take them to the markets in the south.

"Conrado and Jacob will herd the sheep to you." Emmanuel looked at Jacob. "That is, Jacob, if you will work with us until the wagons arrive?"

Tamarron tried to see Petra's face. But in the deep morning dusk he couldn't tell if she wanted him to agree or to decline the request. For many days she'd been quite busy at some task at the hacienda. Probably making something for their new home, thought Jacob. The spring was still young, so he might as well give her additional time for the project.

"Certainly I'll help you a few days more," Jacob told Emmanuel.

"Then it's settled. The shearing corral will need new willow stems added to repair the walls. You men who are shearers work on that this morning so everything will be ready. Conrado and Jacob will begin to bring the sheep in. Keep the corral full so that the shearers won't have to wait."

The days passed, each one cresting at a temperature warmer than the one before. Hundreds of sheep were thrown to the ground and shorn of their long wool. The men labored, sweated, and cursed the contrary, kicking animals. As the mound of gray-white wool accumulated, it was crammed into a huge wooden press, compacted into dense blocks, and tightly bound.

The wool buyers arrived late one day. They spent the night at the Solis hacienda. The next day the big wagons were loaded with wool, and sheep were brought in and run through a counting chute. With armed guards scouting ahead and others bringing up the rear, the cavalcade went off to the south.

The April sun burned unnaturally bright, and a hot wind blew across the Llano Estacado as Emmanuel halted his horse. He dismounted, his legs trembling and the world rotating dizzingly. He tossed the reins down to drag on the earth and leaned against his *caballo*.

"Stand," he ordered the horse.

Weakly Emmanuel lowered himself to the ground and stretched out on his back in the shadow of the horse. He closed his eyes. The well-trained horse looked down at its master, switched its tail, stomped the dirt once, then stood quietly.

As Emmanuel rested, the spinning world gradually slowed, finally stopping and becoming firm. From time to time he opened his eyes to gaze at the high, clear sky.

The perfect blue dome of the heavens arching over him was a beautiful sight.

The periods of weakness were becoming more frequent and severe, Emmanuel reflected. Never before had he been forced to dismount when one of the episodes occurred. He was an ill, old man. His days of riding were growing few in number, and his life upon the earth would be but a little longer.

The pounding hooves of a running horse shattered the stillness of the plains. Emmanuel's hand snaked down for his pistol. Indians or *banditos* had found him. He jerked to a sitting position and raised his weapon in the direction of the drumbeat of the swiftly approaching horse.

Tamarron dragged his cayuse to a quick stop and sprang down. "Are you hurt, Emmanuel?" Jacob called as he hurried to kneel at Emmanuel's side.

"No. Not hurt. I am just getting old, and the heat made me feel weak. So I thought I would lay down and rest in the shade made by the *caballo* until my strength returned. What are you doing here?"

"I was returning to the hacienda when I saw you. Do you want me to help you on your horse?"

"Not now. Sit and talk with me." Emmanuel reclined again on the ground.

Jacob dropped down and took a seat on the grass. He pushed back his hat. "I'll wait and ride back to the hacienda with you when you are ready to go," Jacob said.

"That won't be necessary. We're within eight or ten miles of the hacienda. I can ride that distance after a little while."

"I'm going in that direction. I'll go with you," Jacob said again.

They were quiet together. Jacob scanned the surrounding terrain through the shimmering heat waves. The only things that stirred on the land were a band of antelope on the eastern horizon and a raven that flapped in and landed to sit like a chunk of broken, black obsidian on a mesquite to watch the two men avidly.

The hot sun drifted across the sky. Jacob moved Emmanuel's horse so its shadow would still fall on the old man.

Emmanuel heard the sound of the horse's hooves on the ground and opened his eyes. "Jacob, I am sixty-nine years old. Soon I'll no longer be able to ride with the men. When that happens, Conrado will become the major owner of El Vado. He is much younger than you and will at times need advice. I have watched you these past weeks. You are a hardworking man with sound judgment. The men respect you. The children and women all have grown to like you because you speak gently to them. You are at that stage when a man is old enough to have gathered much experience in the world, yet young enough to be very strong. That is a good time in a man's life. I hope you and Petra will soon bring children into the family."

Tamarron did not reply. Emmanuel had more to say.

"I want you to counsel Conrado when you think he might be making an error in judgment. At the moment he has not decided he likes you. However, he's getting closer to accepting you. I hope he will soon be your friend. Jacob, will you help hold the rancho together after I am gone?"

"Yes, Emmanuel, I'm proud that you have asked me."

"That is good to hear." Emmanuel sat up. "I think I can ride now if you'll help me to mount."

As Jacob assisted Emmanuel up on his horse, he was surprised at the slight build of the man. Emmanuel, with his piercing black eyes, thick beard, big sombrero, and heeled boots, had seemed a much larger man. But then, all men looked small when they neared death.

The two riders touched their horses with spurs, and the animals started off across the Llano Estacado.

"Call out if you need help," Jacob said.

"I will," replied Emmanuel. His spirits had lifted. It was good to have the strong man called Tamarron near. To Emmanuel the sky was more blue, the wind sweeter, and the new spring grass had grown an inch in the last quarter hour.

Emmanuel and Jacob stopped at the hitch rail in front of the hacienda. Jacob watched after the elder Solis until the man entered the door. Then he took hold of the reins of both mounts and led them to the corral inside the compound.

Tamarron began to brush his cayuse. The long winter hair was gone, and the short, reddish-brown coat of the horse glistened in the sunlight. The horse stood with its eyes closed, savoring the scratching stroke of the brush.

The lean, muscular body of the horse pleased Tamarron. As he often did, Jacob had ridden his own mount during the day. The big brute should always be tough and able to cover long stretches of difficult land swiftly.

Conrado rode in and swung down near Tamarron. He tied his mount to the gate of the corral. Somewhat hesitantly he walked toward Jacob.

"Your *caballo* is sound asleep," Conrado said, slowly circling Jacob and his cayuse. He halted in front of the horse. "*Madre de Dios*, that is an ugly beast." Conrado smiled to show he meant no offense or rebuke to Jacob for owning such a mount.

"But one of the very best," replied Tamarron. He grinned back at Conrado. "Would you like to race your gray against him, the winner to take both horses?"

"No bet. I've seen your animal run. My gray is fast but not a match for this long-legged fellow."

Conrado's face became solemn. "Jacob, I am glad you can see past the imperfections of a horse and other things and know what their true value is."

Conrado looked away from Tamarron in an embarrassed manner, as if he had said too much or had spoken of something he shouldn't have. He spun about and walked away hastily, his boots thumping on the dirt of the compound.

Tamarron stared after Conrado and knew the man

wasn't referring to the ugly horse but rather to Petra's imperfection: the scar that marred her face. Conrado was thanking Jacob for taking Petra as a wife. With those words Conrado had come as close as he ever would to welcoming Jacob into the Solis family.

"Petra needs no one to thank me for marrying her. She's more than ample reward in the joy she gives me with her wonderful mind and body," Jacob said to the straight, retreating back of Conrado.

Only the ugly horse heard Jacob's words.

CHAPTER 11

New Orleans, April 24, 1846

The fear of the Negro slaves was an invisible vapor that Senator Simon Caverhill could smell. The bitter, acrid odor that frightened men exuded always amazed him. Never had Caverhill felt fear.

The senator walked along the single row of sixty black men, evaluating the health and strength of each. The slaves had been brought from a warehouse on the docks of the Mississippi River and lined up on the edge of the cobblestone pavement of Chartres Street in the French Quarter. At each end of the line of blacks stood a white man with a pistol in his belt.

Caverhill finished his examination of the slaves. He stopped near several other prospective bidders standing on the street in front of Maspero's Exchange, a large coffeehouse where cotton, sugar, and slaves were sold. He looked to the south toward the waterfront, impatient for the slave broker, Picotte, to arrive.

New Orleans was the greatest slave market in the nation. But he could see little of the city, for it was smothered and pressed down by thick gray clouds lying dense and damp on the rooftops. Though it hadn't rained, moisture was condensing out of the low clouds onto the tile roofs and dripping dismally from the eaves.

The city was old and had been built by the French more than a hundred years before on the flat mud delta of the mighty Mississippi River. Bayous, swamps, and coastal bays surrounded the city. The streets were dirt, except for the main trading district around Chartres Street, with its shops, businesses, and large brokerage houses.

The city was one hundred and ten miles from the sea. Still more than half a hundred oceangoing ships, both sail and steam, were berthed at the docks that extended for a mile along the riverbank. Also tied up were an even greater number of the flat-bottomed riverboats that plied the winding body of the Mississippi. The shallow-drafted vessels, belching smoke and steam, climbed the swift current for a thousand miles north to Cincinnati, and Saint Louis, and beyond.

Caverhill saw Picotte and his auctioneer come into sight on Bienville Street. A group of Negro women followed close behind. As they came closer, Caverhill noted that one was a pretty, yellow-skinned mulatto. The slave broker arranged the women in a single row on the side of Maspero's Exchange opposite the Negro men.

Caverhill let his view wander over the women. Though he wanted strong black men to work his ranch near Austin, he should buy some of the women and start a breeding program—so his ranch could produce more than cotton and livestock to sell for cash.

The riding mounts, buggies, and other vehicles of the bidders were against the curb on the far side of the street. Most of the drivers and slave handlers had gathered in a group and were talking among themselves. Caverhill's three men were alert and watching for any signal he might make. Because of their diligence he decided to reward each of them with a female slave for the long trip to Austin. If he could purchase the yellow girl for a reasonable bid, he would give her to his foreman, Dockken.

A Negro chain gang of a dozen men, trailed by a pair

of guards with rifles and whips, worked their way along Chartres Street. The Negroes moved in a straight-line formation, sweeping the pavement with large, coarse-strawed brooms. Their heads were turned down to the street, and they listened intently to the boss Negro calling out the cadence that controlled the sweep of the brooms.

As the prisoners came abreast of the women the nearest man glanced at the mulatto girl. Immediately one of the guards lifted his whip from where it rested on his shoulder and slashed the offending Negro.

"Goddamn black bastard," shouted the guard, "get you eyes on your work." Almost too fast to see, the white man struck twice more, the whip licking out and cutting the black's back.

The slave seemed to shrink under the brutal blows, and he yelped shrilly.

The Negro next in line roughly jerked the chain that held them all together, reprimanding the man for making the outcry.

Caverhill looked away from the chain gang and out over the foggy town. The plight of the slaves meant nothing. They were merely machines made of flesh, from which as much work as possible was to be wrung.

Picotte opened the door of Maspero's Exchange and called inside. A half minute later two Negro men came out carrying a wooden platform. They sat it on the sidewalk in front of the entrance. At a nod from Picotte the auctioneer stepped up on the dais.

The slave broker leaned on the wall of the exchange and looked at the bidders. Every man had stated his intention to attend the sale. Their bank drafts were from local banks. Picotte was satisfied that payment would be made for any slave bought.

"Gentlemen," said the auctioneer, "please come closer so you can see the condition of the merchandise."

The plantation owners and their managers, warehouse-men, and proprietors of manufacturing companies gathered in a half-circle on the cobblestones around the platform.

"We shall start the bidding now," said the auctioneer. He motioned at the white guard near the lines of slaves. "Bring the first black."

As the guard and slave came forward, the auctioneer continued to speak. "All of the Negroes to be sold today are second-and third-generation slaves from the West Indies. They all speak English, at least sufficiently to understand and be understood."

The Negro climbed up on the platform. At an order from the auctioneer the man faced toward the group of whites.

The auctioneer studied a manifest in his hand. "This fellow is thirty years old and has lived on one plantation all his life. Look him over carefully. He is strong and willing. The record shows he has been whipped only once, receiving ten lashes. What am I bid?"

Caverhill did not bid but rather watched the process to determine what the current price for slaves was in New Orleans. The Negro sold for four hundred dollars.

Another black came to the platform and his pedigree was read. The senator began to bid when the price reached three hundred dollars. He bought the slave for four hundred and twenty-five dollars.

Gradually Caverhill accumulated slaves. Dockken came each time the senator was successful and led the acquisition away to be chained at the tail end of one of the wagons. By the time all the male slaves had stood on the auction block, Caverhill had purchased twelve of them.

One of the black women was called forward. She never looked at the white men, her eyes lowered and locked on the cobblestones of the street.

The auctioneer stated the woman's history, then added, "Those of you interested in a strong woman for work or breeding could do no better than to buy this one. Who will begin the bidding?"

Caverhill again waited for the bidding to finish. She sold for three hundred dollars. He was surprised at the low price. Female slaves had small value. He bid and won the next two women.

When the last black woman had been sold, the auctioneer called out to the bidders. "We have saved the best for last. This mulatto girl. Begin the bidding, please."

The price went to nine hundred dollars and halted. Caverhill waited for a competing bid. None came. He called out, "One thousand dollars."

The previous high bidder looked at Caverhill and smiled. "She's yours, Senator. Have a pleasant trip back to Texas."

"That ends the auction for today," said Picotte. "All those who have made a purchase, please come inside and make your payment to my clerk."

The men moved inside the Exchange. Caverhill stopped by Picotte.

"I understand you have some Negro men that are for sale but weren't part of this auction?" Caverhill said.

"You're correct," replied Picotte. "I have six that I bought from a ship that came straight from Cameroon. They're mean ones culled from the three hundred that were on board. They've been whipped several times and are still troublesome. I wouldn't sell them for field work or house niggers. Also, they speak no English."

"I'd think they would be cheap," said Caverhill.

"For such ornery ones, I have a standing offer from the foundry. The owner will pay two hundred dollars for each slave I bring him. They cause no problems for him because he chains them to their machines until they learn to obey or they die."

"Let's examine them."

"Very well. Come with me. They're just a little distance from here."

"Dockken, come with us," Caverhill called to his foreman. "We may have one more Negro to get."

Picotte led the way two blocks toward the river, crossing Decatur Street and entering a warehouse on Canal Street. Six Negroes, all extremely black and dressed only in tattered cotton trousers, stood chained to iron rings bolted to the thick wooden columns that supported the

roof of the cavernous warehouse. With a rattle of iron
the black men swung around to stare at the three approaching white men.

Trodo straightened to his full height. He recognized
the smaller man, the one named Picotte. The other two
were unknown. One of the white men was as big as
Trodo. That man's eyes were like muddy water. Trodo
sensed that below their surface some evil plan was forming, like slimy water bugs birthing.

Trodo believed the big man could be more dangerous
than any pale-skinned man he had yet encountered, even
those aboard the slave ship that enjoyed using their biting whips. Then Trodo smiled, a fleeting smile that came
and went. He was already a dead man. He was merely
waiting to be killed.

Caverhill saw the brief stretching of the black man's
lips. He thought it was a twitch of fear. Yet when he
moved close, he smelled no fear on any of the men.
There was only a strong musty odor, like Caverhill had
once encountered on the king stud of a band of wild
horses.

One after another the Negro men dropped their stares
as Caverhill walked past, inspecting them. He motioned
with his hand for each to turn. He saw the fresh wounds,
as well as the old ones that crisscrossed their backs.
Indeed they had been whipped many times.

The large black eyes of the last man didn't waver but
stared back, watching Caverhill keenly. Yet at the same
time he seemed to be looking at some other scene, one
entirely within his mind.

Insolent bastard, thought Caverhill. Without warning
he balled a fist into a bony hammer and struck the man a
powerful wallop to the side of the head. The Negro
staggered under the force of the blow. Then he quickly
caught himself and started to spring toward his attacker.
Even as he moved toward the white man his step broke.

He halted, trembling, and his eyes raged as he fought to master and control the hot desire to strike back.

"This one will do," said Caverhill. "I'll give you the foundry price of two hundred dollars." He was greatly pleased with the Negro's reaction.

"Are you sure?" Picotte questioned. "Look at him. He is ready to kill you."

"Exactly what I want," said the Texas senator. "Dockken, go get one of the other men to stand guard while you unlock this fellow and chain him to one of the wagons."

"Here's the key to the lock," Picotte said.

Trodo stared after the three white men as they walked toward the entrance of the warehouse. When he was sure they wouldn't see him, he spat out a mouthful of blood and two broken teeth.

Caverhill looked out from the fire at the West Indies Negroes, chained to each other between two trees. The big Negro that had come directly from Africa was fastened to a tree on the opposite side of the camp. In the darkness Caverhill could not always see his black form.

The three women sat within the light cast by the leaping flames of the fire. The evening meal had been prepared and eaten. Now the women awaited the call of the white men.

"You," Caverhill said, pointing to the women, "go over there and sit."

The slaves immediately rose and moved hastily off to the end of the farthest wagon. When the two other women began to talk, the mulatto hushed them. She cocked an ear back at the white men and listened intently.

Caverhill had waited long enough. For three days he had journeyed with his men and slaves northwest along a well-used road. At a village named Baton Rouge they had crossed the broad, brown flow of the Mississippi River on a ferryboat. Now they were a day west of the river, but still four hundred miles from Austin. Caverhill could travel that distance on horseback in ten days or less. The slaves and wagons would take twice that much time to reach the same destination. It was the right moment to teach the slaves obedience and then go on his way alone.

"What's on your mind, Senator?" asked Dockken.

"I want to ride to Austin, and then on to the ranch as quickly as possible. But before I go, the Negroes must be taught to always obey. It has to be a tough lesson, one that will be told for generations of slaves."

"What do you have in mind?" asked Dockken.

"I want to use him as an example." Caverhill chucked a thumb at the Cameroon Negro in the darkness.

"I thought as much," replied Dockken. "But he hasn't done anything to be punished for. He does whatever he's told. He's strong as an ox, can outwalk all the others, and could even beat the horses if he wanted to."

"I know that. He must do something that the other slaves will know is wrong and deserving of strong discipline. Tomorrow we'll goad him into disobeying. Think of some method to do that. Then we'll finish with him."

"All right," replied Dockken. "We'll make it happen."

"Good," said Caverhill. He stood up, stretched, and walked toward the lead wagon where he would sleep.

Trodo heard the sound of an animal creeping closer through the tall marsh grass that grew around him beneath the tree. Was it one of the large swamp beasts that resembled the crocodile of his native land? Or some other animal he had never seen and whose appearance he could not imagine. He tensed, ready to defend himself.

"Are you there?" A whisper floated out of the darkness.

Trodo jerked with amazement. It was a woman's voice and it was speaking his language. The words came slow and haltingly, as if she were unsure of them.

"I am here," Trodo said.

The yellow-skinned girl, crouched low, came up beside him. "I want to tell you something," she said quickly.

"You should not be here. They would whip you if they knew."

"I have no doubt of that, but you must know what I heard. They mean to kill you tomorrow."

"I have known from the day the one called Senator bought me what he intended. I have wondered why they have not done it before. How is it that you speak my tongue?"

The girl knelt beside Trodo. "My grandmother taught me her language before she died. She must have been of the same people as you."

"That cannot be. Your skin is of the wrong color."

"My mother's father was a white man. My father was also white. That is why my skin is different from yours."

"Then you really are not one of us."

"Yes, I am. I always will be." She was silent for a moment. "Are you not afraid to die?"

Trodo looked at the girl in the faint light of the far-away stars. He saw in her face the torment that the thought of his death was causing.

"Death is not something to fear. It comes to all of us." He wanted to lessen her anguish.

"But it comes with such terrible pain."

"Let us think of other things," said Trodo. He looked at the soft curves and hollows of her face. He reached out and touched her arm. "Would you make love with a man who is going to die soon?"

The girl's head dropped and she studied the dark ground. Then her eyes lifted. "For a brave man I would." Her voice could barely be heard above the noises of the darkness. She lay down on the grass and positioned herself to receive him.

Trodo clasped the soft mounds of her breasts in his hands. "Your love must last me for all eternity," he said.

Trodo lay down upon the yellow-skinned girl.

Caverhill sensed the imminent attack of the Negro. He had come close to badgering the man for that very purpose, but the Negro was becoming the aggressor on his own volition.

The Negro hurled himself at Caverhill. The senator's arms rose protectively. The two big men crashed together.

Caverhill clamped a viselike hold on the black hands reaching for his throat. He felt the powerful muscles of his opponent. One mistake and the slave would crush his throat. He brought his knee up violently into the pit of the Negro's stomach.

Trodo bent forward under the force of the blow. Even as he fought the pain he threw all his weight upon Caverhill's hands and forced them down. He rammed forward, butting the white man in the chest. They fell together to the ground.

The senator wrenched both hands free and slugged the Negro with two hard, stiff punches to the head. Then he leapt erect and danced away beyond the reach of the slave's chains. Trodo regained his feet swiftly and stood poised for battle.

Caverhill called out to Dockken and the other men. "All of you fellows come and string this feisty Negro up to that tree. I'm going to give him the whip."

The three men swarmed over Trodo and beat him to the ground with rifle butts. "Drag him over there beneath that tree," Dockken ordered. "Throw a rope up over that limb. Tie it around his wrist. Now hoist him up."

The task was quickly completed. Trodo hung from the tree, his toes barely touching the earth.

Caverhill swung the whip. There was a muted pop. A piece of skin and flesh half as wide as a thumb sprang from Trodo's back.

"That's for starters," said the Texas senator.

The biting end of the whip marched up one side of the hanging black body, then across the shoulders to continue down the opposite side of the back and over the buttocks. Each time the metal tip struck, a gaping wound was left that ran blood.

Caverhill ceased the flogging and tossed the whip to Dockken. "This should teach all the Negro bastards never to threaten or disobey a white man. Those here today will not forget, and will tell those yet to come. Whip him for another quarter hour. If he's still alive after that, then cut his throat. Leave him to hang right on the tree."

Dockken shook out the whip on the ground behind him. "It'll be done exactly as you say."

"I'm riding to Austin now. You come with the others as fast as possible. There's a lot of work to be done at the ranch."

"Yes, sir. We'll be along right sharp."

"Do that."

Caverhill tied his bedroll and a supply of food behind the saddle of his horse. Without looking at the black slave hanging from the tree, he mounted and rode west.

A quarter hour later Trodo was still alive and watching when the men came with a knife and cut his throat.

Only the yellow-skinned girl cried at Trodo's death.

CHAPTER 12

Jacob entered the hacienda by the rear patio along the wide, cool passageway. He glanced into the *sala*, full of shadows in the corners, and kept going to the rear of the house, searching for Petra.

In the kitchen two sons of one of the vaqueros, tardy in returning from play, were eating a hardy meal of tortillas, mutton fried with onions, and boiled milk seasoned with nutmeg. The boys stopped devouring the food and looked up when Jacob came into the room.

Quietly the youngsters sat holding their spoons and watching the gringo who had married Señorita Petra. They had heard the men say the gringo was a great knife fighter. The boys hoped someday to see him kill many bad Apache.

"Have you seen Petra?" Jacob asked.

The older boy replied, "She is usually off in that part of the hacienda with *las viejas*." He pointed in the direction of the main patio.

"Thanks," said Jacob. "That food smells good. Save some for me."

The boys laughed and again fell to wolfing down their food.

The patio had been enlarged by an adobe wall thirty feet in length. Two doorways stood open in the new structure. Each opening was flanked by a pair of small, single-paned windows. Tamarron smelled the damp clay odor of fresh adobe as he passed into the nearest room.

One of *las viejas* was stamping the earthen floor with the blunt end of a branch of cottonwood with short limbs left on as handles. As she worked forward the floor behind her was hard and flat.

She found a low spot. With an old hand, thin and blue-veined, she took damp soil mixed with straw from a dishpan and filled the depression. Then, with exquisite care, she leveled the place and pounded it solid.

Every wall was straight and plumb and recently plastered with mud. In the corners the plaster was still dark with moisture. Overhead, new cloth hung below the ceiling to keep the fine particles of the roof soil from falling into the room and onto the occupants.

"Do you know where Petra is?" Jacob asked the old woman.

She jerked, startled by Jacob's unexpected voice. She completed her downward stroke with a thump and turned.

"The señora is in the next room," the woman replied in a hesitant tone, as if reluctant to answer.

"Thank you, Mother," Jacob said.

Petra heard Jacob and the woman talking, and she straightened up from unrolling a wool carpet on the floor. She turned to the doorway as Jacob entered.

He said nothing, silently swinging his view over the wide room, the deep fireplace with the iron cooking hooks, the red-and-gray carpet on the floor, and the whitewashed walls. Petra had built an apartment, again expanding the size of the huge hacienda, making ample space for another family.

"Whose rooms are these, Petra?" Jacob questioned. He had seen the four panes of glass in the outside walls and believed he already knew the answer. He recalled that for many days he'd seen blocks being molded and surmised that some form of building was in progress. Busy working long days with the men, he had given the construction little thought.

"For us, Jacob. For you and me," Petra responded in an uneasy voice.

"I had planned to build us a hacienda on our own land," Jacob said in a nettled tone. "Probably to the south on vacant land near the Rio Pecos."

"I know that. But I thought once you saw how nice a home we could have here, you'd be willing to stay on El Vado."

Petra took a trembling breath. Jacob saw her hands shaking. She clasped them together to keep them still. She may have made a terrible mistake in venturing off on her own plan without discussing it with him.

"There is more to this than that," Jacob said.

"Yes. There is more. I have an interest in El Vado to attend to. I own one fourth of all the land and livestock on El Vado. In truth, you and I are one fourth owners of all the land and livestock."

Tamarron backed up a step, dumbfounded at the abrupt news.

"I earned all of it," Petra cried out. "For more than twenty years I worked as hard as any man. It was not merely given to me. I truly paid for every acre and animal."

Petra saw the expression of deep thought come upon Jacob's face, that look she had come to expect when he was weighing an important decision. Her fear at his reaction almost overwhelmed her. "Remember, Jacob, that day when you offered me all that you possessed? Well, now I offer you all I possess."

"Why didn't you tell me about your ownership in El Vado?"

"Because I was afraid you wouldn't marry me if you knew I had so much property."

Jacob's eyes were riveted on Petra. "You are right. I couldn't marry you knowing that."

"And now, Jacob? And now?" Petra's pensive, questioning face was pale and taut. Her hands were gripped so tightly, they seemed to be breaking each other. She thought of the past weeks with Jacob. Not to be his wife would mean a lonely life.

Jacob's countenance softened. "You've captured me completely. It will be much safer for you on El Vado when I'm gone. So we'll live here. I never want you hurt. But we will buy a large piece of land along the Rio Pecos and expand our herd of livestock there."

Petra went swiftly into his arms. "It will also be safer here for our children," she said. "Within the walls where I grew up."

Tamarron hugged Petra. He had accepted this little universe of people as his family. It did not feel bad. He smiled. There was a soft, warm glow deep down where his real being lived.

Tamarron and Tomas spurred their mounts across the plain and struck the ford of the Pecos at a full run. The horses slowed at the last instant and took the shallow, rock-bottomed crossing in long, lunging strides, flinging water from the body of the river in sharp, glistening spears.

The horses reached the bank, and the men raked them again with their spurs, gouging them up the sloping, gravelly bank.

Tomas had found Jacob after two days of searching, far to the southeast at the base of Taiban Mesa. He informed Jacob that Emmanuel Solis had been found very ill near the corrals. The elder Solis appeared to be dying. A rider had been sent to Las Vegas for the priest and *resádor*, men who attended the dying. Emmanuel had asked that a rider be sent quickly to find Jacob.

The horsemen dismounted at the entrance to the hacienda and hastened inside, directly to the Solis quarters. Jacob pushed through the women of the vaqueros and peons, grouped in crouched positions near the door of the bedroom.

The old man lay pale and motionless on the bed.
Señora Solis, Petra, and Conrado sat beside him. The
priest and the *resador* waited expectantly on the opposite
side. Emmanuel's hand clutched an adobe block. The
last rites had been given, and the dying man was touching the earth.

Petra leaned over the still form of her father. "Jacob is
here," she said.

Emmanuel stirred and opened his eyes. His mouth
worked, but no sound would come. He raised a limp
hand, fingers spread. He looked at Jacob, then Conrado,
and brought his index finger against the adjoining one.
The hand dropped. The eyes closed. The chest rose, then
sank with a shudder.

The *resador* was an expert at knowing the last moment
of death. His sight was locked upon the old man's face.
He saw the first veil of final mystery come. He cried out
loudly. "Go with Jesus! Go with Jesus! Go with Jesus!"
The soul must take flight to its savior's name at the
precise time of death. Its destination must be certain. He
thought he had made the call at exactly the right moment.

As the priest reached out and closed the staring eyes of
the dead man, *las viejas* and the other women came
streaming into the room. They began to scream in grief.
They threw themselves from side to side and wailed
formless words. They paused and gazed at the dead man
while their shrieks fell to whimpers, like lost children
staring. Then, shaking their heads, they redoubled their
lamentations.

Conrado stood up and, taking Jacob by the arm, pushed
from the room. His voice was crusty as he spoke. "The
women will wash and prepare father for burial. You and
I must talk."

They walked beyond the walls and stood looking out
over the Rio Pecos and the limitless, grassy reaches of
the Llano Estacado. Far up above the river, a bald eagle
hung motionless, its telescopic eyes boring downward,
seeking fish in the wet depths of the stream.

"Perhaps an omen," said Jacob, pointing up at the great bird riding effortlessly on the wind.

"Father probably would have said the same thing," replied Conrado. "Did you understand his last gesture?"

"He wanted you and me to work together to see that Rancho El Vado survives, and that the people living here are cared for and protected."

"You are exactly right. We talked before you came. He also said you should take thirty thousand sheep to Austin or Houston and sell them. Here in the valley, one sheep is worth less than two dollars. In Texas a sheep would be worth nearly twice as much, for there's a ready market to build the herds of the new Americans settling there. You, being an American, could make the sale. I can't do it, for the Texans hate Mexicans and would steal our herd."

"I'll do that in the fall after the first heavy rain. Then there will be water on the plains for the animals."

"Good," said Conrado.

They stood together for a very long time and said not a word.

Jacob and Conrado built a coffin in the carpentry shop. Emmanuel's body was placed within it and carried to the *sala*. Candles were lit at the head and feet. Then Jacob sat with the others in an all-night wake. Now and again someone would say a prayer or start a hymn, and the rest of the mourners would join in.

At midnight a light supper was served in the kitchen. As Tamarron ate silently with Petra and several others of the household, he heard the shovels of the peons digging in the family cemetery north of the wall.

When the sun rose to lie yellow and round on the eastern horizon, the body of Emmanuel was carried to the chapel. The priest spoke a short sermon and led all the people of Rancho El Vado in prayer.

There was no ceremony at the grave site. The coffin was placed on ropes held by four men and lowered into the ground. Petra and Conrado led the sobbing Señora Solis away.

Tamarron remained by the grave as, without a word, the peons and vaqueros began to fill it in. He noted that several of the man had tears in their eyes. These men held their heads down, trying to prevent the others from seeing their expressions of sorrow.

Jacob raised his view from the raw dirt of the grave and looked at the more than a score and a half tombstones marking other burials. Emmanuel, you had a worthy life and a good death, Jacob thought. Your funeral was held by your family and friends, and your grave is in the soil at El Vado. You were a most fortunate man.

CHAPTER 13

Chihuahua, Mexico, May 15, 1846

Captain Zaldinar counted the scalps. He scowled as he removed the objects, stiff with dried blood, from the sack. Each was examined closely for the coarseness of the hair and the color, then laid in one of two piles on his desk.

Zaldinar could have assigned the unpleasant chore to a subordinate, but he always performed the task himself. One day Kirker might make a mistake and come again with the scalps of mestizos, people of mixed Indian and Spanish blood, gentle citizens of Mexico.

He looked at the redheaded American scalper, trying to read his thoughts. Were there scalps here that were not Indian?

Kirker stared back at the captain. He knew Zaldinar hated him and what he hoped to find. Kirker grinned a crooked, comprehending grin. These scalps were all genuine Indian hair.

You are a loathsome son of a whore, thought Zaldinar. He went back to the grisly task of counting the remnants of once live, breathing humans.

The first time Kirker had come to Chihuahua to collect

the bounty money for scalps, Zaldinar had found ones he believed were not the hair of Apache or Comanche. He had had Kirker arrested and thrown into prison. Reflecting back upon that time, he knew he should have had Kirker executed immediately. Instead he had allowed a trial.

The judge had not found the nature of the scalps to be positive proof of their origin, Indian or mestizo. Kirker had been released after six months of confinement. Zaldinar had insured that those months were very bad for the renegade American. The judge had ordered that Kirker be paid for fifty uncontested scalps.

Kirker watched the Mexican officer closely. He and his band of men had arrived in Chihuahua and gone directly to the military headquarters on the southeast side of the city. Hundreds of soldiers drilled and sweated under the hot afternoon sun. A company of armed cavalrymen were practicing a fast, intricate maneuver on the far side of the flat, dusty parade ground. The garrison of crack fighting men was a trap Kirker placed his head into once each year to sell scalps.

Two soldiers with rifles had escorted Kirker and Rauch into the room of the duty officer. The other Americans were instructed to remain outside. Zaldinar, the man Kirker did not want to meet, sat waiting for him.

The guards halted the two Americans in the center of the room. One guard took the bag of scalps from Kirker and handed it to the captain. Then the soldiers took up their positions, one on each side of the captain. They had been given their orders and stood vigilant.

The captain continued to sort the scalps into two piles, one containing what he judged to be the hair of women or children, and the second those of men. Kirker wouldn't quarrel about the division. Zaldinar would like an excuse to fight with him. But Kirker would never allow himself to be taken prisoner again and thrown in the filthy *calabozo*.

A very young lieutenant came through a rear door and

walked hurriedly to the captain's side. He bent and began to speak into Zaldinar's ear in a low, urgent voice.

Kirker listened warily, his senses whetted. He could
hear the quick, whispered tone but couldn't make out the
meaning of the words.

The captain's eyes swept over the Americans, then
dropped to gaze at the scalps. He asked the lieutenant a
question. The young officer answered in the same quick
tone.

Kirker knew that the information the lieutenant brought
effected him. The expression on both of the men's faces
told him that. It could only be bad news. The weight of
the pistol on Kirker's side was a very comforting thing.

As Zaldinar spoke to the lieutenant, giving him orders,
the American gang leader felt the jaws of a trap closing
around him and his men. But Zaldinar had blundered.
The two army privates would not be strong enough fighters to arrest Rauch and Kirker.

"Rauch," Kirker whispered from the corner of his
mouth, "something has gone wrong and we've got trouble. Stand ready to back my play. You take the two on
the left."

"Goddamn. Don't start anything here," Rauch whispered back angrily. "We'll lose everything. We're two
hundred miles inside Mexico, and surrounded by thousands of soldiers."

"You just be ready or we'll never leave here alive."

Captain Zaldinar stopped speaking. The lieutenant pivoted and headed for the rear door. He stole a look at
Kirker.

The scalp hunter caught the young, inexperienced eyes
of the lieutenant, read the thought behind them, and
knew that his suspicions were correct. By looking at me
you've killed yourself, thought Kirker.

"Lieutenant, wait," Kirker called in a sharp voice.
"What has happened?"

Zaldinar rose to his feet and, leaning over his desk,
bristled at Kirker. "This does not concern you," he

snapped. "And, remember, you are in Mexico. I give the orders here."

The lieutenant had halted. He looked questioningly at his superior.

"What are you waiting for, Lieutenant? Carry out your orders." The captain's command crackled with his anger.

Kirker was certain Zaldinar had instructed his junior officer to assemble a platoon of soldiers to take the Americans prisoners. He and his men must leave immediately and, if necessary, fight clear of Chihuahua and escape across the vast distance of hostile territory to safety in Texas.

"Then we leave now," Kirker growled at the captain. "Rauch, let's go."

Kirker whirled and walked swiftly for the front door. Rauch moved with him.

"Guards, arrest those men," commanded the captain. "They are prisoners of war."

For four years Kirker had wanted to kill Zaldinar, ever since his confinement and horrible treatment in the prison. Now Kirker's pulse raced in anticipation at blasting a bullet through the Mexican.

"Shoot them!" hissed Kirker as he spun to the rear. His pistol slid easily from its holster and rose in his hand. He fired.

The flame and smoke from the revolver drove at Zaldinar's chest. A hammer blow struck the Mexican officer and slammed him backward, crashing him into the wall.

One down, thought Kirker. He swung the pistol to shoot the soldier before the man could raise his rifle.

The private whipped up his weapon, cocking it. The bastard gringo had killed the captain. Now the damn scalp hunter would die.

The private felt his heart freeze. The American was quick beyond belief. The deadly blue eyes of the man were staring directly into his soul. And his pistol was aimed precisely. The private's mind barely had time to

register the beginning of a puff of smoke from the end of
the threatening gun before he died.

Kirker twisted to assist Rauch in battle. Rauch's pistol
roared for the second time. The lieutenant stumbled,
clutched at his chest, and fell. All four Mexicans were
down.

"I'll get the scalps," Rauch cried.

Kirker caught Rauch by the arm and jerked him back.
"Leave the damn things. They have no value to us now."

"Right! Right!"

The two Texans plunged through the pall of gray
gunsmoke to the outside.

The remaining four members of the band stood with
revolvers drawn, ready for battle and watching the entrance to the duty officer's room.

"Mount up and follow me out at a slow gallop," Kirker
ordered. As he went with long strides for his horse, he
scanned the soldiers on the parade ground.

The infantrymen had stopped their drill and were looking toward the Texans. The distant cavalry were continuing their practice maneuvers. They hadn't heard the shots
fired inside the room, the distant noise masked by the
thud of the horses' hooves.

An officer of the foot soldiers broke away from his
company and walked hastily in the direction of the captain's headquarters. He called out over his shoulder, and
a soldier trotted off toward the cavalry.

Kirker climbed astride. In only three or four minutes
some of the best horsemen in the world would be pursuing his band. Still, he must keep his pace at a gallop, a
pace that a group of men would use to travel but not one
that would indicate men fleeing.

The Texans passed through the open gate of the compound. Kirker touched the brim of his hat in salute to the
sergeant of the guard. He lifted his mount to a faster
gallop along the streets of Chihuahua.

Rauch called to the other gang members. "We killed
the Mexican captain and three of his men. Now we've got

the hardest ride to make in all our lives, and with a minute's head start."

"Why did you shoot them?" questioned Connard.

"Hell, I don't know why. Ask Kirker yourself. I think we're dead men."

Connard spurred parallel to Kirker. He called out above the rumble of the galloping horses. "What in hell has caused all this?"

"The captain was going to arrest us. Something happened that made him mad. I don't think it was anything we did. It's bigger than that. He said something about making us prisoners of war. I think Mexico and Texas are fighting again."

Rauch rode up on Kirker's other side. "They're coming a mile back. Half a hundred cavalrymen. We've got to find a place to lose them."

"No," Kirker said. "We'll outrun them. They must never get ahead of us and alert other army patrols or the people along the way. We don't want everybody shooting at us all the way to Texas. If we get stuck in Mexico, they'll do everything to track us down. Especially if Texas is at war with them."

The gang leader let his horse feel the sharp rowels of his spurs. The cayuse broke from a gallop to a run. The rest of the men, drawn after Kirker like iron filings to a magnet, matched his speed.

All the mounts had covered many hundreds of miles and were hard-muscled. The Mexican cavalry couldn't catch them. Unless a Texan's horse became lame or fell.

The riders whipped past the citizens on the streets, leaving a long stream of reddish-brown dust trailing behind. They left Chihuahua and raced along the heavily used road, El Camino Real.

Kirker glanced behind him. The cavalry was gaining. He raked his mount harder with his spurs, raising a welt on the animal's ribs. The steed stretched out into a full run.

The strategy of the Mexicans was plain. They would try to exhaust the Texan's horses. It meant nothing if the

Mexican mounts also were run into the ground. Replace-
ments were available anyplace they asked for them.

The gang leader smiled grimly. He leaned forward
over the neck of his horse. "Run, you bastard, but don't
die until I find a fresh one."

The Texan scalpers ran their mustangs beneath the
yellow Mexican sun. The rocky, cactus-studded hills slipped
past as the brutes held the heartbreaking pace.

At a junction in the road the riders veered onto the
right fork, leaving the El Camino Real behind, and sped
along a road leading northeast. Kirker knew the route
well. It hugged the Rio Conchos for one hundred and
fifty miles to the village of Presidio on the banks of the
Rio Grande.

The sun seemed not to move, hanging endlessly in the
sky as the horses labored onward. Sweat dampened the
coats of the mounts. It thickened to clotted foam that
was flung from the straining bodies.

"We're pulling ahead," Rauch called. "But only a
little."

"Push harder," replied Kirker. "We made need enough
time to get new horses the first time we see some." He
recalled a ranch a few miles ahead where the river made
a wide loop to the west. He raised his arm and began to
lash his mount.

"Horses!" exclaimed Kirker. "A goddamn corral full
of horses."

" 'Bout time. These we've got couldn't go another half
mile," Rauch replied.

The Texans had topped a low ridge and were looking
down on the buildings of a rancho beside the Rio Conchos. They glanced nervously to the rear at a dust cloud
sweeping along the road.

"Five, maybe six minutes, that's all we've got," said
Kirker.

He led the men from the main road and down the lane
to the ranch. He halted at the corral on the bank close

above the river. As the riders swung to the ground the exhausted horses, trembling with fatigue, splayed their legs to keep from falling.

Kirker quickly surveyed the hacienda in a grove of cottonwoods a hundred yards distant. "The people here haven't heard us yet. Rauch, you and Borkan walk partway over there with your rifles. If anybody comes outside, keep them from bothering us while we swap horses.

"Kill them if they put up an argument. We'll catch new horses and pick you up."

The two men jerked their rifles from their scabbards and trotted off.

"Wiestling, you're the best with a lariat. Get in the corral and rope us good mounts. The rest of you change all the saddles as fast as you can. Move! Hurry it!"

The men sprang to their tasks. The long loop of the lariat snaked out and snagged the head of one of the milling horses in the corral. In three minutes six horses were saddled.

"Open the gate," ordered the gang leader. "Run the rest of those broncs ahead of you up the river a ways. Then scatter and hide them in some of that brush." He grabbed the reins of two saddled horses. "I'll get Rauch and Borkan and catch up with you."

At the thunder of hooves from the departing remuda of mustangs, a man ran from the hacienda. "Stop!" he screamed. "What are you doing?"

Rauch fired and the man collapsed to the ground. "The dumb fool should have stayed in the house," Rauch said.

Kirker wheeled up with the spare mounts. Rauch and Borkan leapt up onto the horses. The men spurred north beside the Rio Conchos.

The night was soot-black, the stars small and far away, and the moon's face was turned away from the earth.

"They can't follow us in the dark," said Flaccus, "and I'm god-awful tired. Let's rest for a while."

"They don't have to see our tracks," said Kirker. "Our

destination will be clear to them. We'll be heading for the town of Coyame. In an hour those cavalrymen could have found some of the ponies we ran off, enough for a goodly number of men to keep after us."

"Then let's turn into the hills and let them ride on past," said Flaccus.

"I'm still doing the thinking for all of us," Kirker said with a growl. "If war has started between them and us, then I want to get to Texas. And I say our asses are harder than the asses of the Mexicans and we can stay ahead of them."

Flaccus grumbled under his breath and fell silent.

Kirker continued to speak. "By morning we can be forty miles closer to Texas. We'll take turns with one man guiding the way. The rest of us will sleep in the saddle. Line up and pass your reins to the man ahead. That way your horse won't wander off in the dark. I'll lead first. Rest as much as you can. Tomorrow will be a hard day. I expect we'll do some fighting."

The town of Coyame lay dozing under the noonday sun when Kirker and his band of Texans entered its outskirts. A church with a high belfrey and a bell, two cantinas, and a smattering of adobe and stone houses were hemmed in on one narrow street. Nearly a score of horses were tied along the street. The largest gatherings were fastened in front of the cantinas.

"Time to change ponies again," Kirker said. He stared ahead with tired, bloodshot eyes. "There's not one man, woman, or child on the street."

"You mean, just ride in there and take the horses right in broad daylight?" asked Connard. He chuckled low and mean in his throat. "I've always wanted to shoot the hell out of a Mexican town. Maybe this one will wake up and be the one that gives me the pleasure."

"It won't take but a few seconds to change saddles," Kirker said. "And I'm thinking the people will all sleep or drink beer right through the horse swapping." He pointed. "Don't wake that old man snoozing in the shade of that tree."

The gang leader pulled his hat lower over his eyes. "Pick the mount you like. I'm going to take a look at the ones at the cantina on the right. All of you meet up with me on the far edge of town."

The Texans separated as they walked their weary cayuses along the main street of Coyame. Each man veered aside to stop close to a tethered mount. With practiced hands they removed the saddles from the new horses and cinched their own in its place. Immediately they climbed astride.

At the northern border of Coyame, the Texans mustered. Connard rode in last. "Not one chance to get in a little target practice," he complained.

Kirker inspected the new mounts and spoke to the men. "These ponies are good animals and are well rested. So we'll bypass Presidio, holding to the east of it. If we're at war with Mexico, the news might have reached those places. Sometimes Mexican Army patrols set up a temporary station at the old fort in Presidio. The last thing we want is a new company of Mexican cavalry after us."

"Suppose the bunch of Mexicans that are chasing us now don't stop?" asked Rauch. "I'd like to slow down enough to get a good meal and a night's sleep."

"Then we'll stop them permanently at the first good ambush point east of Presidio," replied Kirker.

CHAPTER 14

I count twenty-three soldiers," Kirker said, staring intently down into the shallow gorge full of the blue-gray shadows of late evening.

He lay with his band of Texans in the brush on the lip of the rimrock where the Rio Terlingua cut a shallow ravine through the foot of La Mota Mountain. Below him at a long rifle shot, a squad of Mexican cavalrymen in red-and-blue uniforms waded their weary mounts across the shoals of the river.

The officer was out in front of his men by fifty feet. He glanced back at the riders and then up at the trail leading through the break in the brown sandstone ledge hemming in the river. His eyes searched the dense brush on top of the rock outcrop.

"Come on, come on," muttered Rauch. "Move, damn you. It'll be too dark to see the sights of my rifle in a minute."

"The officer should have turned his men back before now," Borkan said. "We're miles east of Presidio. He seems bent on chasing us clear to Austin."

"Look at him. He's leery of the narrowness of the trail

up from the river to the plain," Rauch pointed out.
"Maybe he'll quit and go back to Mexico now."

"From his point of view we're the enemy and still in
Mexico," replied Kirker. "He can't turn back. He's made
it safely past a hundred places where we could've ambushed him. He'll think this place is like all the rest."

"You're right. Look, he's coming," Connard said, his
voice filling with anticipation. "He's decided to gamble
again that the path's safe. Soon we'll have some good
shooting practice."

The officer called a command, and the cavalrymen
pulled their muskets from saddle scabbards and held
them ready. At a second command the men reined in
their mounts, allowing the distance between each of them
to open to three or four horse-lengths so that all the
soldiers wouldn't be in the confined neck of the gorge at
one time.

"I'll take the officer and the next man. That's probably
the sergeant," Kirker said as he picked up one of his
rifles. "Rauch, you take the next two. The rest of you
fellows count off two men each down the line. Now don't
shoot someone else's target. Take steady aim and drop a
pair of them.

"When your rifles are empty, use your pistols. The
range is long, but you still may hit something. And the
extra shots should help stampede all the live Mexicans
back south."

Kirker raised the rifle to his shoulder. "Get ready. Fire
when I do," he ordered.

The long-barreled weapon exploded harshly. The Mexican officer was flung backward by the punch of the
bullet. His feet came loose from the stirrups, and he fell
from the back of his horse.

Rifles crashed along the line of Kirker's men. Several
more cavalrymen tumbled from their mounts.

The Texan leader dropped his first gun and snatched
up the second. Below him, the Mexican sergeant was
shouting to his troops. His musket whipped up, and he

fired into the brush that concealed his enemies on the rocks above.

Kirker heard the large-caliber ball smash into the branches near his head. The Texan killed the sergeant with a shot in the chest.

Then Kirker's men were firing a second volley. Five more horses were suddenly riderless.

The Paterson Colts of the scalp hunters began to boom, filling the ravine with rapid explosions. A soldier flung up his arms and toppled to the ground.

The cavalrymen, still astride their mounts, spun them to the rear and whipped and spurred toward the river.

Another soldier was struck by a bullet. He leaned forward and clutched at the neck of his steed. He strove vainly to hold his seat as the frightened beast he rode fled with its mates. "Look at them run," cried Rauch. "They'll not quit until they're back in Chihuahua."

"Wasn't that wonderful shooting?" exclaimed Connard. "We killed more than half of them. Damn, oh, damn, I like to put a bullet in a man and watch him fall."

The last of the fleeing Mexicans vanished into the brush beyond the river. The Texans listened until the sound of the running horses could no longer be heard.

"Let's get down there and see what valuables those greasers were carrying," Borkan said.

"Charge your guns first," Kirker ordered. "Then go check the soldiers' pockets, but watch for live ones," he warned.

The men swiftly reloaded their weapons. Rauch and Flaccus finished first and clambered down from their hiding places.

Kirker maintained a slow pace and came last. Every shot might not have struck true. Wounded men could still kill.

Rauch and Flaccus reached the bodies. Rauch ignored the enlisted men, for they were poorly paid, and went straight to the Mexican officer. The caballeros always had the most money. He kicked his toe in under the body of the officer and heaved upward to roll him over.

As the man flopped onto his back his hand suddenly moved. It held a cocked pistol that stabbed out, pointing directly into Rauch's face. A bright flame flashed from the open end of the barrel.

Rauch, seeing the weapon, tried to dodge to one side to escape the shot. He was too slow. The bullet entered the front of his neck and tore free at the base of his head.

The wounded bandit sat down heavily on the ground. An unbelieving expression washed over his face as he looked down at the blood pumping in great spurts from his severed jugular.

A guttural cry escaped Rauch as he watched the spouting red liquid. His countenance twisted in terror. He shoved his thumb into the hole in his neck, trying to stem the cascade of blood.

"Son of a bitch," shouted Flaccus. He shot the officer twice. "Shoot the others," he yelled.

The Texans, except Kirker, stormed among the corpses, firing into the uniformed bodies. Kirker held his pistol and regarded the dead officer. You were stupid, he thought. You led your men straight into a trap.

Rauch sat for a moment watching the blood flow down his arm and drip from his elbow. He began to shudder. His eyes canted upward into his head. He fell to the side. The blood flow weakened quickly, then ceased.

Kirker walked over to Rauch. "You bastard," he said. "You never would listen to me." But your mistake has saved me the trouble of shooting you, Kirker thought.

The Texans left the killing ground with eight horses and a small handful of gold and silver coins. The dead lay where they had fallen.

Senator Simon Caverhill left the card parlor and immediately moved to the side, out of the rectangle of lamp glow spilling from the open doorway. He had many enemies, but that didn't worry him. His action was merely precautionary. He intended to live a very long time.

He touched his two front pockets, bulging and heavy with paper money and gold coin. Luck had been perched on his shoulder with an unshakable hold, and he had won steadily at poker for hours. Some men with little imagination might even say he had won a fortune.

All around him the night in Austin City was dark under thick clouds. Not one star or glimmer of sky light broke the utter blackness. A quarter mile away, along the main street that lay beside the Colorado River, the single oil lantern at the entrance of the hotel was only a tiny pinprick of fire.

Nothing stirred on the avenue in the small, dreary hours of the morning. Even the night insects were mute and asleep. The hushed quiet lay expectant, as if waiting for something to awaken it.

Caverhill pushed into the yielding darkness. He would retrieve his horse from the stable behind the gambling parlor and ride to the hotel. In a very few hours he had to be traveling to his ranch on the Llano River. Kirker would be waiting.

The stale, musty odor of old hay and horse droppings filled his nostrils when he entered the open door of the stable. He angled to the right in the direction of the stall that held his mount.

Segments of the deep murk abruptly moved, like black specters taking shape. The barely discernible forms became more distinct, and the figures of four men tore free from the wall of darkness. They sprang at Caverhill.

By reflex, he dropped to a low, crouched position. He expected to hear a gun explode, to see the flash of burning powder.

But there wasn't any sound or flame. Only the men charging at Caverhill. They intended to kill him quietly.

Caverhill cursed the stygian gloom. The men must have been hidden in the stable for some time and their eyes would be adjusted to the darkness, but he was almost blind.

He leapt to meet his attackers, the last thing they would expect. His pistol came into his hand. The man directly before him must be blasted out of the way to make an opening for Caverhill to escape.

The opponent on the right was closing in the fastest. His arms rose and he swung a club, invisible to Caverhill in the darkness.

The weapon swept down, missing Caverhill's head as he ducked aside but ripping his ear. The club continued its course and crashed down on the top of his shoulder. Pain, intense as a bolt of lightning, roared through muscle and tendon. The pistol dropped from his numb fingers.

The four men had rushed within striking distance of Caverhill. One slashed at his face. He heard the swish of the blade slicing air. The man's swing had been short by the thickness of a shadow.

Caverhill drove forward into the man who had missed with the knife. He struck out with his good left hand, a solid blow to the head. A gasping moan escaped the man and he sank backward.

A red-hot streak burned across Caverhill's back. One of his assailants had caught him with a knife. He felt no weakness. Only rage.

Caverhill pivoted before the man could cut again. He hurled himself forward and down, rolling once on the ground. His spinning body knocked the legs from under the man. At the same time Caverhill reached and grabbed the man by the front of his clothes and yanked, adding momentum to the crashing descent of his attacker. The man's head hit the earth with a sodden thud.

Caverhill made a hasty sweep with his hands over the floor of the stable, searching for the man's knife. He found nothing except dirt and hay chaff. His fingers closed upon a handful of the debris.

Caverhill's two remaining opponents rushed him again. He came erect, dodging left. As one of the men stabbed at him Caverhill flung the scrapings from the floor into his eyes.

The man's strike missed, and before the hand with the knife could be withdrawn, Caverhill caught it in a viselike grip. Swiftly, brutally, he pounded the man twice in the face. Bones broke under the knuckles of his hammering fist.

He tore the weapon from the man's weakening hand, whirled, and went to the side. The fourth man was close, and his knife skittered across Caverhill's ribs.

As Caverhill spun, he extended his arm to its full length and struck out with his knife. The last man propelled himself backward, desperately trying to move out of Caverhill's reach. He failed. Two inches of steel blade went into his chest.

Caverhill twisted away in the darkness. He crouched, holding the knife poised, awaiting the next attack.

"Let's get out of here," one of the men yelled, his voice garbled, as if he spoke from a broken mouth.

Through the lighter shade of darkness in the doorway, three men ran from the stable in frantic haste. One figure lay unmoving on the ground.

Caverhill straightened. The blood strummed in his veins. He raised his head and laughed. The joy of battle had put the strength of ten in his arms. He was invincible against ordinary men.

He felt around on the floor of the stable until he found his pistol. He holstered the weapon, thinking that the loads must be checked at first light. Caverhill led his horse from its stall and mounted. He left by the small rear door. Men who had failed to kill him with knives might decide to try with rifles.

The senator passed the hotel and, a block farther along, went on by the home and office of the doctor. No one must see him injured and bloody. He had disabled a few of his enemies. There were others, and they, like a pack of coyotes, would gather and try to pull him down if they thought he was badly wounded and weakened.

He looked to the northwest. Out there at his ranch on the banks of the Llano River, his knife cuts would be treated. The mulatto slave he had purchased in New Orleans had great skill as a healer. She had brought with her a sizable pharmacopoeia of natural substances, roots, bark, and leaves of plants from which poultices and salves could be made that would stop infection. And strong teas could be brewed that healed from within. Caverhill had observed her examining the plants that grew on the ranch for their possible curative powers.

He kicked his horse in the ribs. The steed ran the familiar road. Each time it tried to slow, he sent it onward with a thump to its flank.

Daylight was a gray curtain opening in the east when the senator reached the Llano River. Beyond the stream, his slaves were already in the bottomland beside the river. Their axes rang as they chopped the cottonwood and pecan trees, clearing the land for the growing of cultivated crops. Massive piles of logs and brush smoldered and flamed, having burned all night. Horses dragged large sections of trees into more piles.

Caverhill veered from the main road that crossed the river near the slaves. Farther east, he forded the stream. The horse was guided through the woods and up the bluff to the big white house. He stopped the tired mount at the edge of the porch and stiffly climbed down.

Kirker watched the columns of gray smoke slowly rising from burning wood in the valley below him. He sat in one of the wicker chairs on the porch of Caverhill's new house. A rich man's house.

The structure was located on the north bank of the Llano River overlooking far-flung meadows of side oats, grama, and blue-stem grass as high as a man's knees. Patches of live oak were scattered here and there in the wide grassland. On the flood plain of the Llano, large trees made a dense forest. Three to four hundred acres of the bottomland had been cleared. The fields were situated so that the rich, black soil could be irrigated from the river.

To the right of the house in a grove of trees there were squat log cabins, recently constructed slave quarters. The senator had become a slave owner since Kirker had last been there.

Kirker saw Caverhill come up the steps at the end of the porch. He noted with surprise that the senator's shirt was torn and plastered with fresh blood. Even his trousers were soaked with blood.

The senator's step broke when he spied Kirker sitting in one of the tall-backed chairs. With a deliberate stride he then went on to the front door and, without a word, went inside.

For an instant as Caverhill turned, Kirker saw a second mass of blood on the broad back of the man. How badly was Caverhill wounded? Kirker grinned. Perhaps very seriously.

"Millicent, come here at once," Caverhill called inside the house.

Kirker moved to a window and peered through. The light-colored Negress that had come to his knock at the door earlier in the morning hurried from the rear of the house.

"Bring your medicines and needle," Caverhill ordered. "Have Tona bring me fresh clothing and prepare a bath."

Caverhill's movements were strong. His injuries must not be deep. Kirker returned to his chair and again sat staring down at the laboring men and the smoky fires close to the river. But he didn't truly see the activity there. His thoughts were on Caverhill. The man would be hard to kill.

The Texas senator came from the house. He wore a fresh shirt and trousers. He walked with his normal, lithe stride. Kirker couldn't detect one sign that the man had been wounded.

"Kirker, where have you been for three months?" Caverhill spoke sharply. "I paid you good money to gather information for me and you didn't return."

"I came past here to report when I got back from Mexico, but you'd gone, no one knew where. So I went on to Houston to do a job. I needed money. Our luck in Mexico was bad. The damn war between the Mexicans and us started while we were there. We had to shoot some of the greasers' soldiers to get back to Texas."

"Yes, the war started at Palo Alto near the mouth of the Rio Grande," Caverhill replied. "There've been two battles since then."

"I traveled to Fort Leavenworth, Kansas, to check on a rumor that an army of Americans would be assembled at the fort to march on Santa Fe. The rumor was fact. General Stephen Kearny was mustering the 1st Dragoons and one thousand volunteers from Missouri to take New Mexico and from there move on and conquer California. By now he may have marched out from Fort Leavenworth with his so-called Army of the West."

Caverhill fell silent, watching Kirker. The senator had several plans to put in motion. In times of war many opportunities offered themselves for a man to garner great riches, if he wasn't afraid to use force and move quickly. He needed the murderous scalp hunter.

"Come inside," Caverhill said. "I have a plan that will make you wealthy. If you're brave enough to help me."

Caverhill stalked ahead to the library, a huge room with shelves covering two walls and reaching to the high ceiling. Kirker saw that all the shelves were empty except for one row of books and a rolled-up map. Only three pieces of furniture, a round table and two chairs, were in the room. A thick wool carpet covered the floor. Kirker smelled fresh paint. The Texas senator was building a magnificent ranch, with a mansion for his home.

"Sit there," said Caverhill, thrusting a thumb at the table and chairs. He took up the map and spread it on the table. He sat down across from Kirker.

The scalp hunter studied the State senator as the man weighted down the corners of the map. Caverhill had come from New Orleans ten years before to join Houston's army and help defeat the Mexicans. In the years after the victory he had prospered, his wealth accumulating rapidly. He had been elected senator in the first election of the new National Government of Texas.

Caverhill had no opposition for that election. John Towson had campaigned against him at first. Then Towson had made the unfortunate mistake of calling Caverhill a thief. Retribution had come swiftly in the oak woods at the junction of Bull Creek and the Colorado River. Caverhill killed Towson in a duel with pistols.

Other enemies of Caverhill, or men who merely stood in his path, would disappear or hurriedly leave the country. Kirker had accepted gold from Caverhill to kill or harass the senator's opponents. His knowledge of those deeds was dangerous to Kirker. He felt a cold breeze along his spine as Caverhill raised his head and stared at him with his mud-colored eyes. Caverhill was the only man Kirker had ever feared. One day Kirker would leave Texas and get far away from Caverhill. Or kill Caverhill if he could.

CHAPTER 15

"Tell me about the country east of the Sangre de Cristo Mountains," directed Caverhill. "Especially about the ranchos along the Rio Pecos."

Kirker leaned forward. His hand passed over the map from north to south, indicating the course of the river. "It's damn fine grazing country with thick, tall grass. However the river is nearly the only source of water. Almost all the streams that feed the river come from the hills west of the river. From the east the creeks are small and short and often dry, because the Staked Plains are close and slant off to the east, carrying that water toward Texas."

"That Rio Pecos land, and the land all the way to the Rio Grande, is part of Texas," interjected Caverhill.

"I've heard that Texas claim. However, the Mexicans are there on their big ranchos, and I saw no sign that they were moving out."

"That may soon change," said Caverhill. "Go on with what you have to say about the land and the people." He had journeyed from Austin to Santa Fe the year before. During a party at the Palace of the Governors he had met

149

Luis Baustista and Emmanuel Solis. They had talked of land and ranching, and the Mexican caballeros had told him of their large ranchos on the Rio Pecos. Caverhill had decided those ranchos could become his without too much danger, and a plan came to him. He regretted not having taken time to explore the Rio Pecos on his return trip to Austin.

"The Pecos runs all year. It's swampy in places and has dangerous quicksand holes. The valley twists and turns a lot. Often the main current breaks up and flows in three or four separate streams for miles. Then it all comes back together again where hard rock walls crowd it."

"And the ranchos. Where are they located?"

"The Pecos comes out of the Sangre de Cristos about here." Kirker touched the map with a finger. "That's where we struck the river. The northernmost rancho is here at the junction of the Gallinas River and the Pecos. It has a walled hacienda. From its size I judge maybe ten families may live there."

"How many fighting men do you figure they would have?"

"Twelve to fifteen. But at any one time, most likely some of them would be out on the range caring for the livestock, or to Santa Fe or Las Vegas for supplies."

Caverhill studied the map.

"How much livestock did you see?"

"I estimate a hundred thousand sheep and maybe one thousand head of cattle. Those Mexicans like sheep best." Kirker had been watching the senator and now saw the light brighten in his eyes at the mention of the large number of sheep.

Kirker continued. "The second rancho is a long day's ride to the south. The hacienda is on the west side of the Pecos. It also has a defensive wall, and a tall tower in addition. Those two ranchos have been operated for fifty years or more under the ownership of the same families. They must be tough people. If they were warned of an attack and could get behind those walls, they'd be hard to dislodge. But I'm betting none of those places keep

twenty-four-hour lookouts. The haciendas can be taken."
Kirker knew Caverhill would want to know that.

"This second Mexican place has about the same number of livestock as the first. But the other two farther
south along the Pecos are newer and smaller. Their herds
are about half that size."

Caverhill asked many questions and listened closely to
Kirker's responses. The two men talked until nearly noon.
Finally Caverhill leaned back in his chair. He looked out
the window and down at the slaves working to clear the
new ground near the Llano. For several minutes he was
quiet.

"Kirker, I'll pay you twenty-five cents for each sheep
you bring out of New Mexico."

Kirker laughed sardonically. "That ain't anywheres near
a fair price. That's dry country for a hundred miles east
of the Rio Pecos. I'd lose most of the animals if I didn't
happen to hit it right after a good rain. And then there's
another four hundred and fifty to five hundred miles to
drive the sheep. They're a slow-traveling animal. Anyone
chasing his livestock could easily overtake us."

Caverhill turned to Kirker. His eyes were like frozen
spheres of dirty water. "Not if you left no one alive
behind you. Suppose you took a force of men and took
this rancho at the Gallinas River. Then make a sweep
rounding up all the livestock close to the river. Do that
about noon, when most of the animals would be watering
and congregated there. Then send the herd east with five
or six men. With your remaining force, ride south to the
next rancho. Repeat the action you took at the Gallinas
rancho. Capture the hacienda and drive the livestock east
with a few men. And so forth for the remaining two
ranchos."

"Sounds like a bloomin' military campaign," Kirker
said with a growl. "I'm no soldier." He shook his head.

"It is a military campaign, Kirker. And you've been
conducting very similar actions for many years, except on
a much smaller scale. There is a war being fought with
Mexico right now near the Gulf of Mexico. Soon there

will be fighting in New Mexico. Many people will be killed. Why fight and kill for nothing? The Mexican army in Santa Fe will be too busy to come after you. And surely the American army officers won't divert part of their strength to chase you to recover livestock for Mexicans. But the best part of the plan is that no one will find out what happened for days, perhaps weeks. Maybe never. The first rain will destroy any tracks you make. The people and the livestock will have simply disappeared. Even when someone begins to ask questions, I'm certain the deed would be blamed on Indians or Comancheros."

Kirker had slowly bent forward as Caverhill spoke. He looked again at the map, his mind replaying his recent views of the river, land, the ranchos, and the thousands of sheep and cows on the Rio Pecos.

He glanced up, his eyes smoldering as he mentally counted the money that could be made. "I'd need forty men and maybe two months to ten weeks to do it. Would there be enough money in it for that many men?"

"The fewer men you use, the more you make for yourself. Also, the fewer tongues to tell what you did."

Kirker believed he could accomplish the job with thirty men or less. The larger number was strictly bargaining stock to raise the pay from Caverhill. "How many sheep and cows do you want?" he asked.

"All you can drive. You'll be crowding the livestock, and there's rough land to cross. You'll lose one quarter to one half of the animals you begin with. So start with all you can round up in one long sweep along the river at each rancho. Then move promptly to the next place."

"Pay me a dollar a head for the sheep and three dollars for cows, and I'll do it. You got that much money?"

Caverhill grinned thinly. "More than enough. Can you find men to ride with you?"

"I could get a thousand if I wanted to. The people haven't forgotten the Alamo massacre and the slaughter of our soliders at Goliad after they'd surrendered to Santa Anna. Yes, sir. I could get two thousand men."

"Don't hire any men from Austin. Go to Houston and

get them. Have them go directly home after the livestock drive is completed. Tell them to keep their mouths shut. Don't tell them who you work for."

"I'll need some money to pay the men beforehand. Just enough to pay part of what they'll earn. They can wait for the bulk of it until we return."

"How much?"

Kirker quickly calculated. "Say, twelve thousand dollars."

"All right. Twelve thousand dollars. But we haven't settled on the price for the livestock delivered."

"Yes, we did. I told you what I'd do it for."

"Too high. The price for a cow is all right at three dollars. I'll pay you forty cents for each sheep."

"No, sir. Not enough. Say seventy-five cents."

"Fifty cents, and that's my last offer."

Kirker sadly reduced the giant sum of money he'd been envisioning. "Fifty cents it is. I'll have them animals to your ranch before the first frost."

"Don't let one sheep or cow set foot on my land," Caverhill said, his voice turning coarse and threatening. "You deliver the livestock to that hilly land between the Llano and the San Saba Rivers where Wet Beaver Creek and Las Moras Creek head up." He would take his slaves and drive the livestock onto his land. The sheep would be used to stock the ranch. The heavily branded Mexican cattle would be driven to Houston and sold to a buyer he knew who asked no questions about ownership.

"Do you know the place I describe?"

"I know the place," replied Kirker.

"I warn you, Kirker, don't leave anyone alive behind you at those ranchos on the Pecos. Every man, woman, and child must be killed. Bury them where they'll never be found."

"I don't want to be hung, either," said Kirker. "There'll be no sign left for anyone to find. I'll burn down those damn Mexican haciendas too."

Caverhill leapt to his feet. "Don't you damage one

building or any of the furnishings. Do you hear me
plainly? Not one building."

"All right," Kirker hurriedly replied.

"Stop in Austin and get Glen Sansen and take him
with you."

"Why that damn forger? He hasn't ridden a horse ten
miles in ten years and couldn't keep up at all."

"You're wrong. He's been riding every day for a month.
He's up to twenty miles a day. I've had someone riding
with him to be certain he's not lying about that."

Kirker realized Caverhill had been planning this campaign into New Mexico for some time. "We'll be traveling closer to fifty miles a day. He'll never keep up."

"You'll see that he does. Tie him to his horse if you
have to. He must be with you at each rancho. He'll be
collecting every written document that can be found.
You help him. Is all this understood?"

"Yes. It's plain enough." Somehow Caverhill was going
to take the haciendas and land, as well as the livestock.
Now, how would he pull that off? Kirker turned to leave.

"No one left alive," the Texas senator called after him.

Behind a slightly ajar door, the yellow-skinned Negress,
Millicent, hastily withdrew to the kitchen. Her face was
ugly with hate.

Kirker brought his band of men down from the Staked
Plains and onto the wagon road. He halted them beneath
the steep walls of Mesa Quatas fifteen miles north of the
junction of the Rio Gallinas and the Rio Pecos. He rode
out in front and turned to face the bearded, dusty
horsemen.

"That is the road to the Mexican ranchos we've ridden
six hundred miles to find." He pointed down at the
wheel tracks in the dirt. "We start our campaign here so
that no one escapes us and gets to Santa Fe. Every
Mexican south of us must die. Every head of livestock we
can round up will be driven to Texas. You'll make more

money in two months than you can make in two years working for wages."

Kirker ranged his sight over the thirty fighting men he'd recruited. Except for Wiestling, who'd been killed in a robbery in Houston, the four men who had escaped with him from Mexico were here. The rest of the band was made up of the worst thieves and murderers, the toughest men he could find in all of southern Texas.

"If any man here isn't up to spilling a little Mexican blood, then let him turn around and get his ass back to Texas. The ones that stay will do exactly as I say. Who's leaving?"

The men steadily looked back at him. Connard was smiling and fondling the butt of his pistol.

Kirker spoke. "So nobody's leaving, eh? Well, that's good. We'll ride easy for three hours or so until we see the first hacienda. Then we'll camp quiet like, and take the place first thing come daylight.

"Borkan, ride out a quarter mile in the lead and watch for riders on the road or tending the livestock. We don't want to be seen until we're ready. If you spot somebody, come back whippin' and spurrin' and warn us. Then we'll figure out what to do."

"I'll do that," replied Borkan. He spurred his mount from the pack of Texans.

CHAPTER 16

August 15, 1846

Jacob crested the last range of high hills. The green valley of the Rio Pecos lay three miles ahead to the east. Beyond the river, the immense Llano Estacado, perfectly flat and shimmering with heat, stretched away forever. Far to the southeast, thunderheads were building. He pulled his view back from the great plain and spotted the Solis hacienda, a tiny brown dot on the bench above the river.

The horse also saw the familiar land and, sensing the end of the day's labor, increased its pace to a swift gallop. The ground, still damp and soft from a rain during the previous night, muffled the fall of the hooves to a low mutter.

A hidden smile drifted across Jacob's heart as the distance between him and the hacienda narrowed. Soon he would be at the gate, and Petra would come with her bright smile to greet him. He'd hug her female softness and breathe in her sweet woman smell.

Tamarron's smile broke to the surface as he remembered that at first he had thought of Petra merely as a woman. But over the months his mind, unbidden, silently began to call her by name each time she gave him pleasure. Petra had grown to have infinite value to him.

He tightened the reins of the horse suddenly, dragging it down to a slow walk. Something was out of kilter, somehow wrong. He scanned the terrain in all directions. He saw the tall, wild grass, heavy with seed heads, rippling on the hill slopes and in the hollows as a quick wind passed by. Where were all the cattle and sheep?

Jacob brought the horse to a standstill. His sight jumped to the hacienda. There was no smoke from cook fires, nor were there children's voices. In the evening, after the heat of the August day had lessened, the children should be out and running about playing. He'd be able to hear them easily across the few hundred yards to the hacienda.

Jacob lifted his pistol from its holster to inspect the caps and the set of the balls against the powder charge. He guided the horse to the north. Shortly he struck the road that came from Sante Fe. The road held no tracks of either horses or livestock. Nothing had trod here since the rain the previous night. With his worry swiftly intensifying, he rode toward the hacienda.

The gate stood open. The courtyard was empty except for two saddled horses tied to the hitch rail at the front entrance of the hacienda. The heavy main entry door gaped wide.

Tamarron rode partway across the compound. "Hello, house," he called. "May I spend the night? It looks like rain again."

As he waited for a reply Tamarron quickly scanned the courtyard. To his left, thirty feet away on the ground, there was a dark patch as big as a man's hat. A section of the wall of the house near the door was stained with the same brown. The color of dried blood. Men, maybe women, had died here. Looking more closely at the thick adobe wall, he identified fresh bullet marks among the old ones from past battles. The rancho had been attacked.

A cold, empty wind of fear whistled through Tamarron's mind. Was his family still alive? Was Petra alive?

Tamarron swung to the ground. He must search the house.

A heavily bearded white man stepped from the hacienda. "Stop where you are. I didn't say you could dismount." He spoke loudly in a harsh voice.

Tamarron halted. The gringo acted as if he owned the rancho. Damn him. He must be one of the men responsible for the blood spilling. Jacob felt his anger—cold, hard, and determined. He would kill the bastard. But first he needed information. Where was the owner of the second horse?

"I thought nobody heard me call out," Tamarron said. "I could use a night under a roof and out of the rain." He hiked a thumb at the thunderheads moving in.

The suspicious eyes of the man ranged over Tamarron's tight leather pants and high-peaked, broad-brimmed hat. "You're dressed like a Mexican. Where are you from? What are you doing here?"

"I've been in Santa Fe. I trap fur in the winter and then ride as a vaquero in the summer for the Mexican ranchers. I'm looking for work."

A second man, very slim, came from the inside of the hacienda and stopped beside the big man. Jacob noted the smooth quickness of his movements.

"What were you looking at on the ground?" asked the slim man. His tone was hard. Without waiting for an answer, he spoke angrily to his cohort. "I think he saw the blood you didn't cover. Now he'll have to join the others."

Tamarron saw the men shift their stances in readiness for gunplay.

The game had ended. The time for killing was now. There were two against him. Why give them a chance?

"*Die!*" Tamarron cried out as he drew his pistol.

The slim man would be the quickest. Tamarron shot into the center of him. The man crumpled and fell.

The bearded man moved faster than Tamarron thought he could. His pistol came out of its holster and rose to point where Tamarron stood.

Tamarron was moving to the side as he fired, and his second adversary had to alter the aim of his gun to compensate. Which wasted a precious fraction of a second.

Tamarron exploded the outlaw's pounding heart with a speeding lead ball.

The slim man groaned and rolled his head. Tamarron sprang to his side and yanked him to a sitting position. The man had been hit hard in the chest. His lungs would fill with blood. Answers had to be gotten quickly before he died.

"Where are all the people of the rancho?" Tamarron demanded.

The bandit stared at Tamarron, and his mouth twisted in a sneer. His hand came up to feel at the wound in his chest. "You shoot me and then ask me questions. Well, go to hell."

Tamarron slapped the man left and right, rocking his head on his shoulders. "Answer me, damn you!"

The bandit feebly pulled at the strong hand that held him upright. He coughed as his lungs filled with blood. The bright red liquid sprayed into the air. The man saw the blood, and his eyes began to tremble with fright.

"Where are all the Solis people?" Tamarron demanded again. "Tell me and I'll help you die quickly."

"All dead," the outlaw gasped. "All dead and buried, and you'll never find the graves."

"The woman with a scar on her face, what about her? Is she dead?"

The Texan knew he was dying, and his eyes lost their fear. A sly thought came to him: So your woman was here. Then suffer with me.

"She is dead. De—" said the man as his throat and mouth filled and gurgled with his blood.

Tamarron let the slack body of the outlaw fall to the

ground. He rose weakly to his feet. Petra dead! Damn
the cruel God that would allow that to happen.

He pivoted to look at the new adobe walls Petra had
made to build their home. For a moment he could hear
the haunting echos of her voice calling out happily to the
children at play in the courtyard. Then there was nothing. Never again would she press close to him and flood
his being with delight. All the loneliness that had been
banished from Jacob these past weeks came pouring back.
The core of him dissolved into brittle emptiness.

Jacob hastened from room to room in the hacienda.
The possessions of the occupants appeared to be in place,
except for the silver and other small, valuable articles. He
found several places where an attempt had been made to
hide puddles of blood. If he hadn't known what to look
for, they would have gone unnoticed. Not one body did
he discover.

He circled the building, looking everywhere. Many
men and horses had been in the compound earlier in the
day. He followed the tracks to the gate. The horsemen
had ridden south on the wagon road.

Jacob, feeling the pain of his horrible loss, leaned
against the wall of the hacienda. His family was gone,
dead and buried according to the raider. The men responsible for the deed had spent the night at the rancho.
Apparently the sheep and cattle had been driven away
before the rain. But the loss of the livestock had no
significance to Jacob.

He felt his rage building to a white heat in his brain.
He hurried to his bedroom. His vaquero clothing was
ripped away and flung into a corner. Swiftly he donned
his buckskins, a pair of thick moccasins, and his flat-
crowned trapper's hat. Extra powder, firing caps and
lead balls, and a small quantity of food were added to the
pack on his horse.

He would travel lightly, for he had men to catch and
they had a long head start. But he would catch them and
kill every one. All he had left now was a sour revenge.
He would take that revenge any way he could.

He paused half a minute to jerk the saddles and bridles from the bandits' horses. Let them fend for themselves.

Tamarron led his horse across the courtyard to the bodies of the outlaws. He cursed them as he leaned over the corpses and, with swift, deft cuts of his knife, loosened their scalps and ripped them free.

One strong pull of his arms yanked him astride. The horse tossed its head in disapproval as it was guided in the direction of the gate. Then it felt the sure, purposeful tension of the reins and its master positioning himself over its shoulders to help it carry its load more easily. The steed broke into a run from the courtyard.

Jacob did not look back. There was nothing there for him.

The shadows grew long as the steed ran swiftly, directly upon the tracks of the enemy. Miles fell away behind.

On the far-off horizon the Gallinas Mountains devoured the crimson sun. The world turned black.

Jacob thought he knew the destination of the raiders. If he was correct, their tracks would be easily found come first light. So he did not slow but plunged the horse onward into the murk of the Mexican night. The brute between his legs could run many more miles, for it had incredible stamina and determination. With its night-seeing eyes searching for obstacles on the ground, the horse would not fall and throw its master.

The cayuse gradually slowed as its weariness increased and the night aged. It splashed into Carrizo Creek and halted of its own volition. Jacob allowed it to drink a moderate amount, then lifted its head and reined it up the bank. In a patch of buffalo grass he staked the animal out on the end of his lariat.

Tamarron unrolled his blanket under the thin hornlike curve of the dying moon. For a long time he sat in the darkness and listened to the rustling of the grass and the sighing of the wind. Finally he lay down, fretting, grudging the rest the horse must have and the time wasted.

He reached out and gripped the butt of his revolver. He would inflict terrible punishment upon the men who'd slain his tiny clan of people and forever deprived him of Petra and the children that might have been.

Petra saddled the gray mare in the early dawn. Jacob must be found at once. He would know what to do.

Conrado and the vaqueros had left for Santa Fe on the afternoon of the previous day. A soldier, one of Governor Armijo's personal guards, had come with a message from the governor requesting all males of fighting age to assemble in the plaza in front of the Palace. An American army with many cannon was marching from Independence, Missouri, to invade New Mexico. The gringo soldiers were traveling fast and were close to Las Vegas. The governor was telling people that although the garrison of Mexican soldiers might be few in number, now that they were bolstered by the local militia and other volunteers, they would fight the damnable Americans and drive them in a bloody flight back to the United States.

Petra had argued strenuously with Conrado that the men should not leave the rancho. *Banditos* and Indians would learn of the war and that all the fighting men were gathered in Santa Fe. These fierce enemies would launch savage attacks upon the defenseless ranchos. The land of the Pecos was the most isolated and exposed in all of New Mexico and would draw the first raids.

Conrado refused to listen to Petra's pleading. He wouldn't delay even to allow time for Jacob to return from the hills. He said that all the people in New Mexico must run the risk to defend against the invaders. The men armed themselves and rode north.

Leading the mare, Petra walked to the gateway and dropped the strong wooden plank that held the gate shut. She mounted, spoke to the horse, and went west on the path that led through the juniper forest and beyond to the hills.

Petra had passed the corner of the stone wall when the

sharp crack of a rifle reached her. Instantly a hammer blow slammed against her ribs.

The lead projectile, striking a glancing blow, knocked her to the side. A wave of excruciating pain roared through the side of her chest. She teetered on the verge of falling from the saddle as her horse vaulted forward, frightened by the thunderclap of the gun.

Frantically Petra grabbed the pommel and pulled herself back into the saddle. She cast a fearful look behind.

A large group of horsemen had charged up over the edge of the bluff near the river. They were spurring hard for the open gate. Spears of smoke stabbed out from their guns. A bullet zipped past Petra, cutting away a swath of her hair.

She thought for a moment of spinning the mare and driving her back to the gate to bar it against the raiders. But the band of men had almost reached the entryway. For her to return now would be to let them kill her.

Two riders split from the group and rushed toward Petra. She looked to the front and spurred the horse in the direction of the juniper woods on the slope of the hill.

Pistol shots boomed close behind. The mare stumbled, then caught her footing. Petra knew the horse had been hit. But it must not falter now.

She slapped the mare on the neck and screamed into her ear. "Go! Go! Go!" The faithful horse took in the primal call, lengthened her stride, and raced on.

Petra flicked a glance to the rear. The pursuers were gaining on her. However, the dense juniper was less than a hundred feet away. She laid her face in the streaming mane of the horse, and her arm rose and fell as she swung her lash against the heaving flanks of her mount.

The mare plunged into the trees. Petra ran her straight ahead for ten yards, then whirled her left along a trail she knew. Before the *banditos* had entered the woods,

she reined abruptly right and within a few feet had pulled
the mare down to a quiet walk.

The thudding of running horses entered the woods.
Petra knew she had only seconds in which to hide.

The noise of the other horses on her right ceased as
the men halted to listen for her. She hastily reined in the
mare. When the men moved again, she sent her mount
on at a soft walk.

In some ancient time a rock ledge on the side of the
juniper hill had broken loose and come rumbling down.
The jumble of rocks, some twice as large as a wagon,
leaned at a precarious, hazardous angle on the base of
the hill. As a child, Petra had discovered the great mound
of collapsed rock stretching a hundred feet. Unknowing
of the tenuous, unstable hold each rock had upon another, she had crawled into the small passageways, with
their abrupt, twisting turns and, many times, dead ends.
She had only once, willingly, explored those dark, dangerous places.

However, she'd fled to those underground corridors
for safety many years ago when the Navajos raided the
rancho and she had been cut off from the hacienda.
Wounded in the face and terribly frightened, she'd hidden for hours among the rocks. She had not emerged until
the voice of her searching father had reached her through
the crevices between the boulders and coaxed her back
into the world of sunlight.

The monstrous pile of angular boulders lay just ahead
of Petra. She dreaded returning to the cold tomb within
them. The horrible memories of lying injured there welled
up in her mind with fearful clarity. But there was no
other place she could go that the raiders would not
eventually find her.

She halted the mare and painfully climbed down. The
horse was sent away along a path among the trees that
paralled the foot of the hill. Pressing her arm tightly
against her wounded ribs, she took a circuitous route to

the rock pile, carefully stepping on stones to hide her passage.

She squeezed through an opening and crawled deeply into the hard, unyielding embrace of the mound of boulders.

Petra came to the end of a twisting path that had plunged and climbed through the disjointed chaos of the rock. She lay upon a slanting slab and tried to rest. But she could find no position that eased the pain of her wound. Gradually the bleeding from the gunshot ceased.

In the pitch blackness the passing of time could not be measured. Now and then she dragged herself cautiously to a hole and peered out. Twice there was daylight. Then once, darkness.

She thought again and again of her family. Had they survived? *Madre de Dios*, let them live. Do not allow Jacob to ride into a trap and be killed.

A troubled, pain-filled sleep finally overtook Petra. When she awoke, she was shivering with cold among the rocks, and her thirst was awful. Water had to be found soon.

Petra rested a while longer, the hard rock gouging her flesh in many places. Finally, unable to endure the need for water any longer, she made her way to the entrance. The juniper woods lay silent and full of long shadows from a low, westerly sun.

On tottering legs, poor wounded creature that she was, she moved among the trees. The ground was wet from a recent rain. But none of the moisture had reached Petra buried in the pile of stones. She thought of the cold water of the spring. But that water source was inside the courtyard. The *banditos* would capture and kill her should they still be there. She must circle around the hacienda and find the water that came under the courtyard wall.

She reached the border of the woods and stopped. When it grew dark, she would go on.

Two pistol shots rang out ahead of Petra. She flinched,

expecting to feel the sudden hurt of another bullet. Then she realized the gunfire had been inside the compound.

She crouched behind the bole of a thick juniper and peered at the hacienda. Who had been injured or killed with those shots? Please, oh, please, not Jacob.

The growing shadows merged into dusk. Still Petra waited. She dared not go farther until full darkness arrived.

A man on a galloping horse broke from the gate of the compound. Petra recognized the familiar figure of Jacob. She straightened and staggered from the woods.

"Jacob!" she cried. "Jacob, wait! I am here!" The rider didn't slow. He disappeared over the lip of the bluff.

CHAPTER 17

Conrado Solis was exhilarated by the thought of battle with the Americans. Those damnable men, with their crude and insulting manners, were always crowding into New Mexico. Already they owned most of the important businesses in Santa Fe. Now they planned to conquer the entire country. It was time to give them a beating and take Santa Fe back for the citizens. If it wasn't for Tamarron, Conrado could say he hated every gringo.

Conrado glanced to the side at Roberto Bautista. He had stopped at the Bautista rancho and found Roberto and his vaqueros preparing to ride to Santa Fe in response to Governor Armijo's request for volunteers to join the local militia. The two bands of men had agreed to travel together and fight side by side in the battle with the Americans.

Roberto Bautista's face held a slight smile, and his eyes shone with excitement as he caught Conrado looking at him. He winked in good humor. "Soon, soon," Roberto said.

Conrado nodded his understanding of his friend's comment. The conflict would soon begin. However, the Americans were savage fighters. The battle would not be easily won.

He glanced to the rear. Ten mounted men rode directly behind. With their bearded faces, pistols in their belts and rifles in scabbards, they looked very fierce.

A wagon pulled by two teams of trotting horses came last. The war could last for many days. With the governor's treasury always empty of funds to make purchases of supplies, Conrado and Roberto had brought their own foodstuff, ammunition, and bedding.

To Conrado's unbelieving eyes, the left lead horse of the team hitched to the wagon stumbled and fell. In slow motion, the animal slid for two or three yards, propelled by its own momentum and the pull of the other horses on its breast chain. Then the weight of the fallen beast yanked its mate down. The second team tripped on the dragging bodies and toppled to the ground in a jumble of kicking, thrashing legs.

The wagon slithered sideways. The long wooden tongue of the vehicle, chained to the horses, began to bend under the thrust of the onrushing wagon. The strong length of wood broke with a loud splintering sound. The wagon careened to one side and rolled.

The crash of the heavily charged rifle that had slain the first horse registered on Conrado's startled senses. He jerked his pistol and yelled a warning to Roberto.

A blizzard of bullets struck the Mexicans. Conrado fired at men, only half seen in the brush near the road. Roberto's pistol was booming beside him. On Conrado's right, a man was knocked from his saddle.

Roberto cried out. Conrado whirled to look at his friend. A lead ball had hit Roberto in the side of the head, tearing away a corner of his skull. He flung wide his arms, dropping his revolver, and tumbled from his mount.

Cursing wildly, Conrado cocked his gun and fired again and again at the attackers. Bullets flew around him, buzzing and snarling like small, deadly animals, plucking at his clothes, burning his skin.

His pistol snapped on an empty chamber. He slung a look around.

Many horses and all his comrades lay in crumpled mounds on the ground. Two mounts were storming off with reins dragging and stirrups flapping. One of his vaqueros started to rise. A bullet slammed him down.

In shocked surprise, Conrado realized he was the only man still uninjured. Somehow God had kept the bullets from striking him.

He couldn't beat the large number of gunmen alone. He raked the ribs of his horse with the sharp rowels of his spurs. The big brute darted away along the road.

A hurtling chunk of metal nicked Conrado's ear. He shook his head in wonder. So close and yet never seriously wounding him.

A hundred yards, then two hundred separated Conrado from the murderous rifles of the attackers. The horse ran free and strong, swiftly carrying him from the killing ground. The gunfire at his rear stopped. He was safe.

He looked ahead. In front of him on the right in the waist-high brush beside the road, a white man stood up abruptly. Then another and another, until there were six of them. Men had been stationed farther along the road to kill anybody that might escape the main assault. They wore unmatched clothes, not the uniforms of soldiers— *banditos*. Petra had been right. The greatest danger to the people of the Pecos ranchos was outlaws such as these. Forgive me, Sister. I have killed myself. I fear that I have done the same to you and the others.

Bullets pierced Conrado. His world exploded into total darkness.

The broken-edged moon cast a thin silver light down on the Gallinas River. In the brush beside its banks, the band of Texans stole toward the Bautista hacienda.

Kirker grinned inside his shaggy beard as his men

moved with him in a ragged line. This fight with a few sleeping Mexicans should be easy.

The thicket fell away behind, and the men entered a zone that had been cleared of brush and weeds near a stone-and-adobe wall. Kirker felt his breath quicken as he stretched to his full height and looked over the wall at the dark gun ports of the house. How many sharpshooting Mexicans were awake and waiting with guns cocked?

Kirker went swiftly, cat-footing the remaining distance to the wall. His men came hurrying behind him up to the obstacle. Kirker's grin broadened to a wolfish smile. Everything was happening according to plan. He checked the eastern horizon. The black night was graying into morning. The attack must be made quickly.

"Custus, over the wall you go," Kirker whispered to a tall, skinny man near him. Let someone else take the first bullet if a trap was waiting to be sprung.

Custus grabbed the top of the wall, hoisted himself up, and dropped inside. His feet grated noisily on gravel when he landed.

The gang of men tensed in silence and waited. But there was no sound of alarm, and the only thing that moved was the moon slipping across the brightening sky.

"Everybody over," Kirker ordered.

There was a short scuffle of boots and muffled grunts as the men swarmed over the wall. Here and there moonlight glinted in silver sparks off the iron barrels of their rifles. A man fell with a muttered curse.

A large, long-haired dog raced into the moonlight at a corner of the hacienda. He slowed for half a second, his head coming up, questioning. His keen hunting nose caught the alien scent of the invaders. He roared a deep-chested bellow that changed to a savage growl. He launched himself across the courtyard at the nearest intruder.

Custus, in the lead, jerked his rifle to his shoulder. He fired, the rifle booming like a cannon in the confined space of the compound. The dog swerved aside, whining in agony from his wound. Then its savage animal instinct

for battle brought it back to its original course. It leapt at
Custus's throat. Man and dog went down in a struggling
tangle.

One of the men close to Custus ran forward. He shoved
the barrel of his rifle against the ribs of the dog and
pulled the trigger. The snarling creature was blown away
to roll in the dirt. The dog tried to rise, its head lifting
and its lips pulled back tightly as it snarled again. Its eyes
glared yellow hate at its many enemies, and its paws
scratched at the dirt as it tried to crawl forward. The
dog's life drained away in a red tide through the cavelike
hole in its chest. The shining eyes went black with death.

Two dogs, seemingly replicas of the first, tore in the
direction of the Texans. The men shot both growling
beasts before they could cross half the courtyard.

"Spread out!" shouted Kirker. "Some go left! Some
right! Cover all the doors and windows." The damn dogs
had ruined his surprise. The smile in his beard was gone.

"Shoot everything that's alive," Kirker called to the
charging Texans. He raced with a group to the front of
the hacienda.

The men with Kirker ripped the hitch rail loose from
its moorings and began to pound the front entry with it.
The thick timbers of the door held firm against the onslaught. Then all at once it gave way and slammed back
against the inside wall.

The men dropped the battering ram and sprang to
shelter on each side of the opening. They snatched up
their rifles from where they'd been leaned against the
wall. Nervously they looked at each other and at the
open doorway, faintly framed by candlelight. So tempt-
ingly silent.

"Hell, we can't stand here all morning," said one of
the men. He took a quick look inside and ducked back.
"Empty, by Gawd," he said.

"Then let's get this over with," Kirker called, and
lunged into the doorway. He raced along the shadowy
hall.

An old, white-haired man moving with a hobbling limp

came from a side hall. He thrust a short-barreled rifle at
Kirker and started to take aim.

The Texan chief shot the man through the chest. He
sprang over the body, rushed farther along the hallway
and turned around a corner.

A young woman held a double-barreled shotgun pointed
straight along the hallway. She fired both barrels. The
recoil kicked her back a step.

Kirker had seen the danger and was already throwing
himself to the floor. He heard the lead shots tearing past.
His hat was knocked from his head.

To his rear he heard moans and cries. A man cursed
and a rifle roared. An invisible wind seemed to whip the
dress of the woman. A stunned expression froze her
pretty face. She fell backward and lay there quietly.

A half-grown boy stepped partway from a door of a
room to face the Texans. A large revolver bucked in his
hands. He forced it down and started to pry back the
hammer again.

In surprise, Kirker heard the bullet go into the ceiling
above his head. The youth was so rattled, he hadn't
aimed. Kirker shot him.

The boy stumbled into the hall. Slowly, as if very tired,
he sat down on the floor. Using both thumbs, he vainly
tried to cock the gun again. His strength wasn't enough.
He glared at the man who had mortally wounded him.

Kirker saw the same indomitable spirit in the boy's
eyes that had been in the dog's. He shot the boy in the
face, snapping his head cruelly back.

"Goddamn, Kirker," growled a man, "you didn't have
to do that. He was already same as dead."

"No time to waste on him. Can't let them get organized. Let's go and shoot the rest of the damn Mexicans."
Kirker went cautiously along the hallway.

Rifles and pistols boomed in other parts of the hacienda. Every wall shook and jarred with the concussions.
Dirt rained down between the willow-stems of the ceiling. A woman screamed in great agony.

"Halt here," Kirker said as they neared an unlit section. "We'll be shooting each other if we're not careful."

The sound of firing dwindled away. The Texans began to call to each other. A group of men came out of the darkness farther along the hallway.

"Every greaser we could find—man, woman, and child—is dead," called Borkan, who walked in the lead.

"Maybe," replied Kirker. "Light candles in all the rooms and search. When you're done, come outside. How many of you are wounded?"

"Only one," said Borkan. "Some old man shot Jeeter dead center. We didn't see any real fighting Mexicans. Did you?"

"No. That must have been them we shot to pieces yesterday. We've got some wounded. A woman with a shotgun got off a blast. We'll take them outside where there's more light and see what we can do for them." Kirker pivoted and pushed back through the men.

Glen Sansen came in timidly. He had stayed by the river until the firing had ceased. He cursed having ever met Caverhill and the killer Kirker.

He saw the leader of the Texans with other men, some standing and some lying prone on the ground. He slowed even more at the sight.

A short blond man straightened up from the prostrate bodies. "One dead. One shot in the face with a shotgun and blind. He'll die soon. Two others wounded, but they can ride and should heal okay."

"All right, Tumblin," Kirker said. "Not too bad." The first ojbective had been taken with the loss of only two men. That left twenty-eight and himself to complete the job.

Kirker saw Sansen and motioned for him to come close. "Get in there and find every scrap of paper there is," Kirker ordered. "Bundle it up for safe carrying." He gestured for Sansen to hurry.

"Tumblin, I brought you because you've had some

doctor training. Get busy and take care of the two who'll
live."

The shrill, frightened cry of a woman pierced the walls
of the hacienda. A moment later a heavyset man dragged
a buxom woman from the door. He was laughing in a
jovial tone as she struggled futilely to break free of his
hold on her arm.

"Look what I found. She was hiding in a big basket in
the storeroom. Now I'll have me some pleasurin'."

Kirker spoke to Borkan, standing at his elbow. "Back
me. One woman is certain to make trouble. The men will
fight over her."

Kirker raised his voice and called to the man holding
the woman. "Timmins, remember your word. Every Mexican was to be killed immediately, even the women."

The man laughed roughly. "That was two weeks ago.
A man's needs change."

"A man's word to me doesn't change. Now kill her!"

"Not for a little while," Timmins said. His eyes battled
with Kirker.

Kirker drew his pistol with a lift of his hand. He fired.
The bullet broke the woman's sternum, then plowed
onward and shattered her spinal column. Like a rag doll,
she was flung away. With her arm still clutched by Timmins, her body whipped around to land on the ground at
his heels.

Timmins's rage poured into his eyes. His hand moved
to touch his revolver.

With a swift movement Kirker shifted his point of aim
to Timmins. "I need every rider I've got. But just maybe
I can do without you. Do you want to test me?"

Timmins seemed to stop breathing. He'd heard much
about Kirker's skill with a gun. He moved his hand and
hooked his thumb in a vest pocket. "You're right. We'll
do it as we agreed."

"Good. Take all the men except Tumblin and Sansen
and round up every head of livestock you can by mid-
afternoon. You and four others will leave today and take
this first drive to Texas. I want you gone, because I may

still decide to kill you. If you have any argument about this, then spit it out."

"No argument. I'd just as soon go east back to Texas."

"Then do it." Kirker growled, tired of the man. He holstered his gun and stood watching after Timmins until the man had ridden off.

Kirker slept in the giant master bed with its deep feather-tick mattress. It rained hard during the night, and he came awake, listening to the downpour. All signs of the herd moving east would be washed away. The big common grave of the dead occupants of the hacienda was also well hidden. The storm would add even more to its concealment.

Caverhill had been right. Kirker believed he would be a good leader of military campaigns. He kept his mind away from what might have happened if the fighting men of the rancho had been behind the walls and in the hallways of the hacienda.

CHAPTER 18

"Come awake!" a guttural voice speaking in the tongue of the Comanche ordered Jacob. The sharp point of some weapon pricked the flesh of his cheek.

Tamarron sat up with a surge, his hand darting out for his pistol. But the Colt was gone, and so, too, were his knife and rifle.

An Indian squatted close by in the morning dusk. He held a fourteen-foot battle lance, steel headed from half a soldier's saber, pointed directly at the white man.

Tamarron froze in place. The hatred in the Comanche's smoky bronze face was ugly to behold. Only a trifling motion from Tamarron would trigger the Indian to strike with the lance.

The warrior did not stir. The only movement about him was a thick vein pulsing in his forehead just below a twisted, red cloth cord that encircled his head. The cloth was from a Mexican soldier's uniform.

Tamarron ignored the few drops of blood that dripped from his cheek. He held his gaze unwavering, locked on the black liquid eyes of the Indian. Minutes slid past, endlessly long.

As Tamarron waited, he evaluated the Comanche. The warrior's face was broad with a large, flaring nose. He was slightly undersized and leanly sinewed over heavy bones. He wore only a breechcloth and moccasins with leggings tied above the knees.

His left arm up near the shoulder had recently healed from a bad wound. A sunken spot where a bullet or some sharp weapon had deeply punctured the flesh was puckered and purplish, marring the perfect flow of muscle. Yet that didn't seem to lessen the man's obvious strength. Tamarron belived he'd have little chance to get past the war lance and overpower the Comanche.

The Indian arose in one fluid motion. His lance reached out to touch the two scalps Tamarron had placed on a rock in the night to dry.

"White man's hair. Did you kill these men?"

"Yes," answered Tamarron in the Indian language.

"Why? White men do not take other white men's scalps when they kill them."

"Because I hated them for what they did to me."

"What harm did they do that made you kill them?" questioned the Indian.

"They murdered my family and wife while I was not there to protect them."

A momentary flicker of some deep emotion passed over the Comanche's features, then it was subdued and hidden.

"Were they alone, just these two?"

"When I found them, they were. But they were with other men before." Tamarron pointed at the many tracks on the bank of the creek. "These two who lost their scalps stayed behind. Now I'll catch and kill these others who are riding south." Tamarron thought the Comanche knew more than he pretended.

"Are they also your enemies?" Tamarron asked.

"They *are* my enemies. And only because you had two of their scalps did I not run my lance through you in your sleep."

"Why do you trail them?"

The Comanche lowered his lance. "The leader and
some of the men are scalp hunters for the Mexicans. The
governor of Chihuahua pays gold for the scalps of my
people, the Comanche, and also for the scalps of the
Apache. He gives gold even for the murder of children.
How many times has your family been slain?"

"Once," replied Tamarron, surprised by the question.

The Indian held up three fingers. "Three times white
men have destroyed my wife and children. My sorrow is
threefold greater than yours."

The Comanche fell silent a moment. His eyes stabbed
down at the tracks. "This band of murderers, part of them,
are responsible for two of those attacks on my tepee.
They must not be allowed to do such deeds again. I, like
you, will catch and slay them."

Tamarron felt his own poignant sadness. How awful to
lose your woman and be all alone. Yet the Indian had
experienced it three times. Jacob examined more closely
the face of the Comanche. Beneath the hate that glinted
iron-hard from the man, Jacob saw the soul-bending
anguish in him.

"You and I shouldn't fight," Tamarron said. "Together we would be doubly strong and would win the
battle with our foes."

As the Comanche pondered Tamarron's suggestion he
gazed to the south along the fresh traces on the worn
wagon road. He glanced back at Tamarron. "They take
your sheep and cattle and drive them to the land of the
Texans. What will you do about that?"

"The livestock means nothing to me. I must run these
men to earth."

"Before your rancho, they take many animals from the
rancho on the Gallinas River."

"That would be the Bautista rancho. What of the
people at the rancho?"

"All dead. I found the big grave that holds them all.
The scalp hunter thinks he hides it, but I found it."

Tamarron jerked, startled at the news that the Indian
had found a grave. "Did you find a grave at my rancho?"

"I did not search. However, I believe the murderers would do the same thing—hide the bodies."

The Indian studied Tamarron. "I must be the one that slays the chief of the scalp hunters," he said.

"Your grievance against this man is greater than mine. You can kill him. But should you fail to take his life, then I will complete the task."

The Comanche laughed, his mirth hoarse and ghastly, like a raven's croak. "Four moons now I have hunted the man that slays women and children. He thinks me shot and drowned in the Rio Pecos. But, you see, he is wrong. I am alive and healed. Several times I almost catch him when he goes to Chihuahua to sell the scalps. But he leaves there very fast, with the Mexican cavalry after him. So I cannot get near to him. Then I follow him far to the east, among many white men. That was very dangerous for me. But now he has returned to my land of the great Llano Estacado and the Rio Pecos.

"I have only one goal before I die, to take this man's life. I shall not fail to do that."

Tamarron visualized the silent Indian in pursuit of the white man through all the many days and across hundreds of miles of Mexican desert and Texas plains. How had he managed that without losing the trail in the rain and wind, and more difficult still, in the countless horse tracks near the cities? The Comanche must be an unmatched tracker, even among his own people.

"What is your name?" Tamarron asked.

"High Walking. What is yours?"

"Jacob Tamarron."

The Comanche warrior nodded curtly. He strode to his horse, a Mexican Cavalry mount, and climbed into the saddle. He fastened the lance along the horse's side to point upward and backward at a slant. A quiver of arrows, jasper-tipped and winged with hawk feathers, and a powerful war bow were taken from where they hung on the pommel of the saddle. The quiver was slid over his shoulder to hang down his back. He held the bow in his hand. With a touch of rein the Comanche's horse left at a fast lope.

Tamarron hastened to pack his bedroll and retrieve his weapons, lying nearby on the ground where the Comanche had placed them. He overtook High Walking, and under a new sun breaking loose from the far horizon, they sped south beside the Rio Pecos.

The blazing sun tortured the earth and the creatures of the earth. No wind stirred to carry away the heat, and it lay on the surface of the ground like liquid gravity.

Tamarron and High Walking rode doggedly south beneath the fireball. Directly under their feet, the tracks of the raiders always led onward. Through eyelids hammered down to a squint by the brutal sun, they warily watched for an ambush. Both men knew that somewhere ahead, a rear guard of the outlaws could be waiting in hiding to kill them.

The land was changing as they traveled, gradually flattening, the soil becoming sandy. The grass was shorter and beginning to lose its greenness. The flowers of the cacti had died and turned brown. A multitude of yellow bean pods were ripening on the slender limbs of the mesquite.

On the left, the meandering Rio Pecos flowed in a wide, swampy valley choked with water-greedy phreatophyte grasses, sedges, and brush. Large cottonwoods lined the banks, elbowing each other for space in which to sink their roots. The horsemen passed many abandoned oxbows lying half full of dead water, as gray and dull as lead.

Near midday the river curved steeply away to the west, and the road led down to a gravelly ford. The men stopped in the shade of a cottonwood at the edge of the water. The horses lowered their heads and sucked noisily, slaking their thirst.

For several minutes Jacob and High Walking cautiously evaluated the dense stand of brush and trees on the far side of the two-hundred-foot strip of open water. To be caught in that flat, exposed surface by riflemen would mean death. Still, they had to move on. They glanced up and down the stream. The muck and mire and rank grass and brush of the swampy river extended in both directions as far as they could see. There would be quicksand in many places.

High Walking emitted a short, aggravated hiss. "I go. You stay," he said. "Help me with your rifle if our enemies are there."

Without waiting for an answer, he kicked his mount into the water. Jacob saw him unlimber his war bow and draw an arrow from the quiver. He nocked the shaft. Jacob lifted his rifle to a ready position for a quick shot.

The river deepened to touch the belly of the Comanche's horse, then became more shallow.

Suddenly High Walking struck his mount with the bow and let out an earsplitting shriek. The animal leapt forward, throwing water for yards. Indian and steed drove into the trees on the riverbank.

A handful of minutes passed, and High Walking returned to the water's edge. He motioned Tamarron to cross.

"Next time you go first," High Walking said, his face grim.

The hacienda sat in a grassy meadow above the flood line of the Rio Pecos. All the doors and shutters were closed.

Tamarron went silently to the front entry. He tripped the lock and kicked wide the door. With pistol drawn, he burst inside.

His eyes swiveled, scouring the big, shadowy room and the several hallways leading off to the recesses of the hacienda. The echoes of his noisy entrance died away. There remained only the complete quietness of a house deserted.

The structure was less than half the size of the Solis

hacienda, and he finished his investigation in a brief time. As far as he could determine, all of the ranchers' major furnishings and possessions appeared to be intact. However, again, as at the Solis hacienda, he saw none of the smaller, valuable articles that Mexican households normally contained.

Jacob detected some storage chests and drawers askew, as if someone had searched among them. It was odd that the bandits hadn't damaged or carried off more items. The band was organized, with the leader maintaining tight control. Such a disciplined, almost military band of men would be dangerous to attack.

He left the house and began to search the yard. The ground was heavily marked with the fresh tracks of horses' hooves and heeled boots. He found a pool of dried blood. "Goddamn," he cursed.

High Walking rode his splashing horse back across the Pecos. The Indian was little interested in the Mexican people of the rancho and had ridden off to seek out the route the raiders had taken.

"They take many sheep and cows and go that way." High Walking pointed to the east. "The same direction they took from all the other ranchos."

"To Texas," Tamarron said. "Did all the riders go the same way?"

"No, only five or six. The others go down the river."

"There is one more rancho there."

"I know," said the Comanche. "I have seen it, nearly a day's ride from here. It is a small rancho with few people."

"These tracks are a day old. That means the raiders could have attacked that rancho this morning, or perhaps even as early as last evening."

High Walking shrugged his shoulders. "I think we will be too late to warn the people. But the Texas *banditos* are getting farther and farther ahead of us. We must ride swiftly."

"I agree." Jacob mounted his horse.

The two riders crossed the river and swung south. The horses picked up into a trot, a jarring ride, hard on the riders, but a pace the animals could maintain for miles.

The sun grew old, turned blood-red, and vanished into the bottomless pit behind the rim of the world. The shadows of twilight crawled out of the hollows. A million mosquitoes rose up from their daytime resting place in the river marsh. They swarmed upon the horsemen.

Tamarron batted the buzzing black insects from his face with a hand. He glanced at High Walking. The bloodsucking pests were a black fog around the nearly naked Comanche. The man ignored the mosquitoes, his sight picking out the hoofprints of the Texan marauders from the blackness settling over the ground.

Tamarron looked to the west at a hill silhouetted against the darkening sky. He pointed and called to High Walking. "Up there a wind may be blowing and could keep the mosquitoes off us. Let's water the ponies and go see."

The Comanche grunted something Jacob could not make out. He halted his mount and allowed it to drink beside Jacob's.

They traveled directly away from the river, climbing upward to the crown of the small rocky hill. Near the top the Indian angled away, and without a word, he disappeared into the night.

Jacob found a spot where the wind had the mosquitoes swept clear. He hobbled his horse and spread his blanket.

Jacob lay sifting the ashes of his memory of Petra, seeking those bright moments of pleasure with her. But the gloomy thoughts came swiftly and lay heavily upon him. Never again would he be able to hold her and find joy in the comfort she gave him.

He turned from his bleak thoughts and listened to the night. A bird roosting somewhere below in the brush crooned like an old woman. To the east, far out on the Llano Estacado, a desert wolf gave his weird and wavering call. Jacob drifted off into sleep.

Sometime in the night Jacob came awake in a second,

and his hand closed on the butt of his revolver. The echo of a sad, heart-rending cry from the Comanche filled the darkness. He listened for the sound to come again.

The Indian made no further noise. Yet Jacob sensed the man's wakefulness out there somewhere in the blackness. Jacob didn't know where the Indian had finally lain down. That was not good. Whether he liked the Comanche's presence or not, closer attention must be paid to him.

CHAPTER 19

Tamarron awoke at a slow, sliding movement on his chest. The movement ceased, but a solid weight remained. Slowly, ever so slowly, he cracked an eyelid.

In the light of first dawn he saw the tan-and-brown body of a giant rattlesnake coiled on his chest. Jacob flinched, and before he could prevent it, his lungs expelled a short breath of air.

The rattlesnake was awakening from the drugging coolness of the night. Its recovery was being hurried by the heat radiating from the mound on which it lay. Already it felt the elastic strength in its muscles.

The large reptile felt the warm wash of air over it. It sensed a quiver in the mound beneath.

A third of the snake's body lifted, and its venomous, fanged head swung to point straight at the source of warm air. The bulbous, nearsighted eyes stared. The wet, forked tongue licked out to capture the molecules of scent on the air and to deposit it inside the olfactory pits in the top of the snake's mouth.

Tamarron rolled his eyes to the side. The Comanche

185

crouched not three yards away, intently watching Jacob and the rattlesnake. His lance was in his hand. But Jacob could tell by the expression on his face that he was not going to give any assistance.

The reptile sensed the almost imperceptible tremble of the mound again. It pulled back its head and the elevated portion of its body, in preparation for striking at this strange-smelling animal that was so threateningly near. The snake pointed its tail at the sky and began to vibrate its loose, interconnected rattles in a frenzied warning.

Tamarron had to strike before the snake did. He lashed out. His open hand hit the solid, muscular body of the reptile. It seemed to be gripping his clothing. Then it broke loose and slid to the side.

Jacob rolled the opposite direction. He kicked the blanket free and leapt to his feet.

The rattlesnake coiled instantly. It raised its poisonous head, poised to stab out at the thing that had hurt it.

"Goddamn heathen Indian," stormed Tamarron. "You put that snake on me." He rushed at the Comanche.

High Walking sprang erect. He thrust his lance out to meet Tamarron's charge.

Jacob barely halted in time to prevent himself from being impaled on the long steel head of the Indian's weapon. "You bastard, I could have been killed by that snake, or poisoned so badly that I couldn't travel."

Tamarron's fist ached to smash the brown face and the black eyes that watched him without emotion, like marbles of obsidian. All of Jacob's will was required to hold in check the anger that flamed in his mind. "Why did you put the snake on me?" he demanded.

"I wanted to see how brave you are," High Walking said. "I do not want to go with a coward to fight battles."

The Comanche lowered his lance and turned his back to Tamarron. He gestured to the south. "That is the way we must go. We waste much valuable time here," he said over his shoulder, without looking at the white man.

Tamarron stared at the man's back. "One more trick and I will kill you," he promised.

One slight shrug of the Indian's shoulders was the only response to Tamarron's threat. "Do we go now?" asked High Walking.

Jacob pulled on his moccasins and rolled his blanket. "Damn heathen," he said under his breath as he cinched the saddle on his horse.

"Let's ride," Tamarron called harshly.

The rested horses ran easily through low hills studded with prickly pear, cholla cacti, and scattered clumps of bunch grass. As the day wore on, yucca appeared, as well as agave, stabbing skeletal fingers upward. The riders also encountered small sand dunes. Fresh tracks of buffalo and antelope appeared. And always there were the tracks of the Texans' horses pounding on ahead.

The sun reached its zenith, burning the earth with unnatural heat. Horses and men sweated. Strange mirages formed, then melted away and disappeared before Jacob's and High Walking's eyes, to reappear again like monstrous spirits rising from the bowels of the earth.

The Indian and the white man ignored the false images. The Texan raiders traveled somewhere ahead of those things that did not exist. What was real were the men they must find and kill.

The two riders came warily toward the hacienda, which squatted a hundred yards ahead on an old river terrace. At one time the adobe building had been whitewashed. Tamarron thought that an odd thing for the owners to do in this remote location where few visitors would ever come. However, the house was now heavily weathered, the brown adobe showing in many places. The hacienda stood exposed, with no protective walls.

"The Texans have already been here," Tamarron said, raising his sight from the scores of tracks on the sun-baked ground.

"No one will be alive," High Walking said.

"I'll look inside."

"No time for that. Let us go on at once. We cannot help the people who lived here."

"I said, I'll go look around." Tamarron's voice was flinty. "You do whatever you want."

High Walking's dark face turned surly. Perhaps he had made a mistake in journeying with Tamarron. Never could he be a friend to a white man. Always an enemy. However, to kill the scalp hunters, he would use the strength of anyone. He whirled his cayuse and circled off to the left, his eyes sweeping the ground.

Tamarron found the major contents of the hacienda to be in place. The storerooms were partially empty, with open sacks and lids off other containers. In the kitchen, plates and dishes sufficient to feed ten men stood on the long wooden table. Tamarron went quickly to the fireplace and felt the stones. They were cold. No cook fire had burned there that day.

He ran from the hacienda and toward his horse. The men who had attacked this rancho were miles ahead. He yelled out loudly to the Comanche.

High Walking rode up the grade from the river. "They crossed the Pecos just below here, where the water is wide but shallow. Their sign is fresh. Made late yesterday."

"I know. We'll catch them tomorrow if we hurry." Tamarron flung himself onto his mount.

The flat, smooth surface of the Rio Pecos shone brightly in the glare of the hot evening sun. The fish of the river had long ago sought a cool haven in the shade beneath the overhanging banks. Just downstream from the smooth flow of deep water, the river shallowed and became braided, flowing in three swift streams between low gravel bars.

"Damnation, I'm melting," complained Custus. He looked west at the sinking sun. "I hope the night comes quick."

"This is better than riding out there on the Staked Plains herding sheep and cattle with the other men," replied Borkan. "The only shade there is a man's hat brim."

"You're right." Custus turned onto his back. "It's your turn to keep an eye open while I catch a nap."

Borkan and Custus lay in the shadows among a grove of cottonwoods and spied on the road where it forded the wide spread of water at the gravel bars. Kirker had ordered them to keep lookout for two days. If no pursuit came trailing the Texans, the two men were to give up their vigil and hurry after Kirker.

Borkan rose to a sitting position and surveyed the Pecos Valley. On both sides of the river the cottonwoods clung to the banks in a narrow, hundred-foot-wide band. Higher on the bank, the desert bunch grass had finished growing and was turning brown. The hacienda they had attacked the day before, though less than half a mile distant on the old river terrace, could not be seen.

Borkan came to quick attention. Two horsemen, their mounts moving at a fast gallop, had come into sight on the steep road leading down from the hacienda.

"Custus, wake up and get your rifle. Some fellows are coming."

Tamarron and High Walking sat their saddles and watched over the wide expanse of open water at the far shore. At their feet, the Pecos murmured a liquid undertone. High overhead, a buzzard hung ominously on wings that did not move. Jacob saw the bird riding the updraft of hot wind and wished he had that vantage point from which to examine the dense mat of trees on the opposite bank of the river.

The water wrinkled at a strong puff of wind coming from the east, the direction in which danger could lie. High Walking sniffed, turning his head, testing, evaluating. Tamarron did likewise, searching for the odor of sweaty horses and men.

Just for an instant Jacob thought he caught a whiff of scent from something that should not be there. But so faint was the smell, so laden was the wind with the odor of the river mud and water, he wasn't certain.

"You go," said High Walking. "If we circle every

place where are foes could hide, we shall never catch them."

Was there a new and odd tone in the Indian's voice? Tamarron believed there was. But he said nothing. His long-legged horse felt the heels of its master brush its flanks, and it stepped forward into the shallow water of the river.

Tamarron's eyes probed the thicket of cottonwoods he must reach and pass through. The last rancho on the Pecos had been overrun, and the livestock was moving east to Texas. Never was there a better time for the raiders to waylay and kill anyone following them. Nor a better place. If the Texans left as a rear guard were not as strong as the men who hunted them, then they had an excellent retreat to the east up a draw full of trees.

The nearest gravel bar was reached and crossed. The horse entered the middle stream of water. The edge of the bar was steep, and the gravel and cobbles rolled from under the hooves of his mount. The horse began to fall.

Jacob heard the crack of the rifle above the splashing noise of the horse trying to regain its balance. He felt the tug of the bullet cutting at the neck of his shirt. He'd been shot at, and only the movement of the horse had saved him from being hit.

Immediately there came a second shot, just as the horse straightened and tossed its head. The bullet struck the brute in the throat.

The animal lifted its head, curled back its upper lip, and screamed shrilly. It crashed down on its side with a mighty splash.

Jacob vaulted from the saddle as his horse fell. He landed on his feet in water to his knees. His eyes swept the shore. Two plumes of blue-gray gunpowder smoke floated near the base of a large tree.

His rifle jumped to his shoulder. He aimed to the right and low of one of the smoke plumes. The gun roared. Almost before he pressed the trigger, he was scrambling in long, lunging strides at an angle downstream toward the wooded riverbank.

A shrill, undulating war cry sliced the air behind him. He heard a horse running in the river, coming up fast behind him. A rifle boomed from the distant trees.

Jacob cast a fast look to the right. High Walking's horse was breaking stride, falling. The Comanche flung himself into the air. He hit the shallow water hard. Then he was up and still holding his war bow, raced a zigzag pattern toward the riflemen.

A fourth shot rang out. Jacob couldn't tell where the bullet went. High Walking did not slow but continued to run as if he hadn't been injured.

Tamarron won the distance to the grove of trees without being fired on again, and raced full-tilt around its outside border. He had to cut off the escape of the gunmen. But even as he closed upon the band of trees that extended up the draw, two horses, one without a rider, flashed by in the green foliage and were gone.

More than one man had fired. Yet only one had fled. Tamarron went cautiously to the ambush point.

High Walking was already there. A body lay at his feet. He pointed with the end of his bow at a hole in the man's chest.

"You killed a man you could not see. That is very difficult to do."

"It was easy," said Tamarron.

High Walking's face twisted into a crooked smile. "Yes, easy," he replied.

"We have no horses. Now we walk," said Tamarron.

"Nòt walk. That is too slow. Can you run?"

"I can run," Tamarron said. He turned and with long strides waded into the river to his horse. He stood for a moment and watched the dark blood of the dead beast spreading like slow smoke through the clean water of the Pecos. The death of the faithful mount bit at him like acid.

Hastily he dug out a pouch of lead balls, a horn of powder, and a tin of caps from the pack on the horse's back. A canteen of water was hung over a shoulder. He took nothing else.

High Walking came from the body of his cayuse with a
small pack and bow and arrows and joined Tamarron at
the riverbank. He led off at a fast trot.

Tamarron and the Comanche ran, their footfalls measuring the last minutes of the day. All around them the
wild grass shook and shimmered beneath the yellow sun,
like the guard hairs of some giant wolf. Finally the sun
fell behind the western hills.

The men halted in the gray-purple end of the day.
High Walking searched around for a short time, then
began to dig with his knife at the base of some low-
growing plants with fringed leaves. He pulled the roots
loose from the soil and tossed half to Jacob.

"Yampa," he said.

Tamarron grunted his thanks and laid the wild carrots
beside him. He was too exhausted to eat. He lay back,
feeling the sweat drying and crusting into a thin film of
salt crystals on his skin.

Jacob took one deep, weary breath and was asleep.

CHAPTER 20

The soreness reached to the very core of Tamarron's bones, making it difficult for him to move. The strain of the grueling footrace with High Walking, and then sleeping on the hard ground without a blanket, had nearly crippled him. He glanced around to check on the Indian.

High Walking was squatting in the morning twilight and cutting at a spineless, low-growing cactus with his knife. The plant had a round, wrinkled top that was almost flat. Its flowers were dry and shriveled, and their once bright pink had turned brown.

Methodically the Comanche cut the flesh of the cactus into bite-sized pieces. He stuffed a large, double handful into his pocket. The remaining portion he gave to Jacob.

"This is peyote," High Walking said. "Comanche use it in many ways, eat it, drink it as a tea, or breathe its powder up their noses. You must eat some now. Soon you will feel very strong. Also, it relieves the crowded mind and lessens a man's sorrow." High Walking stuffed a chunk of the peyote in his mouth and began to chew.

Tamarron did likewise. The moist flesh of the plant

was bland. And yet, as he chewed, he sensed the narcotic effect, a soothing of his nerves and a strengthening of his muscles through the soreness. The dawn around him filled with a pleasant aroma, a familiar one he recognized. It was Petra's sachet. He started to make a hurried look around before he recalled that Petra was dead. The odor was false, a trick of the peyote on his mind.

Jacob stood up. His thirst for revenge had not been dulled by the drug. He picked up his weapons and turned to the Indian.

High Walking saw the burning light in Tamarron's eyes. "Now you are ready to run. Perhaps you will be able to keep up with me." His face screwed itself into a grimace around his own glowing eyes. "Tonight you will have very bad dreams. That is the effect of the peyote as its power deserts you."

High Walking pointed to the east where a bright swath of red dawn was spreading as the sun burst from below the horizon. "That is an omen. We will spill the blood of our enemies today."

"Or lose our own," breathed Tamarron in a whisper that only he could hear. But he would take many of Petra's killers into the darkness with him.

Tamarron, trailing his long rifle in his hand, ran beside High Walking as they raced through the heat waves pouring from the hot earth. The vast flatness of the Llano Estacado had swallowed them, and they were lost in the tall plains grass that surrounded them mile upon weary mile. A slow wind moved, tossing the grass reeds into thousands of waves, crests pursuing troughs, as though they were part of the surface of a great sea.

The running men easily followed the trail of the stolen herd of livestock by sign both on the ground and in the air. The thousands of hard hooves had tromped the grass into the brown soil, and the raw trail cut like an open wound in the green prairie. In the vortices of the updrafts along the trail, vultures were tracing wide, swinging circles before beginning to drop toward the earth.

Down, down they came by the score, to level off above
the ground and come up on the scent of a dead sheep or
cow.

As Jacob and High Walking approached, the carrion
eaters craned their skinny necks and bald heads toward
them and hopped around nervously with wings half un-
folded. Then, unable to endure the nearness of the running men, the buzzards rose in a cloud, a living black pall
that climbed upward.

The men began to encounter pockets of grasshoppers.
Soon they were fluttering up in swarms, their yellow
wings with black spots clacking and chittering. A coyote
feeding on a sheep darted out of the path of the runners.
He stopped off a way, with just his head showing above
the grass, and watched the men pass by.

In the noon heat Jacob's heart beat rapidly. His tortured breath was rushing with a hoarse sawing sound
through his throat. The hollows of his lungs felt as if they
were being scalded. His legs trembled with exhaustion,
yet he could not stop, for the damn Comanche ran on
and on.

High Walking cut a look across at the gray-bearded
white man. "The sheep and the Texans cannot be many
miles ahead. Can you run some more?"

"You catch them," Jacob called back grimly between
breaths. "I'll be there with my gun."

Jacob saw the Indian put another piece of peyote into
his mouth. Jacob, himself, began to chew on a new
piece.

By mid-afternoon Jacob's breath was sobbing in his
throat as he reached the extreme limit of his mortal
strength. He opened his mouth to call out that he must
rest or die. Then he saw the large gray smudge on the
grass-covered plain ahead.

High Walking also spotted the herd of livestock. He
halted abruptly and fell to his kness, hunkering low.

High Walking flung a look at Tamarron, and his mouth

opened in a great, silent cry of pleasure. He gripped his
war bow and shook it savagely at the enemy.

Tamarron watched the Indian's face, creased and drawn
with fatigue. The Comanche's lungs heaved as he caught
his wind. His copper-colored skin glistened with sweat,
shining like a dark silken cloth. His eyes, sunk in deeply
caved-in sockets, burned with his eagerness to kill.

"The livestock of the Texans makes a lot of dust," said
Tamarron. "By staying hidden behind it, we can go close.
But we must be careful. There are ten or twelve men,
and they have horses to ride us down."

"In the light of the day they are many and strong. In
the night we two are stronger, for then we can attack
when and where we choose."

Jacob looked to the west. The sun was barely a finger's
width above the horizon. "Soon it will be dark. Let's go
on."

The two men moved like ghosts through the dust cloud
that rolled toward them like fog off a winter sea.

The moon slid out of the east, making the faces of the
Comanche and white man oddly animal-like. The men lay
in the tall grass and spied on the camp of the raiders. For
the last two hundred yards they had snaked forward on
their stomachs and now were not fifty feet from a small,
yellow-flamed fire.

Tamarron looked into the bubble of firelight that held
back the night. A covered pot sat boiling in the edge of
the bed of coals and flames. He counted five saddles
lying scattered about. Bedrolls, two packsaddles, and
other supplies were in a mound on the far side of the
fire. Beyond those items, and partially illuminated by the
flames, was a grove of hackberry trees some ten to twelve
feet tall.

A young man with a sheep carcass over his shoulder
walked into the light. He dumped his load to the ground.
He bent and made cuts with his knife between the ten-
dons and bones of the animal's rear hocks. Thongs were

inserted through the openings in the legs, and the body of the sheep hung from a limb of one of the hackberry trees. With deft, quick strokes of his blade the man skinned the sheep down to the head and stopped there to let the fleece hang and drag on the ground.

The Texan cut the tenderloins from both sides of the backbone. He sliced the slender pieces of mutton into chunks and dumped them in the pot. Other ingredients were added from a pouch. He built up the fire around the pot.

The grass rustled at a puff of night wind, and High Walking whispered to Tamarron, "There is only one man." There was a tone of regret in his voice.

"I count five saddles, so there are others. The man that escaped at the river has warned them about us. Somewhere out there in the grass or among the sheep, they're hiding and waiting."

The leader and his lieutenants had gone on to Texas, reasoned Tamarron. They would leave these peons to do the hard work of driving the herd of livestock five, maybe six hundred miles to a place where they could be sold.

"These men don't know how close we might be, or even if we still follow," said Tamarron. "So this fellow cooks a hot supper. We have to be patient, for the others will come to fill their hungry guts. Then we'll kill them."

High Walking turned his black mask of a face to Tamarron. "You talk too much," he said. "I do not need someone to tell me how to fight."

"I don't want any of them to escape."

"None will escape. I will kill more of them than you do."

Tamarron grunted his disdain at the Comanche's remark. "Let's leave the cook till last. That way, if someone should come to eat or check the camp, he won't know we are already here."

"First we must take their horses and hide them. Then no one can ride away from us."

"I agree," said Tamarron. "I heard a nicker off in that direction. There'll be at least one guard."

They crept in a circle to the left around the firelit camp. Tamarron saw the flock of thousands of sheep and a few hundred cows to the east on the moon-silvered plain. The backs of the sheep were barely visible above the top of the grass. The larger bodies of the cows, casting long shadows, were magnified by the slanting rays of the moon, still low on the horizon. A subdued, weary baaing from the sheep reached him.

In the middle of the herd of livestock, moonlight reflected off a shiny surface. The water from the recent rainstorm had collected in one of the depressions sometimes found on the plain. However, the pond would be very shallow and gone in a few days, sucked away by the hot, thirsty sun.

Tamarron saw the indistinct forms of horses. He counted seven of them. Two of those would be pack animals. His judgment of the size of the band of raiders at five had been correct, unless some men were mounted and not in sight. He should be cautious of that possibility.

The two men hunkered lower in the grass and veered farther away. They came up the wind so as not to alert the horses. The moon was behind the grazing beasts, making shadowy silhouettes of their forms.

Tamarron stopped. A man had moved among the horses. He was turned as if watching the faint glow of the campfire.

Tamarron touched High Walking and pointed. The Comanche nodded.

High Walking drew one of the jasper-tipped arrows from his quiver. He nocked the shaft on the gut string of his powerful war bow. He pulled the cord to his cheek.

The bowstring twanged. The arrow leapt toward the man.

Tamarron caught the barest fleeting glimpse of the hurtling bolt. Then the shaft vanished into the chest of the guard.

The man crumpled to his knees and pitched forward in the tall grass. He uttered not a sound.

"One dead," High Walking said.

The men waited, their eyes wrestling with the darkness. The grass bent and bowed in the wind. The moon walked along its ancient, endless path. With low, tearing sounds the horses cropped the rich, ripe seed heads of the wild plains grass.

Tamarron spoke. "The man you killed must have been the only guard. Let's take the horses and hide them."

Quietly they pulled the stakes from the earth and led the cayuses a quarter of a mile west. There the horses were again tied on the ends of lariats.

"Now we will return quickly to the camp of our enemies," said High Walking. "I want to have my revenge. First we will find and kill any rider watching the sheep and cattle."

The two men made a wary turn around the scattered herd. The weary animals took no notice of the skulking figures. Not one guard was located, and Tamarron and High Walking stole back over the plain.

Drawing near the camp, they dropped to their knees and crawled close. The light in the camp had weakened, the fire throwing only a red luminescence from a bed of glowing coals.

The low mumble of voices came from the edge of the darkness beyond the fire. Tamarron caught the words. The Texans were assigning the hours of the night guards.

Tamarron strained his sight to pierce the murk and pick out the targets. The Texans figured themselves to be safe in the night. They were wrong. Tamarron made out the indistinct forms of four men sitting on the ground. Their arms moved as they ate. That is your last meal, he thought.

He leaned toward High Walking and spoke. "You take the men on the left. I'll take those on the right. Don't stop shooting till every man is dead."

He loosened his pistol in its holster, and then gripped

his rifle. He couldn't see the sights of the gun in the dark. But he wasn't worried about that. At this short range he could simply point the long-barreled weapon and hit the center of a man.

High Walking rose to his knees. The bow bent in his hands. The taut string hummed. He released the arrow. The speeding shaft jumped across the bed of coals into the darkness.

A man screamed. Once.

"Bastard!" exclaimed Tamarron. The Indian should have made his assault on the raiders at the same instant as Tamarron. The man was unpredictable and therefore dangerous. Tamarron jerked his rifle up and fired at a dim form just beginning to rise from the ground.

The blackness of the night seemed to ripple from the concussion of the gunshot. The man fell backward with a harsh expulsion of air.

The two remaining Texans were scrambling to their feet. Their hands clawed at holstered pistols.

Tamarron grabbed his revolver and shot at one of the raiders. The man sank to his knees and pitched forward, his face plowing into the hard ground.

High Walking had again bent his bow. He released the string, flinging an arrow at the shadow of the last man spinning to run away. The shaft struck the middle of the shadow, driving it backward. A guttural moan came out of the gloom. Then all was silent.

High Walking looked through the night at Tamarron. Neither man spoke. Tamarron knew their presence together was only a matter of convenience, of joining strengths and weapons to better kill other men. When the battles had ended, the Comanche might decide to fight him.

High Walking pulled his knife and, holding it poised to strike, went from body to body. He checked the last one and called out to Tamarron. "All are dead."

"Then let's see what the Texans have that we can use." Tamarron collected a handful of brambles from under the hackberry trees and tossed them on the hot coals. A short flame burst into life.

In the night Tamarron gathered a rifle, pistol, and ammunition from one of the dead men. He took a section of canvas, a two-gallon canteen of water, and a quantity of food from the pile of supplies. All of the items were stowed in one of the packs. A saddle was selected from the ones the Texans had used.

Satisfied he could leave at a moment's notice and be well provisioned, Tamarron took a tin plate he'd found in the packs and filled it from the pot near the fire. He began to eat.

The mutton stew was delicious. He chewed hard, feeling a strange sense of pleasure at the thought of eating the food of his foes.

"Try some," Tamarron said, pointing at the pot with his spoon. "It's very good."

The Comanche looked at Tamarron with a bitter stare. "The man I had hoped to slay was not one of those," he said, gesturing at the dead bodies. "I have seen him up close enough to know. He is tall with red hair."

"The chief could be a hundred miles east of here. But now we have horses and can ride them down. Eat, for we need to be strong."

In the flickering light of the fire Tamarron saw the haunted, sorrowful expression on the Indian's face. Did his own countenance also show his terrible anguish?

The Comanche spat at the pot of food. He extracted a piece of peyote from his pouch and began to chew it. He stalked into the night. "I will bring up the horses," he called back.

Tamarron had lost his appetite. High Walking and he had killed some of their enemies but not their leaders. Those men had planned the murders and had a higher priority to die. And they had escaped.

He went to meet High Walking and helped stake out the horses. As he worked, he saw a nimbus of hazy mist forming around the moon. A ring of light was visible through the mist close around the yellow sphere. By the density of the high, cold moisture and the swiftness with which it had come hurrying in, he judged that the weather was changing, and that rain would fall within a day.

The last horse was fastened to the end of a lariat. The Comanche, without a sign, turned and walked off, becoming lost in the darkness.

Tamarron picked up a blanket and, selecting a spot near a tall horse, lay down. As he watched the haze thicken around the moon, he sensed that his days remaining upon the earth had a small number, and were of little value. Except for his revenge.

During the night he dreamed of fighting a gun battle with a swarm of Texans on a windy plain. He could see Petra far off, beckoning to him to come to her aid. But the Texans were always barring his way, shooting at him and laughing uproariously, as if it were all some great joke.

The storm wind came running from the east like some giant night animal charging upon Tamarron. He awoke with a jerk and sat up to stare into the wind. He could see nothing, for all around him the night lay congealed in utter blackness, so thick that a man could hold a handful. The grass stems whipped and broke with a brittle sound. Darts of their reedy bodies stung Tamarron's face like biting insects.

He rolled himself back into his blanket. He hoped the stakes would hold the tethered horses so they wouldn't drift away with the winds. He lay listening to the storm wind punishing the prairie with its anger.

At last Tamarron dozed. At times the wind pushing against the blanket brought pleasant dreams of Petra's body moving against him when they slept. He would awaken and realize with sadness that he was not with Petra in the big hacienda on the Rio Pecos.

With the dawn the fury of the storm increased and drove Jacob from his bed. The air was full of dust and flying bits of grass. Overhead, dense, threatening clouds streamed past in the teeth of the wind.

The thousands of sheep and the few hundred cows had vanished. Three of the horses were missing. The animals had gone off to the west, and Jacob thought that their situation wasn't too bad. They could easily end their wind-propelled journey back on the Pecos. Permanent water could be found there.

High Walking came out of the grass. He paid no attention to Jacob, as if the white man did not exist. He saddled one of the horses but touched not one item of the provisions.

You are a damn fool Comanche, thought Tamarron. He hastily shoved his blanket into the pack he had assembled the evening before. One of the horses that had marks on its back from having previously carried packs was again loaded. The long-legged horse was saddled. The others were turned loose and immediately began to wander off in the wind.

Tamarron dipped out a plate of the cold stew. As he wolfed the food he looked at the Indian, a gaunt, brown statue sitting motionlessly on his horse and staring east into the storm. Jacob wondered what the Indian ate. Or if he ate anything except the peyote.

Tamarron swung astride his new mount. The horse immediately grabbed the bit in its big teeth and went stiff-legged. Tamarron saw the cruelty at the mouth, and he had no time to fool with the brute. He jerked its head roughly to the side and slapped the horse hard across the ears with his hand. The brute stomped the ground with both front feet and acted as if it wanted to rear. Jacob cuffed it again. The horse relaxed and accepted the domination of its rider. It went off smartly beside High Walking's mount.

Beyond the trampled zone of the prairie where the sheep had grazed and bedded, Tamarron and High Walking found the tracks of four horses. They stepped down from their saddles and squatted in the whipping grass to examine the imprints in the dirt.

"The riders are ahead of us, maybe two days," High Walking said, and touched one of the horse tracks.

"The gunmen who escaped from us at the river warned the men with the herd. Now the leader and three others ride on ahead. They'll be alert and watching for us."

"That makes no difference to me," growled the Comanche.

The men mounted and guided their cayuses to the east. The storm wind pounded them as it rushed past in a roaring, invisible river. The mighty current often staggered the horses, and they would slow and try to turn from its bite. Each time the horses faltered, the men whipped them onward with cutting blows.

CHAPTER 21

Rio Pecos Valley, Mexican Territory, August 16, 1846

The tuneful sound of fife and drum and the voices of hundreds of marching soldiers singing "The Blue-tailed Fly" reached Captain Paul Spradling, army surgeon. For the first time in many weeks the captain had a short, free hour to ride away from the noise and confusion of the soldiers and wagons, and the needs of deathly ill men.

He sat his mount just below the timber line on the south slope of El Barro Mountain and just above the head of El Cañon de Peña. Las Vegas was fifteen miles off to the northeast, and Santa Fe fifty miles to the west, beyond the steep, high backbone of the Sangre de Cristo Mountains.

General Kearny's Army of the West was strung out below the captain, traveling in detachments of two or three companies each along the Santa Fe Trail. The First Regiment of Missouri Cavalry, under Colonel Alexander Doniphan, was nearly out of sight to the west and approaching the Rio Pecos Valley. The colonel's mounted riders were the scouts and advance guard for the army.

Two batteries of artillery, with twelve six-pound cannon and four twelve-pound howitzers, under Major Meriwether Clark, followed second in line. E. V. Sumner's three squadrons of First Dragoons came next. One of the squads was always riding in a protective position along both flanks of the marching army.

Two companies of infantry under Captain William Angney were just below Captain Spradling. It was their singing that he heard.

Close behind the marching foot soldiers, three hundred wagons rumbled and rattled on the rough road. Within their capacious bodies were transported the sick and injured soldiers, as well as ammunition, food, medicine, harnesses, a blacksmith shop, and a thousand other items needed to keep the army moving and ready for battle. A large herd of livestock came last, walking in a perpetual storm of dust kicked up by their own pounding hooves.

Kearny's soldiers had grown tough over the six weeks of the march. His total army at the beginning when it had left Fort Leavenworth, Kansas, had consisted of one thousand four hundred and fifty-eight men, four thousand horses and draft mules, and fourteen thousand nine hundred cattle and oxen.

Most of the men had been unaccustomed to long marches, especially in the heat and dust of the arid plains. But the general had pushed them hard, up to thirty-two miles a day. Regulars and recruits alike had cursed and moaned, but they made it, outpacing the horses at times. In twenty-nine days they had covered five hundred and fifty miles and reached Bent's Fort on the Missouri River.

On August 2, the soldiers left Bent's Fort and started southward toward Raton Pass. For four days they marched almost without water, the temperature climbing to one hundred and twenty degrees, the wagons falling back, the horses collapsing, and the men burying their weaker comrades who could not survive. Packs of wolves followed the columns, feeding on the dead livestock.

Water was the most difficult thing to find. When a

water hole was found, the lead men usually rushed to use it, spoiling it for those behind. Often when the wind was right, the livestock would smell the water, bolt ahead, and plunge into it, fouling it for all.

Captain Spradling had been moving constantly from one infirmary wagon to the next, tending the ill and injured. Then the days had grown cooler as the army climbed into the higher elevations of the foothills of the Sangre de Cristo Mountains. Fresh mountain streams were found. Men began to crawl out of the sick wagons and fall into formation.

The hardships and deaths had been more than the young captain had bargained for. Still, now that the goal of Santa Fe was within striking distance, he felt a wonderful exhilaration.

As the marching soldiers below him began to sing "The Girl I Left Behind Me," Spradling turned his mount and rode parallel to the column. He passed through a mile of piñon pine and juniper, and came out on the northwest point of the mesa above El Cañon de Peña. The valley of the Rio Pecos, cutting apart a series of short, grassy hills, was within sight three miles ahead.

More than a quarter of a mile distant, an animal came into view, moving up from a swale between two hills. Spradling thought the beast a buffalo, for there seemed to be a hump on its back. It limped as if its hindquarters were badly injured.

The animal moved northeasterly, a course that converged with Spradling's route. Soon he could tell that it was a gray horse with a pack on its back. Or was that a man lying far forward and clinging to the neck of the horse? Spradling spurred his mount to a run to intercept the strange horse.

The gray mare heard the thudding hoofbeats rushing toward it and started to turn and run. Its wounded right rear leg gave way, and it almost fell. It looked back over its shoulder and whinnied in alarm.

Spradling reined his steed down to a walk and came up

slowly. The person on the back of the mare made no movement and seemed either dead or unconscious.

Spradling spoke in a low, soothing voice to the horse. "Easy there, old girl. Who are you carrying?"

He saw the blood on the person's side. And then the long black hair and the smooth, beardless face. "A woman, by God!"

The captain sprang down from his horse and hurried to the woman. Her arms were locked around her mount's neck. A rope was fastened around her waist and tied to the pommel. She must have secured herself to the horse, knowing that to fall and be left behind was surely to die.

Spradling lifted her head and felt for the pulse in her throat. The heart throbbed, low but firm. He saw the scar on the side of her face. You've been badly hurt before, and still you lived through it, he thought. He parted her bloody shirt. The wound on her ribs had mostly stopped bleeding but still oozed a pinkish lymph fluid. Her injury was not so bad that its treatment couldn't wait until he reached his operating wagon.

He pulled the bridle reins from off the saddle horn and led the horse to his mount. He swung astride and briskly started off, towing the limping mare.

In noisy, ordered confusion the American army made camp on the east side of the Rio Pecos at the base of El Barro Mountain. The wagons were halted and the teams of mules unhitched, hobbled, and turned loose to graze on the lush grass along the river's edge. Under heavy guard the cattle and oxen were herded to a large meadow on a bend of the river below the encampment.

The tents of the enlisted men blossomed in patterns of dirty gray squares, each company separated from the next. The officers' area was established on a rise of ground on the north border of the bivouac.

Captain Spradling entered the camp and immediately spotted the red flags on the fifteen-foot staffs attached to the infirmary wagons. He nodded his approval at the location of the mobile hospital. Sergeant Atkinson had chosen a site just below the officers' area and near the river. The water would be purest there, and the noise least. An excellent place for the ill men to rest.

The busy soldiers halted their work and stepped aside to allow the captain to pass. They stared at the woman lying over the neck of the limping mare.

"Is she dead, Captain?" a man called.

"She's alive," Spradling replied without slowing.

"Got yourself a female patient this time, eh, Captain?" another soldier said in a jovial tone. A chuckle ran through the men.

Sergeant Atkinson saw his captain break free of the crowd of soldiers and start up the slight grade toward the hospital wagons. He spoke to the two medical orderlies helping sick and injured men from the wagons and onto blanket pallets inside the newly erected tents.

"Stanbro, Cordell, Captain Spradling's coming and he's got a patient. Stanbro, go to the river and bring back two buckets of water. Cordell, help me get the operating table and surgical instruments set up. Move fast now."

The sergeant began to take the segments of a long, narrow folding table from the bed of a wagon. Cordell hurried to help. Soon a sturdy table was assembled and leveled.

An assortment of probes, needles, and sharp steel cutting instruments were arrayed on a smaller table close by. A pan of water and a bowl of soft soap was placed beside them.

"Good work, Sergeant," said Spradling as he reined in his horse and viewed the preparation for surgery. "You guessed correctly. We have some work to do. Come help me get the woman down."

"Sir, will you need one of the other surgeons?" asked the sergeant. "They are just up there in the officers' tents."

"No. I can handle this without their help."

The captain sprang to the ground and swiftly untied the rope holding the unconscious Petra in the saddle. The fingers of her clasped hands were pried loose, and her arms removed from around the horse's neck. Gently she was laid on the table.

"God!" exclaimed Atkinson. "She sure is a scarred-up woman. She'd be pretty except for that."

Spradling had given the old wound little attention in his first quick examination of the woman. Now he bent and felt the thickness and width of the mass of scar tissue on the side of her face. A thoughtful expression came to his eyes.

"Do you want her strapped down, Captain?" asked Atkinson.

"No. You and Stanbro wash up. Then hold her on her side so I can work."

With soap and water the surgeon scrubbed Petra's wound until the gaping flesh was raw and bleeding. He inserted a thin thread into a curved needle. "Hold her tightly," he ordered.

Petra flinched and moaned at the punch of the needle. Her eyelids fluttered. Her hands tried to come up to protect her ribs.

"Hold her still," the surgeon snapped at Atkinson and Stanbro. "Cordell, mix a dose of laudanum in water."

With neat, precise stitches the captain sewed the red lips of the gunshot injury together. Finishing, he evaluated his handiwork. In a year only a slight scar would remain. He applied a generous covering of salve and fastened a bandage over it all.

For a long moment he stared down at Petra's face. He leaned and again felt the coarseness of the scar on the mutilated cheek.

"Cordell, bring me the laudanum," said the surgeon. "What we are about to do will be damn awful painful and will take a long time." Cautiously, so as not to strangle the woman, the surgeon got a heavy dose of pain-deadening narcotic down her throat.

"Turn her on her back and strap her down," he directed. "Strap arms and legs and head. Then I also want Atkinson and Stanbro to hold her. Cordell, you stand by close in case you, too, are needed. Though she's unconscious and the laudanum will soon take effect, she'll feel hellish pain.''

The captain picked up a gleaming scalpel. "She must not jerk while I am operating. This is going to take delicate cutting, so pay attention to what you're doing. And hurry. The sun is almost down and I've got to have strong light to see by.''

The orderlies inserted leather straps through slots cut in the wooden top of the table. Petra's arms and legs were encircled and cinched firmly down.

"Put a soft pad of cloth beneath her head first,'' said the surgeon as Atkinson placed a strap across Petra's forehead.

"Yes, sir," said the sergeant. He completed his task and nodded at the surgeon.

The captain tested the tightness of the bindings. "Good. We start now.''

Petra twitched and cried out as the scalpel entered her flesh. Her body strained at the leather fastenings. The strong hands of the orderlies pushed down hard upon her.

The surgeon worked swiftly, skillfully, cutting away the scar tissue. The edges of the freshly severed flesh were white for an instant, before the blood welled up to fill the new wound and overflow down Petra's face and run in a tiny red rivulet across the boards of the table top.

"She's bleeding badly, sir," said the sergeant.

"Dammit, Atkinson, I can see that,'' the captain's voice crackled. "Hold her mouth shut and her jaws clamped together. Stop her head from moving. Use more force! More force!''

The opening widened as Spradling peeled away the damaged skin and carved the tissue beneath, sculpting and shaping the contour of the cheek. The operation was much more extensive then he had thought it would be. The sharp object that had caused the injury had struck the face at an angle, then skidded along the bone of the skull, tearing and mangling the full thickness of the flesh of the cheek.

The woman's body arched upward and trembled violently. It was forced down by the weight of the two orderlies. Cordell stepped forward and added his strength to hold Petra motionless.

Spradling hastily felt for the pulse of the patient. The heart had a speeding, ragged beat. His hands shook for an instant before he brought them under control. He had removed men's arms and legs, and sometimes had even seen them die from the shock of his cutting knife and saw. Still, this woman's agony affected him more deeply than any other patient he'd ever had. Had he been right in trying this operation? He went back to the delicate task.

At last the shape of the cheek satisfied the surgeon. He replaced the skin across the raw, bleeding flesh. The finest thread was passed through the eye of a slender needle. With the greatest care the captain began to sew. When he had finished stretching and stiching the skin together, there still remained an area broader than his thumb between the edges in the center of the wound.

A shadow fell over the woman's face. Spradling looked up.

"The sun's going down, sir," said Atkinson.

Spradling wiped at the sweat running down his forehead. He did not want to try to complete the operation in the dimness of lantern light. Quickly he measured the open section of the wound. Then, above the woman's breast on the left shoulder, he made an incision and stripped away a section of skin.

With fine, even stitches Spradling sewed the skin patch into place to complete the covering of the cheek. On the shoulder, the soft, pliable skin was pulled closed over the exposed flesh, and the needle again did its work.

"I've never seen skin removed from one place and put in another," said the sergeant.

"Neither have I," said the captain. "Let's hope it will grow there."

"She looks prettier already," commented Atkinson.

"Really quite lovely," said Spradling. He reached to check her pulse. The laudanum was coursing through Petra's veins, and her heart throbbed slowly and steadily beneath his fingertips. "She is a strong woman. She should heal if infection doesn't set in."

He applied salve and carefully bandaged both sites. He breathed a sigh of relief, letting it out slowly so that the orderlies could not hear it. For the first time he allowed himself to wonder where she had come from. How many miles had she traveled? Who had wounded her so cruelly?

"Put her in a tent by herself. Be sure she's not bothered by anyone. I'll look at her in a couple of hours."

"Yes, sir," said the sergeant. "Will she be able to travel with us tomorrow?"

"She must be. The general will wait on no one."

CHAPTER 22

P etra came back to life slowly, floating up layer by
layer out of her drugged stupor. The rise was full of
ever-increasing pain. She almost surfaced to full
consciousness, but the laudanum in her blood held her
just short of complete wakefulness.

Her mind began to function in her narcotic, twilight
world, reaching out to test the hurt body. The soreness
of her ribs—she remembered the cause of that. The
bandits had shot her during the attack on the hacienda.
But the terrible ache in the side of her face and the lesser
one on the front of her shoulder—those she could not
explain. Had she been wounded again?

A frightening thought more important than her own
wounds came surging forward. Where was Jacob? She
recalled only that he had ridden away as she called to
him. He must be somewhere searching for her. Or perhaps the *banditos* had found and killed him.

That first night after crawling out of the rocks, she had
wandered, weak and frightened, through the corridors
and rooms of the big hacienda calling out for members of
the household. The spaces echoed back ghostlike and

empty. She had found a loaded rifle and carried it with her. Finally she had slept, alone and clutching the weapon in her hands.

In the morning dusk Petra had found the two dead men in the courtyard. The mare had been at the gate but would not enter because of the smell of death.

Petra had mounted the faithful mare and started up the Rio Pecos to the Bautista hacienda to find someone to tend her wounds. She'd found the hacienda deserted. Nearing unconsciousness, she had tied herself to the horse and continued north toward Las Vegas.

Where was she now? Was she safe?

Not uttering a sound, Petra opened her eyes. Directly overhead were ceiling poles supporting an earthen roof. The diagonal pattern of the poles was somehow familiar. She rotated her eyes downward and saw a crucifix gilded with gold. Below that, a statue of the Holy Mother rested in a small alcove in the wall. Her view darted about at the rocking chair near the window, a picture on the wall, the washbasin on a stand. In startled amazement she realized she was in her own bedroom in the Solis house in Santa Fe.

"Aunt Teofila," Petra called. Her voice was cracked and dry and came as a coarse whisper. She swallowed and called again. "Aunt Teofila."

The quick patter of footsteps sounded in the hall, and the door burst open. A tiny woman, very old, swept inside. The web of wrinkles in her worried face crinkled and rearranged themselves into a happy smile at the sight of Petra.

"Oh, Petra, it is so good to see you awake," Teofila cried.

"I am home! I am home!" Petra wanted to laugh, but it hurt too much.

"You certainly are."

"How did that happen?"

"The American, Dr. Spradling, brought you."

"What do you mean? I know no Dr. Spradling."

"He is a surgeon with the American army. You were

in one of the army wagons when they came to Santa Fe. Dr. Spradling told everyone in the city that he had found a woman with a scar on her face, riding a gray mare near the Rio Pecos. When I heard the story, I went to see the doctor. Even with all your bandages I knew you. The doctor helped me bring you home. He gave you laudanum and left. He said he had many other ill people to care for, but he would be back."

"Then the Americans have captured Santa Fe. The battle must have been very fierce. Did they kill many of our soldiers?"

Teofila stamped her small feet, her eyes flashing. "Our great Governor Armijo showed the true coward he is. Colonel Piño had our soldiers ready for battle in Apache Canyon. But even before the Americans arrived, Armijo ordered a withdrawal of all the men and told them to go home.

"Many of the angry soldiers surrounded the governor in the plaza. I could hear them shouting at him. They demanded he fight. The governor's troop of personal bodyguards could not get him free of the men. Then he opened a bag of silver and threw many coins on the ground. While our poor soldiers scrambled to grab a portion of the money, Armijo and his guards spurred their horses through them and went south toward Chihuahua."

"Then there was no fighting."

"Not a shot fired."

"I am ashamed we didn't fight to stop the Americans from taking Santa Fe. Yet in a way I am glad, for that means Conrado and our vaqueros are safe. Ask Conrado to come and see me, for I want to tell him about the *banditos'* attack on the rancho."

"I have not seen Conrado."

"But he must be here. He left the hacienda . . ." Petra paused. How many days had passed since he had ridden off toward Santa Fe?

"Tell me about the *banditos*," Teofila said.

"I believe all the people at the rancho are dead. I

could not find their bodies, but I feel the worst has happened."

Teofila began to cry. "I never liked that place, so far away on the Rio Pecos. Either the Indians or the *banditos* are constantly causing trouble. I'm glad I always stayed in Santa Fe." Her sobs increased. "All dead. Just you and I still alive. Oh, Petra, what shall we do?"

"Stop that crying, Aunt. Conrado is not dead. Go and find him. Ask questions of everybody." Petra did not believe her own words. Conrado, had he been in Santa Fe, would have stayed at the family house. She felt the moistness of tears gathering. She blinked them away. It would change nothing to cry.

Teofila stifled her sobs. "Do you want anything before I leave?"

"The largest, coldest drink of water possible. And when you return, fix me some of your delicious soup." Petra must regain her strength quickly so she could deal with the conquering Americans and somehow keep Rancho el Vado from being lost to the invaders.

Captain Spradling examined Petra Tamarron's wounds. Every stitch had held. The flesh was still red and somewhat swollen, but the graft was taking. Best of all, there was no infection.

"It's been four days since I operated, and you are healing quite well," Spradling said. He looked into the black eyes of the Mexican woman. She had flinched only once as he removed the bandages, but he knew the pain must be very great, especially from the severed nerve endings on the sensitive face.

"Do you want some laudanum for the pain?"

"I need nothing. It does not hurt that much."

"Very well. Do you want to see your face?" asked the surgeon.

"Yes," replied Petra. How much skill did the American doctor have? She thought it strange that he had operated merely to remove a scar. Never had she heard of such a thing.

Teofila handed Petra a mirror. The old woman smiled in a pleased, anticipatory way.

Petra lifted the mirror. For all the many past years she hadn't liked what she saw reflected back at her. With a skeptical bent to her mind she looked at the person staring at her from the looking glass.

The cheek that had been so badly scarred now had been contoured to resemble the opposite one. A portion of new skin had been inserted, to replace a damaged area. The addition was a perfect oval in outline. She believed the surgeon had deliberately shaped the new skin so that any scar that remained would not be jagged in form and thus displeasing to view. The stitches were very small, as precise and neat as a most practiced seamstress could sew.

"The light-colored skin graft from your chest will tan to the same color as your face," said the surgeon. "I'll remove the stitches in a few days. During the next months the scars will gradually grow less noticeable."

"You will be beautiful, Petra," said Teofila.

I would give all my chances at beauty just to be sure Jacob was safe, thought Petra. She spoke to the surgeon. "You have done a wondrous favor for me, Dr. Spradling. I am greatly in your debt. Why would you be so kind to an enemy?"

"You are not my enemy," Captain Spradling replied gruffly. "I have no enemies."

"I believe what you say, and know that you are a kind man. You have made a friend in Santa Fe."

"Friends are gold." The surgeon backed away a few steps and looked at Petra, evaluating his handiwork. He nodded. The old woman was right. Petra Tamarron would be beautiful.

Petra wanted the day to end. When the darkness of night came, she and the band of vaqueros she had gathered would ride into Texas.

Her wounds were healing rapidly, and the bandages and the stitches had been removed by the American surgeon. The pain that remained was but the slightest of annoyances. Now she waited only for the long journey to begin.

She crossed the plaza, her boot heels thumping on the hard-baked August ground and her leather pants whispering with her stride. *Los pelados*, the town loafers, had vanished from the Santa Fe streets with the invasion of the Americans. A vaquero passed her, his expression sullen and his eyes lowered. He carried neither pistol nor knife. It was odd, and also sad, to see one of the proud riders without his pistol.

One of the primary ordinances issued by General Kearny was to prohibit the Mexican citizens from carrying weapons. That restriction was harshly enforced. Kearny's soldiers had filled the *calabozo* with offenders on the first day of occupation. Petra had moved her stiletto from her belt and hid the sharp blade inside her shirt.

American officers came and went at the general's headquarters located in the Palace of the Governors. Nearby on the drill ground, where Armijo's personal guards had so recently ridden their prancing horses, an American captain was giving orders to the lieutenant of a company of dragoons. When the captain finished speaking, the lieutenant saluted and, with a command to his troops, led them from the plaza.

The heavily armed horsemen in their blue uniforms passed Petra at a gallop, heading south to patrol and guard El Camino Real. Any Mexican expedition that marched to recapture Santa Fe would come along the El Camino Real from the large army garrison at Chihuahua. Petra did not believe a relief column would ever come.

Some six hundred yards northeast of town, the two-foot adobe-and-stone walls of a large fort were being swiftly erected by the Americans. The two-acre enclosure could hold a thousand soldiers and many cannon. The conquerors meant to stay.

The fine, lush meadows along the Santa Fe River were crowded with gringo horses and mules. The pastureland had been confiscated, and the Mexican livestock forced to move far down the river or to the wooded hills to the west.

Wagons were being repaired on the broad bench between the river and the town. Nearby, in a fenced pasture, scores of horses and mules were waiting for the blacksmith to nail on new iron shoes. It was no secret that the gringos were preparing to march on California. Already a group of vaqueros mounted on fast horses had slipped away to warn the Mexican officials at Sacramento of the imminent invasion.

Petra turned away from the town and walked toward Atalaya Mountain, climbing leisurely upward through the pine and juniper on the steep slope.

She followed the path Jacob and she had taken back in the spring. She recalled that happy day as she paced along. But the evening shadows fell before she reached the high shoulder of the mountain where they had stopped. The time to put her plan into action had arrived. She turned around to retrace her steps to the town.

Petra saw something move, a fleeting glimpse of a gray form vanishing among the pines. Had that flicker been the back of a man, or only the rump of a deer? She shivered as if someone had drawn a feather along her spine. Though her conscious mind couldn't determine if danger existed, her subconscious primal instinct knew it was there. She veered away from the point and hastened down the slope on a different route.

Unger crouched behind the bole of the bushy juniper and watched Tamarron's woman hurry off the mountain. For a moment he was angry that she had spotted him, then his wide mouth opened and he chuckled silently. Now she was scared. That was good. Let her worry.

She and Tamarron had made a fool of him in front of the other trappers. Tamarron had bluffed him from a fight with knives. Now he would repay the man tenfold, a hundredfold, for that insult. Unger would take Tamarron's woman. Nothing could hurt the gray-bearded man more than that.

*   *   *

In the late evening the plaza was full of off-duty American soldiers. They ambled about or leaned against the walls of the buildings and talked among themselves. To Petra they appeared quite youthful.

She was surprised at the large number of the town's young women, who, bedecked in brightly colored clothing, paraded past the soldiers. The Americans often spoke and smiled to the girls who came close. The young women would laugh back and flash their eyes at the fair-skinned men.

Petra saw a Mexican man in the doorway. He was also observing the young women flirting with the foreigners. His face was clouded with disapproval. Petra could not untangle her own mixture of emotions regarding the women's interest in the Americans. Petra had married one of them.

With a shrill, scolding cry an old woman dashed past the man in the doorway and grabbed one of the girls on the street. A leather strap rose and fell as the old woman whipped the protesting girl through the door and out of sight. Petra heard the angry voice of the man join that of the woman in berating the girl. The soldiers on the plaza were no longer smiling.

Unger crept through the darkness to the wall of the Solis hacienda. Silently, on moccasined feet, he moved to an open window and listened for noise inside. Satisfied that the house was empty, he leapt up to grab the edge of the roof. He muscled himself up and swung over the low parapet. He crawled across the dirt rooftop to a position where he could see down into the broad patio.

He had stalked the Solis home before and knew the location of the patio, enclosed with a wall higher than his head, on the west end. At the rear of the house were stables for several horses. He waited, watching the stables and listening for footsteps as the dark sky brightened and shadows formed on the lee side of objects as a round, full moon rose above the Sangre de Cristo Mountains.

A growing excitement built in Unger. Soon he would take his vengence against Tamarron's woman. That would be a much anticipated pleasure.

He came instantly alert as a boot grated on sandy soil on the path leading from the street. Below him, Petra Tamarron entered the patio. Unger's blood raced. Woman, I have you now!

He rose to his knees and spied on the woman as she moved to the center of the patio. She did not sit down in one of the seats but walked around restlessly and looked often at the moon and the patio entrance.

With a swift motion Unger swung down from the rooftop and sprang to block Petra's escape from the patio. He changed directions and closed in on the woman. His eyes swept her body. He saw no weapons.

Petra backpedaled rapidly. Her heart thudded as if it would break every rib in her chest. She recognized the American, the man called Unger. Her hand darted for the knife within her shirt. A puny weapon, for the man would also have a knife, and he was twice her size.

"Stop! Stop!" Petra cried, and held up her left hand as if warding off the man. "What do you want?" She must slow the man, for the buttons of her shirt were stubbornly resisting her frantic attempts to undo them and get to her knife.

Unger did not reply. Words were unnecessary.

Petra bumped into the wall. The deep shadows cast by the structure fell over her. A button broke off. Her hand grasped the handle of the knife.

Hoping desperately that the man wouldn't see the weapon in the darkness, she drew it and let it hang beside her leg. She must have an opportunity for one cut with the sharp blade—a good deep cut, for one chance would be all she would have. She froze, as tense as a hummingbird watching a snake.

Unger was within three steps of the woman. She was bent silently forward and as immobile as a statue. Why didn't she scream or cry out for help? Very strange, thought Unger. But this way suited him best. He sprang at her.

Petra stabbed out with the knife. It plunged deeply into Unger's body, severing muscle, then stopping hard against bone. She twisted away abruptly, tearing free of the grasp of his clutching hands.

The blade sliced with ice-cold heat into Unger's stomach. He felt the shock and the sudden weakening of his strength. Goddamn her, she must have had the knife hidden inside her clothing. I'm hurt, you bitch, but I'll kill you.

Unger pulled his long-bladed skinning knife and lunged after Petra.

CHAPTER 23

Vincente Alvarado had reached the corner of the stables when he heard Petra's frightened voice cry out in English. Though he understood none of the language, the tone of the words told him of the danger to her. Vincente rushed to the gateway to the patio.

He saw Petra and a man struggling at the far end of the enclosure. Then Petra broke free. The man, a large American, spun around to pursue her.

Vincente hurled himself across the patio, yanking his pistol as he bore down upon the man. He sprang between Petra and her assailant. With a quick swing he hammered the knife from Unger's hand. A savage blow of the iron barrel of the gun broke the American's jaw, knocking him flat on his back on the ground.

The Mexican put the sharp heel of his boot beneath Unger's chin and his neck. For a moment Vincente stared at the half-unconscious man. Then he thrust powerfully downward, twisting his heel, crushing the man's neck.

Vincente felt good at killing the gringo who had abused Petra. The deed seemed to lift part of the overwhelming shame that had burned his soul ever since the Mexicans had retreated from Apache Canyon. To run from the enemy before you can see him and test his strength—how cowardly that was. Vincente should have fought them even if that meant fighting alone against the whole American army. Even to his death.

"Petra, are you all right?" Vincente asked.

"Yes. Just scared. But, *Madre de Dios*, we have killed one of the Americans. They will hang us."

"No, they won't. I'll take his stinking carcass into the forest and hide it. I'm glad I got here in time to help you."

"Listen!" said Petra. "Someone is coming now."

"Probably our vaqueros. It is time for them." Vincente held his pistol ready in his hand.

Nineteen men warily filed into the patio. Every man had a pistol on his belt. Their eyes sharply examined the body on the ground.

Gomez pointed at Unger's body. "Who is that?"

"A gringo that thought to harm Petra. He is nothing now." Vincente turned to Petra. "We have chosen the best horsemen and marksmen in all the Rio Grande Valley. They know only that we have a very difficult job for them to do and that we leave tonight."

"And that we will be paid in gold," added Gomez.

"Yes, in gold, Gomez," agreed Vincente. "Petra will tell you the rest of what must be done."

Gomez took off his hat. "Señorita Solis, it is an honor to help you. I knew your father and brother."

The other men doffed their big hats and nodded in agreement with Gomez's words.

"My name is Señora Petra Solis Tamarron," Petra said, correcting Gomez. She was pleased to see the pistols on the men's belts. That showed their bravery and daring and a willingness to fight the Americans. She went directly to her plan.

"Two weeks ago, Rancho el Vado was raided by gringo bandits. They killed my family and drove away our sheep and cattle. With your help I mean to trail them into Texas and take back what belongs to me. We will kill as many of the bandits as we can." She did not mention that she hoped to find Jacob. A horrible fear cramped her heart that he might think her dead and never return. However, he would be in pursuit of the Texans, so she had a chance to encounter him if she hurried.

"It will be very difficult to trail the bandits after half a month has passed and rains have fallen," said a heavily bearded man standing near Gomez.

"Not too hard for a good tracker," responded Petra. "Vincente is the very best."

Vincente spoke. "We know the direction they must take, and it isn't south to Mexico where most bandits take their stolen animals. There is not one man there that would buy livestock with a Mexican brand from an American now that the two countries are at war. The gringos will go east to Austin. They must cross the Llano Estacado to do that. Water is very scarce. So the animals will be driven on a route that will strike the headwaters of the Colorado River and then follow that live stream to Austin. I know that country, for I traveled it ten years ago when I fought with Santa Anna against the Texans."

"They could go to Missouri," said Gomez. "That isn't much farther than Austin."

"I've thought of that. We will track the herd. These *banditos* stole perhaps eighty thousand sheep. Many will die. We'll see the white fleeces of the dead ones marking the way for us."

"We must not waste more time talking," Petra said. "The Texans can drive the sheep twelve, maybe fifteen miles each day. Already they could be two hundred miles from Rancho el Vado. On our horses we can travel fifty miles a day or more. If we push hard, we should catch them in six or seven days."

"What is to be our pay, Señora?" asked Gomez.

"Each man shall receive three hundred pesos in gold, even if we can't find the *banditos*. If we are lucky and get my livestock back, the pay shall be one thousand pesos in gold."

Petra saw the pleased expressions of the vaqueros. "I

am glad you ride with me," she said. "Now go get your
horses and rifles. Watch carefully and don't get caught by
the American patrols. Meet Vincente and me in half an
hour at the edge of the woods just south of the road to
Las Vegas."

The men left the patio, the big rowels of their spurs
jingling. After the last vaquero had passed from sight,
Petra spoke to Vincente. "Do you have the extra horses?"

"As you directed, I have two riding horses to replace
any that become lame. Also, I have three packhorses
carrying provisions. They, too, can be used as mounts if
we need them."

Vincente studied Petra. "What we plan to do is very
dangerous. Not only will the *banditos* fight us for the
livestock, but every Texan we meet will try to kill us. We
are only twenty-one against many thousands."

"They have robbed us and killed our people. So do we
have any choice except to pursue them?"

"No." Vincente was pleased at Petra's answer. He
wanted to kill more Americans. Killing Texans would be
best of all.

"Then let's ride. I will get my rifle and blanket from
the hacienda and meet you at the stables."

Five minutes later, astride a long-legged gelding, Petra
rode beside Vincente toward the forest covering the flank
of the Sangre de Cristo Mountains. She glanced back at
Unger's body, tied across one of the spare mounts. He
was but the first American to die by the hands of her and
the vaqueros.

Far to the rear, Santa Fe was only a scattering of pale
points of light. Then that vanished as she and Vincente
entered the dark wall of the forest. The other vaqueros
had been waiting, and now, touching their steeds with
spurs, they fell into position to follow.

The cold wind that came down from the high, stony
crown of the Sangre de Cristo Mountains washed over
Petra. She shivered. She knew the shiver was not all
from the wind. Vincente was correct. Texas was a hazardous land. The men who lived there even more danger-

ous. How many of these fine vaqueros was she leading to
their deaths?

The winds hurtled themselves at Tamarron with the
noise of a maniacal flute, then raced onward past him
toward the curve of the horizon, as if trying to blow
themselves off the earth. He yanked his hat down more
tightly and turtled his neck deeply into his collar. This
was the evening of the second day of the storm wind.
Now he smelled the moisture of impending rain. Damn
his bad luck.

High Walking rode on Jacob's left. The Comanche was
starving, his body shrunken and his ribs sticking out like
ripples in brown sand. His long hair had escaped from his
headband and flicked and danced in the wind like a
hundred young blacksnakes.

On all sides, the Staked Plains was a flat expanse of
tall grass, whipping and bowing and springing erect, only
to be knocked down again. The storm clouds, their dark
bottoms boiling and churning, streamed by so close overhead that they seemed to touch the men and horses
driving forward into the invisible force of the wind.

Jacob saw the streaked, grayish wall of falling rain
speeding in on the back of the wind. "High Walking,"
Jacob called out above the tumult, "rain's coming."

The Indian raised his face and looked ahead. He halted
his horse and sat without moving.

Jacob jumped down and hastily hobbled his mount and
the pack horse. The pack was dumped to the ground,
and a section of tarpaulin was extracted from it. He laid
the pack on one edge of the canvas to anchor it. The rain
hit as he dropped down on the tarpaulin beside the pile
of provisions and pulled the covering up over his head.
The raindrops, slanting down at a tremendous speed,
rattled like rocks on top of the tarpaulin.

Jacob squirmed around until he was somewhat comfortable sitting with his back leaning against the pack. He
rested, listening to the storm tearing and clawing its way
over the plains.

After a time Tamarron parted the canvas and looked for the Comanche. The man crouched beneath the front legs of his horse. His shoulders were humped, as if the shape of his body would ward off the rain. Jacob shook his head in disgust. The stubborn Indian should have brought himself one of the white men's waxed canvases, for there was no protection on the open plain. Jacob's cover would shelter only one person. The Indian would just have to hunker down and suffer.

Jacob went to sleep, listening to the fury of wind and rain. Now and then, when the cold wetness found a way in, he would awaken and rearrange his cover. He tried to see the Indian once again, but night had fallen on the plains like a big black dog, hiding everything.

Tamarron awoke in the drippy, misty, no-man's-hour of dawn. The storm was gone, and utter stillness lay everywhere. He looked at High Walking, sitting wet and hunched in the wan light. The Comanche's lips were moving, and his brow furrowed, as he argued with a crazy creature in his dreams.

Tamarron studied the sad and tormented face. He understood, for he, like the Indian, felt the full depth of man's loneliness in the universe.

High Walking shook his head like shaking off a bothersome fly, and his black eyes opened. He stood up slowly, his cold, stiff muscles stretching reluctantly. The reins of the horse fell from his clawlike hand.

Jacob evaluated High Walking's emaciated body. He was dying. His deep sorrow was destroying his will to live.

"You must eat," Jacob called to the Indian. "I'll fix some food."

"I want nothing of the white man's." High Walking's voice was slow, like a glacier moving.

"You have to eat something so you'll be strong enough to fight the scalpers."

The Indian showed his teeth in a ghastly caricature of a

smile. "I shall be strong enough. Even if they should shoot me in the heart, I would still kill them."

They left without eating, riding through the fog that rose like slender ghosts awakening in the grass. Then, as the sun crested the curve of the earth, the gray fog-forms unraveled away to nothing.

Jacob and High Walking rode hard beneath the sun that climbed the blue wall of the sky and blasted the plains. The miles slid past under the hurrying feet of the horses. By mid-morning the sky was bleached to a shimmering gray by the intensity of the sun's rays. The two horsemen did not stop to rest but drooped lower in the saddle, their bodies sweating in the scorching heat.

The buffalo and the antelope and all living things seemed to have vanished from the land. The only thing that moved was a flight of crows driving its dark gang south. They became a single black smear on the sky, and then even that disappeared.

In late afternoon the riders came upon the headwaters of the Colorado River. On the south side of the stream they found the tracks of the four bandits. As they hounded the trail, the evening waned, the sun sank, and the day became night.

The days seemed to blend together for Jacob. Always there was the river running to the southeast, and the plains stretching endlessly north and south. With the sameness of the terrain, time could have been flowing backward and he would not have known it.

They traveled swiftly, riding the sunlight of every day into the gloom of night. They halted where the darkness overtook them. But their enemies also rode fast, and Jacob and High Walking gained only a little on them.

The land along the river was full of game. Buffalo were always in sight. Flocks of turkeys could often be seen, and beneath their roosting trees, the ground was carpeted with their droppings.

Tamarron watched the night fall like blue-gray mist on

the far, flat horizon and come hurrying upon them. He signaled to the Comanche, and they halted and began to make camp. High Walking had not spoken for four days, refusing even to reply to direct questions, and Jacob was worried.

The Indian finished his few chores and walked toward the river. Soon he was digging among a patch of cattails at the edge of the water. At last he was going to eat.

Tamarron spread his blanket and lay down. Overhead, the big desert stars came out bright and hard and close to the earth. In the nearby brush there was the brief chatter of sundown birds settling in for the night. Crickets began to click their incessant tune.

The moon broke free of the horizon and swam into the star-studded sky. The mighty yellow globe of the moon conquered the stars, dimming them to mere pricks of light.

Jacob saw movement against the sky, and a giant owl swooped in low, its underfeathers glowing silver in the moonlight. The bird saw Jacob, and it screeched menacingly and snapped its bill, the sharp sound echoing through the quiet night like small bones breaking. It darted away into the gloom and did not return.

Jacob heard a sound on a distant breeze that reminded him of Petra's bedtime whisper. He couldn't stop his mind from filling with the memory of the woman. God! How he would miss her infinite tenderness for all the remaining years of his life. Every man lived on the edge of the great deep of death. But that was not so bad if your woman stood near you. His woman never would again.

Jacob went to sleep cursing the darkness that slowed his pursuit and delayed his revenge.

Tamarron awoke to High Walking singing in a low, quavering voice full of pain and yearning. After a bit the song ceased, but immediately the Indian's voice rose in a woeful wail that held and held at an unbelievable peak of sorrow. The wail stopped, and the voice descended in a series of weakening moans to silence.

Jacob knew that High Walking's sorrow and the peyote he ate were doing something to his mind. He was deeply concerned that his companion would become completely demented.

Jacob lay watching the cold, uncaring moon for a long time before he could once again find sleep.

CHAPTER 24

Tamarron and High Walking ran their mustangs in the light of the orange sun, inexorably mounting the eastern horizon. Their foes were only a few hours ahead of them, and the battle was near.

The Colorado River had eroded the plains into rolling hills covered with oak trees. The valley bottom was crowded with large pecan, sycamore, walnut, and cottonwood trees. However, the running horses weren't slowed by the change in terrain, for they followed the ancient, deeply worn buffalo trails that cut through the woods and held to the more gentle contours of the land.

The sun climbed to its zenith and the heat became fearful. To lessen the loads on their mounts, the riders dismounted and ran beside the tired beasts.

The river valley widened to nearly half a mile. On the deep, rich soil of the bottomland there were meadows interspersed among the trees. The wild grass was dense and reached to the stirrups of the saddles. A score of reddish-brown cattle jerked their heads up from the grass and stampeded off a quarter of a mile, then turned to watch the men and horses race by. They passed a small flock of sheep. Not one rider was seen.

The hot sun went off to the west, and long shadows gathered in the low swales and in the woods. The men's breathing grew labored and once again the men climbed astride the horses.

The woods thinned, and a large house, painted bright white, came into view on the far side of the narrow river. Several men were leaving the fields near the river and climbing the slope toward some cabins that were half hidden in the trees to the right of the house.

Tamarron and High Walking halted at the fringe of the forest and studied the terrain and the men.

"Negroes, most likely slaves," Tamarron said.

"That means nothing to us," replied High Walking. He pointed ahead. "The horse tracks we have followed go down to the crossing."

Jacob ran his eyes over the ford. It was less than a hundred feet across, and the gravely bottom was visible through the shallow water. He could see where the tracks went up the far bank.

"They go straight up to the house. This is the destination of the bandits." He twisted to look at the Comanche.

The Indian's eyes caught rays of the lowering sun and shined like lights in a skull. He laughed a weird and hollow laugh. "The scalp hunters are in the house. I feel it. Let us go find them."

"It'd be better if we waited for dark. That won't be long." Tamarron stepped to the ground and squatted with his back resting against the bole of a tree.

High Walking also dismounted. He began to examine the sharp flint tips of his arrows and to sight down the wooden shafts and then bend and straighten them for perfect flight. He often stared off across the slow-moving river at the house.

The river glowed dull silver in the last of the sunlight. The sheen vanished as a wind came along the valley and started to write a mysterious script in swiftly changing patterns on the surface of the water.

The heads of the horses lifted, their nostrils sucked at the air, and their ears thrust forward, listening. A gray hound came in sight at the edge of the trees near the river and lapped at the water. Getting his fill, the dog ambled back into the trees. The horses relaxed and began to crop the grass at their feet.

The men waited through the time between sundown and star shine. Frogs began to croak in the shoaly, green-scummed water below them. A pair of nighthawks lifted up from their daytime roost in the broken snag of a dead walnut tree. They began to dive crazily and cry out in a whimpering tone, and then suddenly they would call shrilly and raucously into the darkening sky. The birds gradually drifted downriver, where a second pair joined them in their queer acrobatics and unearthly screeching.

High Walking stood up. "I go now. Do you come with me?"

"Yes. Let's leave the horses here."

"You are right. We will make less noise without the cayuses."

The two men moved to the ford. Their feet went into the water like an animal's, sure and quiet. They crossed to the far side and walked quickly into the edge of the woods. They stopped and let their senses expand, searching to detect other men prowling about or standing silently on guard duty.

A man's voice called out in a conversational tone at the cabins. Someone answered. No sound came from the big house.

"They must feel themselves safe. I don't think they have guards posted," said Tamarron.

"They are very foolish. We are here," responded High Walking. He raised his bow, and his face twisted into a grim, wolfish smile.

In the murky light among the trees, the gray hound growled low in his chest. The scent of the two men was unknown to him. The strange intruders creeping toward his master's house in the night must be driven away. The dog made a short rush from his hiding place and sprang directly at the smaller man.

High Walking acted instantaneously, dropping his bow and lunging to meet the leaping dog. He reached out to catch the growling beast in midair. One hand grasped the pointed snout and shut off a bark. The other hand caught a front leg. Without hesitation High Walking spun, adding his strength to the momentum of the dog's body. He curved the trajectory of the dog and, with dreadful force, swung the beast into the trunk of a tree with a drumlike thump. Bones broke. The body of the dog went limp. The Indian slung the dead creature away from him.

"Now all shall remain quiet," High Walking said. He led off without a sound among the trees toward the big house.

Glen Sansen, the master forger, was weary from the long, arduous journey across the Texas plains. Still, he was confident of his skill and satisfied with the finely formed words of script that flowed from under his quill pen.

Sansen had arrived with Kirker, Flaccus, and Connard at Caverhill's home a few hours before. Caverhill had immediately led them to the library and directed Sansen to prepare several legal-looking documents.

Sansen was nearly finished, but the light was failing. He stopped writing and lit two oil lamps, placing one to the left and the other to the right on his desk so there'd be no shadows on the paper to impair his writing. As he reseated himself, he glanced briefly at the four men talking earnestly on the opposite side of the room. He dipped his quill and began to write again.

Sansen had expected that Caverhill would want false deeds prepared for the ranchos on the Rio Pecos. Instead, the documents were mortgages stating that large sums of money had been borrowed from the senator by the owners of the ranchos, and the land put up as collateral. Now Sansen knew all the details of the scheme. With New Mexico conquered by the Americans, Caverhill could make his claim for payment. There'd be no one alive to contest the honesty of the mortgages. A damn fine plan.

The quill pen moved swiftly. Sansen wanted to be finished and gone from the senator's presence. The man was dangerous, and Sansen was afraid of him.

The forger copied the exact words Caverhill had given him. The documents were in Spanish words so that they would appear official and legitimate, since the transactions were supposed to have taken place in New Mexico. False dates were affixed, so that it seemed as if the agreements had been made the year before.

Caverhill had told Sansen the names of the landowners on the Rio Pecos, and now the forger researched until he found examples of their signatures on the various papers he had brought from the haciendas. He practiced the handwriting of each a few times, and then, with a flourish, applied precise copies of the signatures to the documents.

The senator listened to Kirker describe the attacks on the ranchos along the Rio Pecos. He didn't like the fact that only a small number of fighting men had defended the haciendas. Perhaps it was as Kirker said, that all the menfolk had been killed in the fight that had occurred on the road leading to Santa Fe. It was logical that they had assembled to ride and join with Armijo's defense of the capital city. Still, he doubted that the raid had been completely successful and that all the people of the ranchos were dead.

Caverhill had anticipated only a partial success and had designed a plan to serve in that event. He'd soon travel to Santa Fe and investigate the situation for himself. With the Americans in control of the country, he could easily find out if any of the owners of the ranchos had survived. He would lodge a claim only against the land that was truly abandoned.

Sansen finished his preparation of the mortgage documents and closely proofread them. He was proud of his handiwork. Nobody would ever be able to detect that they were false. Now he'd collect his pay from Caverhill and leave quickly for Austin.

"I'm through, Senator Caverhill," Sansen said.

"Very good, Glen," replied Caverhill. He rose and, taking the sheets of paper from the forger, seated himself near the lamps. Meticulously Caverhill evaluated every detail of the documents. At last he looked up.

"Well done, Glen. Well done. They are perfect."

Sansen smiled, pleased at the man's praise. "You have a smart plan with these papers. The American army will help you take possession of the Pecos land."

"You are a talkative fellow," said Caverhill. He frowned, then grinned at Sansen. "I suppose you're ready to go to Austin. Or will you be traveling to Houston?"

"To Austin at first," replied Sansen.

"And there you will get drunk and catch up on all the dry days you've had on the trail to New Mexico."

"I do have some drinking to do," agreed Sansen.

"In a day or maybe two, you'll be telling stories in your drunken stupor of how you forged some papers for Senator Caverhill."

The smile left Sansen's face. He sensed the threat in the big man.

"I'd never do that, Senator," Sansen said quickly.

"I agree. You'll never tell what has happened in these last days of your life. Flaccus, Connard, take this gifted forger down to the river and help him drink a barrel of water. Then bury him deep. Get a shovel from the toolshed."

Sansen stood petrified at the sudden pronouncement of his death. Then he let out a frightened curse and bolted for the door.

The long-legged Kirker caught Sansen halfway across the library. He jerked the smaller man to a halt. "Come and take him," Kirker said to Flaccus and Connard.

"Let me go," pleaded Sansen, his feet anchored and pushing back from the river. "I'll leave Texas and go to

Philadelphia or New York. You'll never see me again. Caverhill won't know."

"We can't do that, Glen, ol' boy," Flaccus said, setting the lantern down on the bank near the water's edge. "Caverhill would find out, and he'd plant us in your place. You've got to drink the river dry, just as he said."

Sansen let our a scream and tried to jerk away. The two men dragged him kicking into the river.

"Down he goes," said Flaccus.

The man slammed Sansen face first into the water. Connard placed a knee in the center of the man's back, plowing his face into the mud of the river bottom.

"How long does it take for a man to drown?" Connard asked, adding more weight onto the kicking, struggling Sansen.

"I don't know. Two or three minutes," replied Flaccus.

High Walking and Tamarron went into the river as silently as water snakes. They crept up behind the two men holding a third man under the water. The victim no longer struggled, the water over his body was quiet and placid.

Tamarron gripped his long knife and drove it savagely forward into Flaccus's back. High Walking thrust twice with his sharp blade, and Connard collapsed.

"Shove the bodies out into the deep water," said Tamarron. He lifted Sansen up from the river and shook him like a large, limp doll. Then, splashing in long strides, Tamarron rushed with the body to the bank.

He laid the man on his stomach, stepped astride him, and, grabbing his belt, hoisted him nearly a yard off the ground. Water and mud gushed from the man's lungs. Tamarron dropped the body, only to jerk it up forcefully and hold it there while muddy liquid drained out the open mouth.

Tamarron worked for several minutes, trying to bring life back into the body he had dragged from the river. Finally he backed away from the sodden figure. "It's no use," he said to High Walking.

"He's dead?"

"The mud killed him. He sucked too much of it into his lungs. He'll never tell us anything about the bandits and the people at the house."

"We wasted our time trying to save him," said High Walking. His eyes swiveled and locked on something past Tamarron. He grew as taut as his bowstring at full draw.

Tamarron pivoted to look in the same direction. A light-skinned Negro woman stood in the far, weak fringe of the lantern light. She seemed frozen on the tips of her toes, ready for flight.

Millicent remained alert, poised to run, studying the heathen Indian and gray-bearded white man. They were fierce-looking men, made into ghostlike creatures by the rays of lantern light flickering upon their faces.

She had been stealthily eavesdropping on Caverhill and his cohorts ever since the horsemen had ridden in. When Caverhill had ordered Sansen's death and the two men had hustled the forger from the house, Millicent followed. Anyone who was Caverhill's enemy might be of help to her. But Sansen had died, and now, watching the two strange apparitions before her, men who killed so quickly and showed no remorse, Millicent thought she may have made a mistake in showing herself.

Then her resolve to destroy the terrible Senator Caverhill flared up hotly, and her bravery returned. "I can tell you about the bandits," Millicent said to the men.

"Speak, woman," Tamarron said. "Tell us all you know."

"Only if you promise to kill the senator."

"Senator? Don't try to dicker with us and waste time. The Indian will surely kill you. Talk fast. Who is at the house?"

Millicent took a quick breath. "Senator Caverhill and a man he calls Kirker. They are both horrible men. The senator makes the plans and has the money to pay Kirker for carrying them out. I've been listening and know that

Kirker has just come back from a place called Rio Pecos. He killed all the people, and now his men are bringing to Texas the sheep those people once owned.

"The senator will be very rich with all the sheep. More than that, this man"—Millicent pointed at the corpse of Sansen—"is what they call a forger. He writes things on paper that will give the ranchos on the Rio Pecos to the senator. He says the American army will help the senator take possession of those lands."

Tamarron evaluated the woman for several seconds. He spoke to High Walking. "She says the scalp hunter you're chasing is in the white man's house. Also, there's another man who is responsible for the murder of my people."

"Then let us go and kill both of them."

"Who else is at the house?" Tamarron questioned Millicent.

"Another woman. She will be in her room in the rear of the house."

"Black or white?"

"Like me."

"And the black men?"

"They are not allowed near the house. And even if they were, they wouldn't help Caverhill."

"Lead the way," ordered Tamarron. He kicked the lantern into the river, and the world went black.

CHAPTER 25

Millicent warily led the way from the woods and up the hill across a broad stretch of newly cleared ground. Several times she glanced at the white man and Indian to be certain they were still with her, for they made no more sound than two floating shadows.

She allowed her hate of Caverhill to soar and flare. Now she believed she might have found in these strange men someone strong enough to help her destroy Caverhill.

They reached the porch and climbed the steps. She whispered to them, "This way. The senator and the other man are in the big library at the far side of the house."

She guided them inside, across a large room with a thick carpet, and down a wide hallway. Near an open door that spilled light, she stopped and put her finger across her lips. She held up two fingers and gestured inside.

As the two men stepped into the light of the room, Millicent slipped off along the dark hallway.

"I'll put these documents in the safe," said Caverhill. He rose from his chair and walked toward an iron vault in the corner of the library.

Kirker also stood up. He looked at the broad back of the senator. Caverhill would kill him with just as little thought as he'd ordered the death of Sansen. Unless Kirker acted first.

Kirker heard the footsteps of two men entering the room behind him. That would be Flaccus and Connard. With the help of their guns, especially the fast Connard, Caverhill could be slain regardless of his skill at fighting. Kirker's hand went to the pistol on his side. When Caverhill opened the safe, the three of them would fire on him. Kirker turned to signal his intent to his men.

The senator rotated the dial of the safe left and right to the correct combination. He twisted the handle and swung wide the thick iron door.

"Goddamn!" Kirker's voice was a guttural whisper behind him.

Caverhill whirled around. Kirker stood staring at two men near the door to the hallway.

The newcomers were a strange pair of intruders. A gaunt Indian, his bronze skin stretched tight over angular bones, held a powerful war bow nocked with an arrow and drawn to full arc. Beside him, a gray-bearded white man aimed a cocked revolver.

Caverhill rapidly measured the intruders. Their eyes bore back at him, hostile and yet with a pleased cast, as if the men were glad to see him. Caverhill primed himself to pull his pistol. He thought he could kill the Indian before the man could hit him with the arrow. The senator was not so sure there would still be time to kill the man with the handgun.

"You can't beat either one of us," Tamarron said. "But go ahead and try. We would like that." His hate of these men who killed women and children burned like fire in his veins.

"What do you want?" asked Caverhill, surprised at the accuracy of the American's reading of his intentions.

"To see both of you die."

"What have we done to you?"

"My rancho was on the Rio Pecos. My friend's wives

and children were murdered for their scalps." Tamarron's words were crusty and brittle.

High Walking spoke in a harsh tone. "We talk when we should be putting the steel of our knives into them. I am going to scalp the redheaded man while he is still alive and make him eat it."

"What did he say?" asked Kirker, seeing the Indian's hot eyes upon him.

"That he plans to scalp you alive and feed you your own flesh. Unbuckle your gun belts and throw them against the wall. You go first." Tamarron motioned to Caverhill.

"Do it damn slow," warned Tamarron, observing the sudden tightening in the senator's face.

Caverhill pulled the buckle of the belt free and tossed the holstered pistol aside.

"Now you get rid of your gun," Tamarron ordered Kirker.

The scalp hunter did as directed. "Now what?" he asked.

"I think this Comanche intends to start carving on you," said Tamarron.

"Don't I get a knife to make it an even fight?"

Tamarron interpreted the words for High Walking. The Comanche laughed at the question, a weird, cackling laugh so full of unquenchable hate that Jacob felt his own soul cringe.

High Walking slid his long-bladed knife from its sheath. He poised on the balls of his feet. In a fury of muscled speed, he hurled himself at Kirker.

The Texan dodged to the side. High Walking veered to meet the change in the Texan's position, and his knife reached out. The sharp blade slashed into Kirker's upper arm.

The Indian stopped and pivoted. He swung the hilt of his knife in a backhanded blow. The hard butt of the weapon crashed into the temple of Kirker's head. He fell to his knees.

High Walking instantly sprang upon the dazed man,

hammering down with the butt of his knife. Kirker collapsed to the floor.

The Comanche's knife flashed as he encircled Kirker's head, cutting through to the bone of the skull. He clamped a powerful grip on the man's hair and yanked. The scalp came loose with a tearing sound.

High Walking flopped Kirker onto his back. The glazed eyes of the half-conscious scalp hunter looked up at the dark visage of the Indian above him.

High Walking held the scalp over Kirker. "Look," said the Indian. He shook the hairy object, and blood dripped in large, slow drops into Kirker's face. Kirker moaned, and his eyes rolled up into his head.

The Comanche squatted beside his hated enemy and stared at his bloody face. He recalled all the wives and children, beautiful wives and children he had lost because of this man. High Walking wished for a way to kill him a hundred times, a thousand times. Oh! If only that were possible.

He dropped the scalp and, taking his knife in both hands, raised it high above Kirker. With every ounce of his strength High Walking drove the steel blade into the scalper's chest to the very hilt.

The Comanche stood erect. "It is done," he said. "The man is dead and will never slay my people again."

Jacob looked at his comrade. The man's body that had once been so strong and vibrant now seemed to have shrunken in on itself, and the fire of revenge in his eyes was gone, the dark orbs vacant and dead.

Tamarron turned to Caverhill. There was a sneer on the man's face. "I won't die so easily," Caverhill said, chucking a thumb at Kirker's corpse.

"You will die just as easily," Tamarron said. His desire to kill the man was like molten metal in his brain.

"Are you a coward that you'd shoot me without giving me a chance?" demanded Caverhill. There was something deadly and implacable about the two men facing him. He felt a new emotion being born in him. At first he hadn't recognized it, but now he smelled his own fear.

But why did he fear this pair? He had faced two men before and always won the fight. He needed a weapon, and then he would show them.

"You aren't worth fighting. You must simply be killed."

"You aren't like this heathen Indian. You're a white man. Fight me with knife or pistol. Take your choice."

A cold wind seemed to blow through Jacob's mind and calmed him. The man was full of fear. Jacob could see it moving below the muddy surface of his eyes. Jacob knew with certainty that he could kill him.

Caverhill's face suddenly exploded, shreds of flesh and fragments of bone torn loose and flung away. He was knocked backward by some titanic force. The room filled with a tremendous roar.

Tamarron's senses reeled under the jarring concussion of the noise. He spun around to locate the cause of the sound.

The Negro woman stood in the doorway. Her face was pinched and taut, and blood leaked from her lips and nose. She held a double-barreled shotgun gripped in her hands. Smoke curled from the large, open bores of both barrels.

She dropped the shotgun to the floor with a clatter. Absently she wiped at the rivulets of blood coursing down her chin. The recoil of the heavily charged weapon firing both barrels at one time had rammed the hard wooden stock into her face.

"Why did you shoot him?" demanded Tamarron.

The woman began to tremble at the terrible thing she had done. And now this white man yelled angrily at her. His pistol was gripped so tightly in his hands, she thought it would go off at her.

Millicent spoke quickly. "I was afraid you would fight him. He'd win, for he always wins. I knew he had to die now, this very night before he killed you, and then the many others later who do not deserve to die."

"She did the correct thing," High Walking said. "You were a fool to consider giving him an even chance. Tell her that so she may have peace in her mind."

Jacob realized the Comanche spoke the truth. Some men should be shot like the savage beasts they were. "You did the right thing by shooting him," Jacob told Millicent.

She smiled, a tentative, fragile curve of her mouth. She brushed at the blood on her lips. "I'll go tell all the others." She backed from the room and was gone.

Tamarron went to the open safe and raked the contents out on the floor. There was a pouch of gold coins and a packet of paper money. He kicked them aside and scanned the various written documents. His anger boiled anew when he read the false mortgages that had been drawn up against the ranchos on the Rio Pecos.

He took the sheaf of papers to the hearth of the fireplace. Lifting the glass globe from one of the lamps, he lit the papers and watched the black ashes curl and then break into fragments as they cooled.

High Walking spoke to Jacob. "Now, my friend, the battle is finished. My enemies are all dead. It is time for me to go and meet with my three good wives and all my children." He turned the long blade of his knife to his stomach and angled it to point upward at his heart beneath the ribs.

"Don't do it," cried Jacob. "There are other women. You can make more children."

"I have lost my family three times. I believe the same thing would happen should I try again. That would make me a crazed man. It is better that I go where I know they wait for me. There we all will be safe.

"But you are a brave man, Tamarron. You must go and try again. I have a feeling you will succeed and die with your wife and children around you."

High Walking pulled mightily on the knife, driving it inward. The powerful muscles of his body quivered at the horrible injury. For a moment he stood erect. His eyes were locked on Jacob, but his sight was turned inward.

High Walking began to smile. "I was right," he whispered. "They are there waiting." His smile broadened to encompass his entire face.

The Comanche warrior fell upon the thick carpet of Caverhill's library.

Jacob's heart anguished at the death of High Walking. But he could help the brave Comanche make a proper journey into the next world. Jacob would burn Caverhill's mansion, that would make a fitting funeral pyre for a friend.

He grabbed one of the lamps and hurled it against a wall, where it broke, splashing oil in every direction. The burning wick ignited the oil and spread outward in a yellow wave of flame. Jacob threw the second lamp into the opposite wall and watched the flames take fiery possession. Tamarron took the gold and paper currency and went out to the yard. A group of blacks had gathered in front of the entrance. They shouted out in happy voices to him.

Jacob called the woman Millicent to him and handed her the gold and paper money. "Divide this among you."

"Thank you very much, but it will do us no good. It will be taken from us by the first white man we meet because we are slaves."

"Bring me paper, pen, and ink and I'll write you freedom papers."

With a joyous laugh, Millicent dashed into the dark end of the house and returned with the requested items. Jacob found a seat. In the flickering flames of the burning mansion he wrote, one by one as the people spoke their names, the declaration of release and freedom for each slave. He signed the documents with his name, and for his place of residence he stated Rancho el Vado, Rio Pecos Valley.

Jacob finished his task and rose. He would return to Rancho el Vado. Perhaps High Walking could see things that other men could not.

The crashing volley of rifle fire exploded in the murky darkness of the morning twilight. A ragged popping of pistols followed. The pistol fire swelled to a crescendo of shots that rapidly blended one into another until they could not be counted.

Jacob sprang from his blanket and stared to the west. He judged that the battle was a mile or so distant. He knew what was happening as if he were there.

Gunfire so early in the morning meant that an attack had been sprung upon a night camp. An enemy had crept close in the darkness and at first light had fired rifles into sleeping men. The defenders not killed by the first volley had replied with their handguns. But only a weak defense had been mounted.

The attacking force, their rifles empty, had replied with many pistols. Even as Jacob drew his conclusions, the firing ceased and the silence of the morning came rushing back.

Tamarron hastily rolled his blanket. He tossed the saddle on his horse and hurried toward the battleground.

He was six days and three hundred miles west of Senator Caverhill's burned mansion and High Walking's burial place. He'd been expecting to encounter one or more of the stolen bands of sheep at any time. Someone had beaten him to them.

Tamarron slowed as he drew close to the place from which the gunfire had come. He rode the swales and stayed below the low ridge tops. Soon the baaing of many sheep reached him. Buried in the surf of sound were the whistles and calls of men. He walked his mount to a rise of ground and looked ahead into the breaking day.

In the half-light the plains were alive, moving, undulating as thousands of sheep moved to the west. A score of Mexican vaqueros were pushing and prodding the animals, snapping laggards into a run with their quirts.

On a nearby point of land a man shouted a shrill warning and fired his pistol in the air. A rear guard had been posted by the Mexicans, and Jacob hadn't spotted him.

Immediately the five nearest vaqueros spun their horses and raced toward the lookout. He sped down to join them. In less than a minute the Mexicans were lined up in a shield to protect those men still driving the sheep in the direction of New Mexico.

A slender figure on a tall horse circled the north edge of the flock of sheep at a reckless run. The rider slid his mount to a fast stop beside the formation of vaqueros. He spoke to the men, and they pulled their rifles from scabbards and rode forward, ready for another battle.

The slender rider stood up in his stirrups and peered intently ahead at the new arrival. Then the rider cried out, "Jacob," in a clear, ringing voice.

Petra spurred hard, and the horse leapt forward. She jabbed him hard again, and the steed seemed to fly over the ground.

Jacob's heart did a drum tattoo high on his ribs. Never could he forget Petra's beautiful voice. He slapped the neck of his mount with the flat of his hand, a sound that could be heard a mile, and ran down to meet her.

Petra swept up to Jacob. A wonderful smile wreathed her face. She began to laugh happily.

Jacob felt his own happiness surging, and he laughed with Petra. God! What a woman. He reached out and lifted her from the saddle and enclosed her in his arms. He pressed Petra tightly against him.

Jacob's world was once again complete.

AUTHOR'S NOTE

James Kirker is recorded in history as a scalp hunter.

Greg, author of *Commerce of the Prairies*, has this to say about the Mexican bounty on Indian scalps: "This traffic was not only tolerated but openly encouraged by the civil authorities, as the highest functionaries were interested in its success—the governor himself not excepted."

In 1840, the governor of Chihuahua engaged the services of one hundred American trappers, freighters, teamsters, hunters, and Shawnee and Delaware Indians who happened to be in the state at the time. Led by a soldier of fortune named James Kirker, the band rode out to "go barberin'," as they called it. They brought in so many scalps that the governor refused to pay the full bounty.

This nonpayment for scalps seems strange, since it would appear that the greater the number of Indians killed, the more satisfied the governor would be. Kendall, in his *Narrative of the Texan Santa Fe Expedition*, may have explained the reluctance of the governor of Chihuahua to pay Kirker for all the scalps he presented.

251

Kendall says, ". . . a well known American, named Kirker, had been engaged in the business of scalp hunting, and with a party of his countrymen had been very successful, but it was soon suspected that he was in the practice of bringing in counterfeit scalps—or in other words, that he did not scruple to kill any of the lower order of Mexicans he might meet with where there was slight chance of being discovered, and pass off their topknots for those of true Apaches."

James Kirker's death is not recorded in history.

ABOUT THE AUTHOR

F. M. Parker has established himself as the most exciting Western writer in years with such triumphs as *Nighthawk, Skinner, Cold-iron, Shadow of the Wolf, The Searchers, The Highbinders,* and *The Far Battleground.* In addition to his writing, F. M. Parker has worked as a land manager in Southeastern Oregon, where he was responsible for vast herds of cattle, sheep and horses. He now lives in Arizona.